LEGACY OF
BLOOD

SPARTAN WARRIOR

LEGACY OF BLOOD

MICHAEL FORD

BLOOMSBURY

LONDON BERLIN NEW YORK

Bloomsbury Publishing, London, Berlin and New York

First published in Great Britain in 2009 by Bloomsbury Publishing Plc
36 Soho Square, London, W1D 3QY

Pages 59, 60 Lines adapted from Samuel Butler's translation of
The Iliad by Homer

A CIP catalogue record of this book is available from the
British Library

ISBN 978 0 7475 9859 6

The paper this book is printed on is certified independently in
accordance with the rules of the FSC. It is ancient-forest friendly.
The printer holds chain of custody.

FSC
Mixed Sources
Product group from well-managed
forests and other controlled sources
Cert no. SGS - COC - 2061
www.fsc.org
© 1996 Forest Stewardship Council

Typeset by Dorchester Typesetting Group Ltd
Printed in Great Britain by Clays Ltd, St Ives Plc

1 3 5 7 9 10 8 6 4 2

www.bloomsbury.com

For Rebecca, as ever

PROLOGUE

'The hour is late, mortal,' said the Oracle, from her tripod stool. 'Why do you wish to wake Apollo from his slumber?'

The man before her wore a red cloak, dripping from the rain that lashed the mountainside beyond the cavern. In his hand was a laurel branch, to show that he came as a supplicant across the God's threshold. He wasn't sure why the Council had sent him, an Ephor, to consult the Oracle. All this was smoke and superstition, nothing more.

'I hail from Sparta,' he said, kneeling before the old woman – the priestess of Apollo, the Pythia. Her eyes were hidden behind matted strands of grey hair, but he felt her gaze burn into him. 'I am sent by the Council. We have a problem . . . a boy.'

The Oracle's cackle echoed off the cavern walls.

'A boy! What danger does a boy pose to mighty Sparta?'

The man bit his lip and forced himself to stay

1

patient. He was here now; he had to go through with this.

'Please,' he said. 'You must tell me what the future holds. How can we meet this young threat to our city?'

'I am obliged to tell you nothing, Tellios,' replied the Oracle. 'If the God wishes to speak, he will speak.' She turned to her attendant priests. Both men were cloaked in white and stood beside the sacred egg-shaped *navel* stone – said to be the place Zeus had marked the centre of the world. 'Has this man made the sacrifices as the God decrees?'

'He has, Pythia, mistress of the bow,' intoned one of the attendants. 'A black ram's blood stains the springs of Apollo.'

'Then prepare the fires.'

Lighting a taper from the torch hanging on the wall, one of the men placed it among the dry tinder beneath the Oracle's cauldron. The Spartan watched the flames sizzle and flare, first green, then yellow, then orange. Soon the air was filled with strange-scented smoke, and he felt his head swim.

The Oracle leant over her cauldron, staring into the water.

'What can you see?' coughed the Spartan.

The Oracle sucked in a deep breath of the air.

'Fire,' she whispered. 'A building ablaze. Flames climbing wooden walls.'

'Anything else?'

'I see a boy in rags, in a foreign land. He plunges his

hand into the flames. What pain!' She gripped the edges of the cauldron. 'Not rags. A cloak made of red wool. A Spartan!'

Tellios narrowed his eyes; this might be interesting. 'Tell me more.'

'I see a jewel amidst the flames – it speaks to me.'

'And what does it say?' asked the man, his mouth turning dry.

'*The Fire of Ares shall inflame the righteous.*'

The Spartan rushed over to the cauldron. The water inside was as still and clear as a mountain lake. There was no vision here!

'What trickery is this?' he demanded.

A deep moan rose in a crescendo from the Pythia's lips. Tellios nervously looked round at her minions.

'What's the matter with her?'

'The boy! The boy!' wailed the Oracle, swaying dangerously on her chair. The two attendants rushed forward and took an arm each to steady her. She convulsed in their grasp. 'The boy is in danger. What pain, what agony!'

The Spartan backed away. 'Will he die?'

'Oh, oh, the God is thrown into confusion. The boy is a danger to himself and to Sparta. Sparta's shields will tremble. Go, Tellios of Sparta, go and warn your people. Go!'

The Oracle's eyes rolled back in her head and she collapsed in a faint. Tellios gathered his cloak around his body, and left the poisonous fumes of the cave.

Outside, the rain had stopped. As Tellios picked his way down the mountainside, his head cleared. He had to admit that the details the Oracle had given him were satisfying; the boy was a danger, not just to Sparta, but to himself too. *There's hope then*, he thought.

The sun broke over the mountains to the east and a smile crept over Tellios' face. Thank goodness old Sarpedon was gone. The other Ephors couldn't ignore Tellios any longer – the boy, Lysander, could be dealt with now. He was a danger – the Oracle had said so. Any threat had to be removed.

He untethered his stallion at the bottom of the slope and swung himself into the saddle. A day's hard riding should get him back to Sparta.

He pressed his heels into the horse's flanks and the stallion leapt forward. With the clouds above clearing, Tellios never stopped to think how the Oracle had known his name.

He'd never said who he was.

CHAPTER 1

One of the boys in the barracks coughed in his sleep. Lysander's head was heavy with dreams of battle – images of slaughter chasing each other through his brain. Ares, God of War, snatching men's lives by sword and spear.

A floorboard creaked.

Lysander shot out an arm, his eyes snapping open, and grabbed a thin wrist. He drew his dagger from beneath his rolled blanket.

'Who are you?' he hissed, holding the blade to a stranger's throat. Blue eyes looked back at him, a pale face threatening to crumple into tears. The boy looked so young.

'My name's Idas, Master Lysander,' he whispered.

'How do you know my name?' said Lysander, keeping his voice low as the boys around him lay deep in slumber.

The boy frowned. 'Everyone knows your name, master. You saved Sparta from the Persians.'

Lysander snorted. 'You've heard wrongly. Hundreds died to save Sparta. I was just one of the few who remained standing. What have you got there?'

'They're your clothes, master; I'm your new servant.'

'My *new* servant.'

'They said your old one . . . that he died.'

Lysander released his grip on the boy's arm.

'He wasn't a servant, he was my friend.'

'Yes, master,' said Idas.

'And stop calling me "master". I don't need a slave.' Lysander lay back on his thin mattress. 'Go away.'

Idas stood awkwardly on the spot, then placed the folded clothes on the table beside Lysander.

'Very well, master,' said the boy.

Lysander listened to his footsteps fade away. Perhaps he shouldn't have been so hard on the boy. After all, his own first day at the barracks had been terrifying. What was it – six moons ago? He remembered standing waiting with his grandfather's slave, Strabo, on a warm summer morning. His best friend, Timeon, had stood at his side.

And now?

Now they were all dead. Timeon, murdered in the night by the Krypteia, Strabo, killed in the battle against the Persians. All gone. Even his grandfather had descended to the land of the shades, slain by his own hand so that Lysander might live.

What a price to pay to be a Spartan.

He didn't need another servant. No one could

replace Timeon. He didn't want to be responsible for anyone ever again.

Lysander slipped back into a doze, trying to keep the images of blood and battle from flooding his mind. He remembered his life as a Helot, working for the Spartans in their fields. Was it really as bad as it had seemed at the time? He and his mother were slaves, with little to eat and only a leaking roof over their heads, but at least they had had each other. Now she too was rotting to dust in the earth.

Somewhere a bell sounded, and around him the other boys began to stir. As Lysander climbed off his rush mattress, every muscle in his body throbbed with a deep ache. The battle had lasted for almost half a day for the regular troops, but Lysander's fight had gone on for another day on board the Persian ship, ending with a plunge into the freezing sea.

Lysander hobbled stiffly towards the side door. Beside each of the beds were piles of armour, discarded in the exhausted return from the plains: breastplates dented from Persian swords, and arm-guards crusted with dried blood. Each scattered piece told a tale of death.

The sky outside was bright with winter sunlight, but the air was cold. Lysander drew a deep breath and squinted up at the sun. From its position in the sky, Lysander saw it was well into morning.

'Greetings, Lysander,' called a boy, rubbing the sleep from his eyes. Other boys wandered out into the courtyard. They had been permitted to sleep longer than usual, and why not? The whole of Sparta would be recovering from the battle, or from the celebrations that had followed the victory.

Lysander wandered over to the communal well, about a hundred paces – half a stadion – from his barracks building. He let the bucket splash into the water below, and drew it up to the ledge. Then he stripped down. A huge bruise spread out from underneath his right armpit where he'd fallen during his mountain survival exercise. The centre was green, spreading to yellow around the edges. His arms and legs were covered in angry welts and purple-black marks, reminders of the battle he and his fellow trainees had undertaken.

Finally he took off the pendant, a family heirloom, that hung around his neck: the Fire of Ares. What did it mean to him now? Surely it was the cause of all the misery he had suffered. Without the jewel and the chance discovery of his parentage, Timeon would still be alive. And Sarpedon would never have made his dreadful sacrifice.

I used to be proud of this trinket, Lysander thought bitterly. *Now it feels like a curse.*

Lysander cast the amulet on his cloak that covered the ground and drew up a bucket of water. He poured it over his head, washing the grime from his hair and doing his best to clean the dried blood and dirt from his body. He noticed two of his toenails had turned

8

black, from where a shield had been rammed down on his foot by a Persian.

'You look dreadful,' said a voice behind him.

Lysander turned to see Demaratos, his fellow student. When he'd first entered the agoge, Demaratos had bullied him relentlessly. Now, his once mortal enemy was a trusted friend in the barracks. They'd survived together in the mountains, and after fighting shield by shield against the Persians, they were bonded by trust and bloodshed.

'You've not fared much better,' said Lysander. Demaratos had a gash across the side of his head and ear, a black eye and his thigh was bandaged with a piece of dirty gauze where a Persian arrow had gouged the flesh.

Demaratos raised another bucket of water, and knelt on the ground scrubbing his chest and arms. 'They let us lie in,' he laughed. 'We'll be soft around the middle like Athenians with such bad habits.'

Lysander took a sponge offered by Demaratos. 'Do you remember,' said Lysander. 'You once tried to push me down this well?'

Demaratos had unfastened his bandage and was gingerly cleaning his wound. It had been roughly stitched the previous evening, but some of the thread must have come loose in the night. Lysander could see bright red flesh breaking through the black scabs.

'You were lucky,' Demaratos grinned. 'Diokles caught you in time.'

9

At the mention of their former tutor, Lysander lowered his eyes. He had watched the Spartan die on the plains south of the city, with two arrows buried in his chest. Just after he'd saved Lysander's life. In peacetime, Diokles had made Lysander's life unbearable, but in battle he had been steadfast.

A few slaves were milling around the barracks doors now, carrying water, and fresh clothes for the tired students.

'My Helot tells me they've planned a feast in our honour,' said Demaratos, shaking droplets of water from his hair. 'It's at River's Rush.'

'The elite mess?' said Lysander, tying his belt around his tunic.

Demaratos nodded and grinned. River's Rush was an area to the east of the villages where the River Eurotas narrowed in its channel and swept over a series of low rocks, churning white water. Beside the banks was a set of barracks that housed the cream of Spartan infantry. They had been away fighting the bulk of the Persians in the north, while Lysander and Demaratos had met the secondary invasion at Gytheion on the south coast.

'Are you coming?' Demaratos called back over his shoulder as he walked towards the barracks. Lysander was looking at the Fire of Ares, lying on his cloak in the dust. The burden was too much for him. For now at least.

'Of course,' Lysander replied. 'But wait a moment.'

Demaratos turned around. 'What is it?'

The rest of the boys were emerging from the barracks, coming towards the well. Many were limping, or wearing bandages over their wounds – scars they'd carry proudly for years to come.

Lysander held out the pendant on its leather thong and lowered his voice as he approached Demaratos. 'I can't wear this any more.'

'Don't be silly,' said Demaratos, his eyes darting uncomfortably from the jewel to Lysander's face. 'It was your father's. When I took it before, I didn't know what it meant to you.'

It was true that Demaratos had taken it when Lysander first entered the barracks, but their previous squabbles seemed alien to him now.

'That's in the past,' he said. There was laughter as the boys threw buckets of water over each other. Since Diokles' death a new tutor had yet to be allocated, and the trainees were enjoying their brief spell of freedom.

Lysander took Demaratos's hand, and dropped the Fire of Ares in his palm.

'I don't even know what this means to me now,' he said. 'I'd rather it was in the possession of someone I trust. Keep it safe for me, will you?'

Demaratos nodded slowly. 'If you wish.' He bowed his head and looped the amulet around his neck. The sight of it resting against his friend's chest brought a sense of relief to Lysander.

'Stop being so glum,' said Demaratos. 'This feast will

be one to remember.'

Lysander fastened his cloak and ran inside to find Idas standing dutifully beside his bed.

'I hear someone's been summoned to River's Rush,' Leonidas called over, as he dressed. 'Congratulations.'

Lysander had been unsure about Leonidas, second son of the Spartan King Cleomenes, when he first came to the barracks. He'd mistaken the prince's lack of aggression for cowardice, but after the battle against the Persian general, Vaumisa, those doubts had been pushed aside. Leonidas had fought like the lion after which he was named, taking his place at the front of the phalanx.

'Don't be too quick to cheer him,' said Prokles.

'What do you mean?' asked Lysander.

'Well,' said Prokles. 'I hear that their leader, the Phylarch Peleus, doesn't suffer fools, or youngsters, gladly.'

'Nonsense!' said Leonidas. 'You have earned the right to sit with the bravest of Sparta.'

Lysander dried himself by his bedside, and ran an ivory comb through his hair. When Idas held out his tunic to him, Lysander noticed the boy's hands were shaking.

'There's nothing to be scared of,' he said, pulling the tunic over his head. 'Just because some of the others beat their servants, it doesn't mean we're all the same.'

Idas managed a small smile, but didn't say anything.

12

He offered Lysander a new red cloak – the old one had been torn apart and lost in the battle with Vaumisa's army.

Something about the cloak, which previously had filled Lysander with pride, now made him unsure of himself. The coarse red wool was heavy, and uncomfortable.

'Which settlement are you from?' he asked the Helot.

'I'm from Messenia,' said Idas. 'My people were shepherds west of the mountains. We came here after my father died, and worked on a settlement.'

'Which one?'

'Near Amikles,' said Idas. 'It belonged to an old Ephor, but he's dead now.'

Lysander took a sharp breath. The boy was talking about Lysander's own grandfather.

'My family came from Messenia too,' he said, forcing himself to ignore the stab of loss that returned with the mention of Sarpedon. The Helot boy didn't reply; he was staring at Lysander's red cloak, his jaw tensing.

'I'll be back later,' Lysander told his new slave. 'Keep yourself to yourself, and no one will bother you.'

Idas gave a small bow. Then Lysander strode out of the barracks again.

Demaratos was waiting for him by the track that led into the villages. With no tutor to give them orders, they were free to make their own way to River's Rush. Lysander's stomach growled. He'd managed only a few scraps of food after watching his grandfather's body consumed by the funeral pyre the previous night.

'Let's hurry,' he said. 'I'm starving.'

They strode through the outskirts of the city, past the remains of the previous day's feasting: spitted carcasses of roasted sheep and pigs, stripped to the bone, wine jars toppled in the dust. Lysander saw a few Helots sweeping, or chopping wood, but for the most part it was quiet – none of the free-dwellers would be working today.

Lysander spotted a servant carrying a water skin. Unusually for a Helot, the muscles rippled across the man's broad back and he didn't look as starved as many who worked the fields. He noticed Lysander watching him and gave him a suspicious look. Even a day after the city had been spared, the old distrust between Spartans and Helots was growing back, like a mould infecting the city.

Roars of laughter and shouting carried across the river. Lysander crossed the bridge with Demaratos and inspected the massive barracks building. It looked like it had once been a two-storey stable block.

'Are you sure they're expecting us?' he asked Demaratos.

'Stop worrying,' said his friend. 'We're the toast of Sparta now.'

Outside, shields were resting against the walls, and eight-foot spears bristled in a rack.

Suddenly the door flew open and a Spartan soldier stumbled out. He pushed past Lysander and ran to the railings, before vomiting over the side. Demaratos pulled a disgusted face.

Once the man had emptied his stomach, he turned and wiped his mouth with a thick forearm.

'Greetings, young ones,' he slurred. 'Forgive me – Peleus mixes the wine too strong for my stomach.'

Demaratos stepped forward. 'We've been summoned for the feast,' he said.

The Spartan raised his eyebrows in a look of mock surprise.

'Have you now? This is River's Rush, you know. What makes you two boys think this is a place for you?'

Lysander was annoyed at the tone in the Spartan's voice.

'I took Vaumisa's life with my spear,' he said.

The smile dropped from the man's face, and he seemed suddenly sober.

'It was you? Yes, I recognise you now. You initiated Sarpedon's funeral rites. Lysander, isn't it?'

Lysander nodded, and then gestured to Demaratos.

'This is Demaratos; he rescued the granddaughter of the Ephor Sarpedon from the Persian ship.'

'I am Phalerius,' said the man. 'Peleus is expecting you. Follow me.' The words were spoken as an order, not an invitation.

The Spartan led them to the double doors of the

dining hall.

'If Peleus is expecting us,' Lysander hissed to Demaratos, 'why all the questions?'

'It's the Spartan way,' said Demaratos, hurrying after Phalerius. 'They like to see what novices are made of.'

The Spartan threw the doors open, and a blast of warm air, thick with the stench of sweat and food, reached Lysander's nostrils.

About a hundred men sat along three long tables, while others walked between. Many of the men had scabs on their faces and arms, or scraps of their cloaks tied around their heads and limbs. On the table were loaves of bread, great wooden platters of sliced meats and several jugs.

One by one, they fell silent and turned to scrutinise Lysander and Demaratos.

Phalerius took his seat beside a man part-way along the bench. He wore a prosthetic wooden nose strapped across his face, and his eyes were black as charcoal.

Peleus, thought Lysander.

Slowly rising from the bench, Peleus turned to face them. Silence swept through the room. 'These are the two mighty warriors who took on the Persian general,' he said.

The men stared.

'Make them welcome, then!' yelled Peleus.

Suddenly the hall was filled with shouts, and the men shuffled down one bench to make room.

Lysander and Demaratos took a seat, and were

offered food. Lysander chewed on the ribs of a sheep. The men were soon absorbed in their conversations again.

Good, thought Lysander. *The less fuss the better.*

'So, how many was it, Phalerius?' said one of the soldiers.

'Six, for sure,' replied the Spartan. 'But I took both arms off another, so he probably didn't make it through the night.'

'He won't be much good in a shield wall, then.'

'Not unless they use him *as* a shield.'

Laughter rippled along the table.

A Spartan with a jug under his arm walked along the table, and stopped by their side.

'A drink for you boys?'

Lysander held out a wide drinking cup. The man poured the red wine clumsily.

'Make sure you mix plenty of water with that,' said Phalerius. 'Many a battle-hardened warrior has been floored by Peleus' brew.'

Lysander poured water into the cup, and lifted it by the two handles.

'All of it!' shouted a Spartan. 'In one!'

Lysander was thirsty, but the wine was fiery and he had to take a breath before tipping all the dregs down his throat. As he placed the cup on the table and wiped his mouth, the soldiers cheered. The wine seeped along his limbs, and his aches and pains dulled to a soft throb.

'Your friend's turn,' said Peleus. Demaratos grinned

as the cup was refilled.

Demaratos lifted the cup to his lips and took a long draught as two rivulets dribbled down each cheek and on to his cloak. He let out a loud belch.

Typical Demaratos, Lysander thought, smiling. He was always happiest surrounded by others.

'The boy is Dionysus in the flesh,' said Phalerius.

'The God of Wine never held a spear,' said Peleus. 'And from what I have been told, these boys acquitted themselves like Ares himself on the plains of the Eurotas.' He looked hard at Lysander and Demaratos and the room fell quiet. 'They say you braved Vaumisa on his own vessel. Is that the truth?'

'We did,' said Demaratos. 'We took on ten men, and prevailed. We swam out through freezing seas, climbed the anchor rope, and rescued the Lady Kassandra. If you had seen Vaumisa's face when we . . .'

Peleus grinned widely. 'What about you?' he said, pointing at Lysander. 'Anything to say?'

Lysander lowered his eyes. He did not feel ready yet to find glory in the events that had unfolded on the Persian ship. 'It happened just as Demaratos says.'

'A quiet one, eh? Well, Spartan valour is not measured by words,' said Peleus. 'We already know what deeds you have performed. Raise your cups, men, and salute these young men. They are true Spartans!'

A deafening raucous cheer filled the hall. A cup was thrust into Lysander's hand, when a sudden hush descended.

Idas stood at the door of the hall, his gaze darting from face to face as he stood before the gathered soldiers. Lysander couldn't help but notice that one of his Helot's knees was quivering.

'I . . . I . . .'

'Come on, boy,' said Phalerius. 'It'll be night by the time you get your words out.'

Lysander saw a flash of contempt pass over his servant's face. *What's he playing at?* Lysander thought. These men would flog him to death him in an instant.

'He's my servant,' Lysander called, scrambling to his feet. 'I'll deal with it.'

He marched Idas to the door, beyond the gaze of the Spartan soldiers.

'I was told to come and find you.'

'What is it?' asked Lysander, shaking Idas by the arm.

'A messenger from the mistress Kassandra's villa. You are wanted there straight away.'

'Does she know that I'm here?' said Lysander, feeling a flash of annoyance.

'No, sir,' said Idas. 'Her messenger came to the barracks to find you. He said it was urgent.'

'Very well. Now go back to the barracks, before the soldiers in there decide to have sport with you.'

Lysander watched Idas leave, then went back into the dining hall, where Demaratos was leaning back, some sort of brown sauce dripping down his chin.

'I've been called away,' he said, loudly enough that Peleus could hear.

'Where are you going?' demanded the Spartan.

'To my cousin's villa,' he said. 'If I may be excused.'

Peleus stood up and spoke quietly. 'May you be excused?' He looked up and down the rows, then pointed to Lysander. 'We invite you to our barracks, you accept our hospitality, then you ask to leave.' His voice had risen to a roar. 'Have we offended you, Spartan?'

Demaratos's face was white.

'No, of course not,' said Lysander. 'My cousin . . . she said it was urgent.'

The table was silent, and Peleus glowered at Lysander, then drew a knife from his belt. Lysander swallowed.

Peleus' mouth broke into a smile, and with the knife he carved a leg off the goat carcass that lay on a platter in front of him. He threw it to Lysander.

'At least enjoy some of the food.'

'Thank you,' said Lysander, catching it clumsily. He turned and left to the howls of laughter from behind.

Lysander set off in a jog back towards the village, limping from a wound to the back of his leg. He had been with Kassandra only the day before. Was something wrong?

He retraced his path as far as the turning to Amikles. The temporary stalls that normally lined the road were all vacant, and he passed a few more Helots, mostly scavenging for food among the ruins of yesterday's feasting – fighting for scraps with the dogs that roamed the streets.

Lysander saw a Helot coming towards him with a large water jug. He was moving quickly, Lysander thought, as though the jug weighed almost nothing.

Wait a moment – he recognised that face. Wasn't it the same slave he'd seen earlier, watching him with Demaratos? Perhaps it was just a coincidence. As they drew level, the Helot tripped, and the jug smashed on the ground. Lysander bent down to help.

'Are you hurt?'

A curved blade, single-edged, was pressed into Lysander's tunic under his ribs. Another hand gripped the back of his neck.

'One move and I'll spill your guts over the road. Understand?'

CHAPTER 2

'I understand.'

'Good, answered like a true Helot. Now we're going to take the alley you see on your left. Go.'

Together, they made their way off the main track and into a shady side street. Lysander's mind was reeling. This was no ordinary Helot. The hand that gripped him was strong and assured.

Lysander felt a blow to the back of his calf and fell to his knees. The blade was whipped across his stomach and for a moment he expected to feel his innards spill into the dirt. Instead the man brought the heavy hilt of the dagger hard into Lysander's face.

The bridge of his nose cracked, and light and pain exploded across his eyes as a cry escaped his lips. He felt blood pour over his mouth. The slave's face was close to his, swimming in and out of focus. Lysander tried to stand but his legs gave way and he crashed against the wall.

As his vision cleared he found himself staring at the

slave's feet, encased in their sandals. It didn't make sense. The leather soles and straps were brand new – way beyond the means of a mere Helot.

Understanding dawned.

'You're not a slave, are you?' he asked quietly.

'And you're no Spartan,' replied the man, seizing Lysander by his tunic. 'On your feet!'

Lysander still felt too weak to fight back, and without a weapon it was risky. He was marched a few steps further down the alley. A door opened into one of the buildings, and he was pushed inside. The man slammed the door behind him. The shutters were closed, and it took a few moments for his eyes to adjust to the darkness.

It was a tavern – the remains of a broken-up straw bale were scattered on the floor among roughly-made stools, benches and tables. A row of empty wine jars, cracked and discarded, lay at one end. Lysander's eyes were drawn to the men who sat together at a table near the closed entrance. He noticed their faces were lean and sober, and they all wore identical rough grey cloaks. These were no ordinary free-dwellers, overindulging.

Lysander's blood ran cold.

One by one, the men stood up. They fanned out across the empty tavern towards him. Their height, not a man under six feet tall, and cold stares, left him in no doubt: these were the Krypteia. They looked like wolves stalking prey.

23

Lysander wouldn't let his life end like this. He saw a stool to his left and toppled it, then brought his foot down twice, breaking off two of the legs. He snatched them up, holding their splintered ends out in warning.

'I'd think twice before you try anything,' he said. 'I'm not afraid.'

One of the Spartans laughed. 'What are you going to do with those sticks, boy? Stitch me a new cloak?' The others sniggered as well, and one drew a short sword.

The pieces of wood felt pathetically small in Lysander's hands, but they were all he had. Even if he could take one of their eyes out, it would be better than dying quietly. A drop of blood from Lysander's broken nose splashed on the floor.

'Come and get them, then,' he said.

Lysander backed away as the Spartan with the sword approached.

He drew back his arm and hurled the leg at the Spartan. It thudded into his jaw. The man howled in pain and fell backwards, as Lysander scanned the room for another weapon.

A sound rang out behind Lysander and he spun round. A grey-haired Spartan, with a familiar face, stood gazing at him. He held a sword straight out in front of him, and brought the blade to press against Lysander's neck.

'Enough!' barked the man. 'Telamon, get to your feet.'

Lysander heard the fallen Spartan scramble up. He

glanced round to see the man pick up his sword. He spat a mouthful of blood on to the ground.

'I'll teach you a lesson . . .' he hissed at Lysander.

'No, you will not, Telamon,' said the Elder. 'You can't even fight off a boy armed with a chair leg. I'll have you flogged by your compatriots before the day is out.'

Telamon growled and backed off.

Lysander looked at the old Spartan again.

'You're an Ephor,' he said slowly, as recognition dawned. 'I remember you from my grandfather's house. Tellios of Limnae.'

The old man smiled. 'Yes, I haven't forgotten your insolence, either.'

Lysander felt a chill pass down his neck. Was it the cold blade, or the memory of Tellios before the battle with Vaumisa? Back then he had looked into Lysander's eyes with the same hatred.

'If you'd had your way, Sparta would lie in ruins,' said Lysander.

'Mind your tongue. I may be over sixty summers old, but I could still remove your head with a flick of my wrist.'

'Then why haven't you?' said Lysander. 'That's what the Krypteia do, isn't it? Kill people who cannot defend themselves? Like Timeon.'

Tellios' face tightened. 'He was nothing.'

'He was my friend.'

Tellios' glance darted over to the other Spartans, and he lowered the sword. 'Tie him up.'

A strong arm slipped around Lysander's throat and a hand grabbed his wrist as he was dragged backwards. He was thrown on to a chair, gasping for breath and struggling as his ankles were tied to the chair legs and his arms were bound. Lysander's heart hammered in his chest. Something was puzzling him.

'How did you know where to find me?'

Tellios' eyes narrowed. 'I make it my business to know such things. Your slave should be more discreet.'

'What do you want from me?' he said.

The Spartan called Telamon slapped the back of his hand across Lysander's cheek. Then he crouched on his haunches and brought his face close to Lysander's.

'We ask the questions from now on.'

Lysander strained against the bonds, feeling them cut into his wrists.

'Tell us about the Persian ship,' said Tellios. His voice was quiet, pregnant with threat. 'Tell us everything you remember.'

Lysander continued to struggle. 'Why do you want to know?'

'Humour me.'

'Is that what all this is for?' said Lysander. 'To ask questions? Why not bring me before the Council?'

'I told you once before, half-breed, don't meddle in politics. The Council like to debate until dawn, but there are those of us who prefer a more . . . direct approach.'

Lysander couldn't believe it. His own countrymen

were torturing him for information? 'I would have volunteered the information without being tied up,' he said.

'Well, talk quickly then. Or I'll have Telamon start removing little pieces of you.'

Lysander saw Telamon grin through his bloodied teeth. If the Krypteia were working without the Council's knowledge, they would be like a rabid dog off its leash. Lysander needed to give up everything he knew – now.

'The ship – Vaumisa's – was moored off the headland west of Gytheion. We followed Vaumisa and his riders there after they kidnapped my cousin . . .'

Lysander went on to tell Tellios how he and Demaratos had swum out to the Persian ship. He shuddered as he recounted their capture. Recalling Sarpedon's brave sacrifice almost brought tears to his eyes, but he managed to hold himself together to describe the moment when he killed Vaumisa with his spear. The members of the Krypteia shared looks with one another, and one or two scoffed when he spoke of nearly being hung on the deck of the ship.

'Is that all?' said Tellios when he paused.

'You know the rest,' said Lysander. 'The Spartan ships came to our rescue, the Persian vessel was sunk beneath the waves.'

'That was regrettable,' said Tellios, leaning back against a table, and drawing a dagger from a second sheath that was fastened opposite his sword. 'No

Spartan has ever stepped on board a Persian vessel before – it would have benefited us to know more. What weapons were on board?'

Lysander eyed the dagger warily. Its blade glinted silver in the cracks of light that came through the closed shutters.

'Only those the men carried, I think. Curved blades, wicker shields, and bows and arrows.'

'You think?' sneered Tellios. 'Who was Vaumisa's second in command?'

Lysander's throat tightened as he remembered the rope thrown around his neck by Vaumisa's lieutenant. 'His name was Cleeto.'

'What happened to him?' Tellios used the point of his dagger to delicately clean beneath his fingernails.

'We thought he'd drowned, but after the battle, he was captured.'

'And?'

'The Ephor Myron asked me what should be done with him. I let him go.'

'You let a prisoner of Sparta live?' said Tellios, his voice suddenly rising. He rammed the dagger hard into the table. 'You should have killed him on the spot!'

'One man means nothing if an army is defeated,' said Lysander.

Tellios snorted in disgust. 'You know nothing of our ways.'

'I know the shame of defeat is a heavier burden than death.'

28

Tellios pulled out the dagger, and jabbed it towards Lysander.

'How many oarsmen were there?'

'I . . . I don't know,' said Lysander. 'They were on the deck below.'

'Pathetic. You're of no use at all.'

Tellios went over to the other men and began a whispered conversation.

There must be something I can tell them, thought Lysander. *Something else useful.*

'I do remember Vaumisa's armour,' he said, an image flashing into his mind.

Tellios' head snapped round. 'What's that, boy?'

Lysander didn't like the tone in his voice.

'The Persian's armour. It wasn't like anything I'd seen before. It was made of polished metal discs, like a snake's scales.'

'Perhaps you're not as stupid as you look,' said Tellios. 'And what happened to this armour – did it sink with the ship?'

'I can't remember,' said Lysander. 'After my grandfather took his own life, Kassandra and I . . .'

A fist crashed into his jaw and knocked him sideways from his chair. He hit the ground hard. Tellios gripped his face between powerful fingers and turned his head towards him.

'You will never mention this again,' he said quietly. 'No Ephor of Sparta would take his own life. It is a coward's way. He would fight to the death.'

29

'But he did it for us,' pleaded Lysander. 'He did it to give us time to escape.'

'Silence!' shouted Tellios. 'Who do you think you are, boy, spitting on the memory of a Spartan? Listen carefully to my words, and take heed. You were never on that Persian vessel. You never laid eyes on the general, Vaumisa. Sarpedon died fighting like a warrior, not by his own sword like some coward . . . like some Athenian.' He spoke the last word as though it tasted rotten in his mouth. 'Do you understand, Lysander? Keep your *stories* to yourself.'

Lysander wanted to shout out, but he felt his strength sap away. He nodded. 'I understand.'

'Sparta must never know how close she came to defeat. If our enemies get wind of it, they will think us weak.'

Tellios released Lysander's face and turned to the men. 'Let's leave the half-breed to think things over. He must learn to honour his grandfather with more respectful . . . memories.'

Lysander was in no doubt what Tellios meant. He was asking him to rewrite history.

With a swirl of their cloaks, the Krypteia were gone.

Lysander was alone.

CHAPTER 3

Lysander waited for his heartbeat to slow, then squirmed on to his knees. He managed to push himself back into a sitting position, but the ropes were still tight on his wrists and ankles.

Rocking back, he could feel that the chair was loose where the upright slats met the seat. He leant back hard, arching his spine, and the supports creaked. He strained against the cords and used all the weight of his torso to try and break the chair.

Finally he heard the wood splinter, and the back of the chair fell away.

He was dripping with sweat, but almost there.

'Come on,' he muttered. Kassandra would be wondering where he was! He tried to bring his bound hands over the top of his head, but couldn't – not without dislocating his shoulder. Then he saw the candle burning on the table. Of course. With the base of the chair still attached to him, he dragged himself over to it.

With his back to the table, and craning behind him, he lowered his hands slowly above the candle. Straight away the rope started to blacken and give off a noxious smell. It sizzled a little, then gave way. Yes! Lysander immediately bent over to grapple with the knotted rope that tied his ankles.

He was free!

Pushing open the door, he peered into the alley. No sign of Tellios, his henchmen, or the man disguised as a Helot. Lysander headed back quickly into the bright street and found it eerily quiet. The fragments of the jar in the middle of the track were the only sign of his capture. Lysander suddenly felt dizzy and placed his fingers to the bridge of his nose. It gave a little from side to side – definitely broken.

He splashed some water from a nearby trough against his face, and washed away the blood that was already beginning to crust. Catching sight of his reflection in the rippling water, he saw a dark cut across his face, and managed a smile – just another war wound.

Lysander soon reached Sarpedon's villa. Outside, a cart was half-loaded with bolts of linen, and wooden crates. His footsteps slowed as he approached the doorway and a sense of unease washed over him. It was only three days since he'd last been here, and interrupted the *gerousia* – the Council of Elders – but already change was all around. No armed guard stood watch over the front gate, and Lysander walked through unhindered.

The courtyard was deserted, and Lysander remembered the many mornings he had come here to train as dawn broke, how Sarpedon had paced the mosaic floor, observing his stances and sword drills from every angle. The tiny tiles that were set painstakingly into the ground depicted two symmetrical horses' heads, one black, one white, facing each other. When Lysander had first come here, he thought nothing could match its beauty, but now the image seemed to be one of wretchedness and faded glory.

Half the colonnade that ringed the courtyard gleamed white in the afternoon sun. The other columns were buried in shadow. Lysander stood against the pillar where he and Kassandra had hidden to watch the Council debate. He remembered bursting with pride at Sarpedon's authority before his peers.

On one side of the courtyard, Lysander saw a spear resting against a column. The first time Lysander held an eight-footer had been right here, an exercise of strength and balance.

But Sarpedon would never teach Lysander again.

Lysander walked over and grasped the spear in his right hand, just back from its centre as his tutor had showed him, then assumed the position Sarpedon had taught him. Lifting his left leg to the horizontal behind him, he extended his right arm so the spear was vertical, its point a foot from the ground. He almost laughed – it was so easy now, but that first time he remembered it felt like his shoulder was being torn apart with hot irons.

'I thought you'd have had enough of weapons?' said a voice.

Lysander relaxed his posture and turned to see Kassandra standing under the portico that led to her chamber. She looked tired, with dark smudges beneath her eyes. For once she wasn't wearing an ornate dress, but instead a simple grey *peplos* – a draped tunic fastened at the shoulders and girdled at the waist. Her arms were bare and her hair was loose.

Lysander rested the spear back against the column and walked over to his cousin.

Her eyes widened as she looked into his face.

'That looks like a fresh wound. We parted just before dawn. You can't have managed any more battles between then and now.'

'Not quite a battle,' said Lysander. 'But . . .'

He paused. No good could come of involving Kassandra in his private struggles. Now he was closer he saw that her eyes were bloodshot as well. He took her hand. 'Enough of that. You summoned me.'

'Is that any way to greet your cousin?' she asked. She opened her arms, and Lysander embraced her. She squeezed him tightly, and he winced where she pressed against his rib. When she pulled back again, he could see fresh tears gathering in her eyes.

'The villa seems full of ghosts,' she said, looking about. 'Memories of Grandfather.'

'What will you do now?' Lysander gently asked. 'Is that why you summoned me? To talk about the future?'

'The future depends on you,' said Kassandra, as servants brought out a linen sack and placed it by Kassandra's feet. Lysander noticed two more carrying a chest between them under the colonnade, then out through the front gate. He recognised it from her bedchamber.

'What's going on? Wasn't that your dress box?' Alarm darted through him.

Helots scurried back in and Kassandra discreetly waited for them to disappear before continuing.

'I'm leaving,' she said. 'For my mother's family near Thalamae. There's nothing here for me now.' She turned as one of the Helots came out carrying a double candlestick.

'No, Hylas, leave that here.'

She walked towards the servant, but Lysander gripped her arm. 'What are you talking about? You can't leave. What about the villa?'

Kassandra shielded her eyes against the sun as she gazed at Lysander. It was impossible for him to see what expression lay there.

'This place, it belongs to you now. You're Grandfather's heir, Lysander. A male descendant always takes precedence over a female one. The lineage passes to you as Thorakis's first and only male child.'

Lysander released Kassandra's arm and snatched up the bag, shoving it into Hylas' grasp.

35

'Take this back where it belongs,' he ordered, then turned back to his cousin. 'Don't be foolish. Until this summer, Thorakis never had a son.'

'It's the Spartan way,' said Kassandra.

'You sound like one of them!' said Lysander, breaking away and pacing across the courtyard. His heart was in turmoil.

'I am one of *them*,' said Kassandra. 'And so are you. Accept it.'

Lysander lifted his hand to the sky.

'What will I do with a house like this — I have to train in the barracks.'

'It's not just the house,' laughed Kassandra. 'It's everything! The land, the wealth . . . even the Helots who live on his estates.'

'I don't want any slaves,' said Lysander, slamming his hand against a column. 'I could never treat anybody the same way I was treated.'

Kassandra approached and placed her hand on his shoulder.

'Don't you see?' she said. 'This is a chance to show the other Spartans that they don't have to be cruel to their slaves.'

Half a year ago, Lysander had been a slave in the fields without a possession to his name. Now he was richer than he had ever dreamt. But he'd lost everything that was precious. And now Kassandra was leaving him as well. He'd be alone, just another ant in the Spartan colony, expected to lay down his life for a system he could never wholly accept. He felt caught up in the whims of the Gods.

'But this is your home,' he said desperately. 'I'll give it to you.'

'You can't do that,' she said. 'Sarpedon would not have wished it.'

'Sarpedon's dead!' Lysander whispered, shrugging off her hand. 'He does not wish for anything.' He strode away, but then guilt plunged through him. None of this was Kassandra's fault.

He turned to look at his cousin; the only other person who could know how he was feeling. Her face had turned pale, and for a moment he thought she would cry. But then she held out a hand.

'Come with me,' she said. 'I need to show you something.'

Lysander followed her under the colonnade and into the room where he'd watched his mother die that summer. Now the bed had been pushed up against the far wall, and beneath the open shutters of the window, a tripod was set up. In its centre burned a shallow bowl of scented oil, releasing the smell of jasmine. Around the outside of the tripod, candles and various objects had been arranged by a caring hand.

'This was Grandfather's favourite room,' said Kassandra. 'I've gathered some of his possessions together, things that meant a great deal to him.'

Lysander went towards the shrine, and inspected the objects more closely. There was a soft woollen garment

37

that might have been a cloak.

'That's the gown our fathers were swaddled in as babies,' said Kassandra. 'It's made from Phoenician fleece. And that's his favourite drinking cup, and some of his vellum scrolls.'

Lysander ran his fingers over the smooth cured skin. Since his old tutor Anu had moved on to another barracks, Lysander hadn't had the chance to learn more reading and writing. *One day I'll read these things too*, he promised himself.

Kassandra crouched beside him and picked up a roll of leather held by a square gold ring. She spoke softly.

'Open it.'

Lysander slid the ring over the leather.

'What is it?'

'Hold out your hand.'

Lysander did as she asked, and Kassandra took the leather and unrolled it. A lock of brown hair, paler than his own, fell out into his palm.

'It belonged to Thorakis,' she said. 'Your father. I think Sarpedon would have wanted you to have it. I have one from my father, Demokrates.'

Lysander ran the hair through his fingers. He couldn't believe it belonged to the father he'd never met. Even after all this time, the shafts of hair were thick and strong, and caught the light like gold thread. Lysander looked forward to the day when he reached adulthood, and would be permitted to wear his hair long once again. Carefully, he rolled it back up inside the leather and replaced the ring.

'Thank you,' he said.

'I thought that you could leave the Fire of Ares here too,' said Kassandra. 'Just for the period of mourning. They say the dead in Hades can feel our kindnesses like sunshine on their faces.'

Lysander's hand went to his chest, then froze as memory pulsed through him. He'd given the family heirloom to Demaratos.

'What is it?' asked Kassandra.

'I don't have it,' Lysander admitted. Kassandra's eyes searched his face, confused. 'I gave it to Demaratos.'

'You did what?' Kassandra gasped, scrambling to her feet and staring down at him.

Lysander struggled to find the right words. How could he ever make her understand how he was feeling; his sense of dislocation and loss? Until he felt worthy again, how could he wear the jewel passed down his family, from one brave warrior to the next? Lysander didn't know if he was a brave warrior – he still didn't know *who* he was.

'Demaratos saved my life,' he said after a pause. 'It seemed the right thing to do. He'll look after it until –'

'It's an heirloom,' interrupted Kassandra, gathering her skirts around her and stepping away from him. 'It's been in the family for generations – how could you?'

She sat on the edge of the bed and buried her face in her hands. Her shoulders shook as she sobbed.

39

Lysander put his hand on her arm, but she pushed it away.

'Leave me alone,' she said. 'I want to be by myself.'

Lysander got to his feet.

'Kassandra, I . . .'

She leapt up, wiping her hands hastily on her gown. Her face was red and mottled, twisted with grief.

'Get out!' she hissed at him. 'How could you? Do you still know so little about our family?'

Lysander wanted to argue, but he could see how upset Kassandra already was. *I'll wait for her to calm down*, he thought, reluctantly walking towards the doorway. Pain twisted like a knife in his heart; he had never wanted to hurt his cousin. All he had been thinking about after the battle with the Persians was that his spirit felt too sullied to deserve the Fire of Ares; he had wanted to be rid of it. He would take it back when the time was right, but how did he explain that to Kassandra now?

As he made his way down a corridor back towards the courtyard, a slave approached. It was Hylas, one of the Helots who helped run Sarpedon's household.

'Master Lysander,' he said. 'There are visitors. I must announce them to the Lady of the house.'

Lysander pointed back towards the chamber. 'Kassandra is in there, but is not to be disturbed. I'll meet the guests.'

'Very well, master,' said Hylas, and led Lysander out into the courtyard.

Waiting for him was Tellios, flanked by two soldiers. He smiled, but Lysander could see the edge of cold in his eyes. The Ephor came forward. Speechless, Lysander took his hand.

'Greetings, you are Sarpedon's grandson, are you not?'

Clearly Lysander was to behave as though nothing had happened, even though his jaw still ached from the punch Tellios had given him earlier.

'I am,' said Lysander coolly. 'Kassandra is . . .'

'I'm here,' she said. Lysander turned to see her behind him. Her hair was tied back now, and her face composed. 'What can I do for you, Ephor?'

Tellios' smile reminded Lysander of a snake. 'Kassandra,' he said. 'I hope we are not intruding.'

'No, Ephor, but if you have come to pay respects to my grandfather, our family tomb is on the southern road.'

A muscle in Tellios' cheek twitched, but his smile did not falter.

'I come with regards to Sarpedon,' he said, 'but on a matter of business rather than mourning.'

'Very well,' said Kassandra. She clapped her hands, and Hylas appeared at one of the doorways. 'Hylas, some refreshments for our guests. Follow me, gentlemen.'

Lysander followed Tellios and the two soldiers to the dining room, where three couches were laid out around a low rectangular table. Tellios took one, his

41

soldiers standing guard either side of him. Lysander stood behind Kassandra, who seated herself opposite Tellios. Hylas entered with a tray of drinking cups and a jug of water with slices of lemon. He set it down upon the table and poured.

'As you know, Sarpedon died without a male heir,' Tellios began.

'What about Lysander?' Kassandra asked.

Lysander caught the flash of impatience that darted across the Ephor's face. 'His lineage has never been proved,' said Tellios. He didn't even look in Lysander's direction. 'And now all those who can attest it are dead. In whatever case, his "mothax" status – his impure blood – prohibits it.'

'He is stood before you,' said Kassandra evenly. Two red spots appeared on her cheeks. 'And unless you've forgotten, he just saved the whole of Sparta from the Persians.'

Lysander moved forward, but the two soldiers stepped together at once, both with hands on their swords.

'Do you defy the Council?' asked Tellios.

Lysander let his hands drop to his side.

'I defy nothing and no one,' Lysander said. 'You should know that, Tellios.' What was happening here? A sense of unease prickled beneath Lysander's skin.

'As I was saying,' said Tellios. 'Lysander was a bastard born of a Helot woman. No, in the absence of a male heir, the estate must pass to Kassandra . . .'

42

Kassandra gave Lysander a look of confusion.

'But,' continued Tellios, 'the management of such a large estate is clearly not the job of someone so young, so the Council has decreed that the estates must be placed in the hands of a guardian.'

Tellios gave the first genuine smile Lysander had ever seen from him.

'And that responsibility is mine.'

CHAPTER 4

Tellios watched them carefully. 'I take it there are no further objections to the Council's edicts?' His voice was rich with threat. Then he nodded to Kassandra and Lysander in turn. 'Good. I will leave you to mourn your grandfather.'

He marched from the room, his cloak sweeping the floor. The guards followed.

'What shall we do?' asked Lysander. He hadn't been sure about being the master of Helot slaves, but faced with Tellios tearing away his inheritance, disregarding the fact that he was of Sarpedon's blood . . . No! Lysander would not allow that to happen. He hadn't fought like this to be labelled *impure*. Not by someone like Tellios – not by anyone!

'There's nothing we can do,' Kassandra replied, looking down at her hands. 'If the Council has voted, the decision is final. And I'm too tired to fight.'

How could she be so defeatist? Lysander sprinted out of the dining room, almost colliding with Hylas on the way, and caught up with Tellios as he strode across the courtyard. Lysander snatched at his arm, and swivelled the Ephor around. The older man stumbled slightly.

'What in the name of Hades . . .'

The two soldiers brought down their spears at once, and in a heartbeat their points were pressed into Lysander's chest. One move, and their blades would slice through his flesh.

Tellios raised a hand to the men.

'There's no need for that.'

'He dares to lay his hand on an Ephor,' said one of the soldiers, curling his lip at Lysander.

'The boy isn't a threat,' said Tellios. 'And he's ignorant of Spartan ways. Leave us – I will see you outside.'

The soldiers lowered their spears and backed away.

Tellios waited until they had left, then turned to Lysander.

'Do you dispute the Council's authority on this matter?'

'Kassandra could manage the estates herself. You must be busy enough already with your Ephorate duties . . .'

Tellios raised his eyebrows. 'My Ephorate duties? You will make a fine orator one day, Lysander. But, you've misunderstood me. I am only Ephor until next summer. Sarpedon's land is vast and fertile. If I work the Helots to the bone, the estates will yield me great riches . . .'

'That wealth belongs to Kassandra!' hissed Lysander.

Tellios waved his hand through the air. 'She will have some, certainly. But with my overseers in place, and some *imaginative* counting, I can take enough to ensure a comfortable retirement. By the time Kassandra gains possession of the land, all it will be fit for is burying the slaves who've worked it.'

Lysander fought the urge to drive his fist into Tellios' face. He didn't care for a single Helot life.

'Why are you doing this?' Lysander asked quietly. A breeze rustled through the branches of a pine tree as he waited for an answer.

Tellios shrugged his shoulders, then looked around the courtyard with an appraising eye. 'I never did like your grandfather,' he admitted. 'He was so . . .' Tellios gazed up, searching for the right word, '*self-righteous.*'

'Sarpedon was as honourable as a Spartan can be.'

'He was trouble, and so are you. I'm glad to say that after some . . . persuasion . . . the Council agrees with me.'

'What do you mean?'

'Your days in Sparta will come to an end, Lysander. With your grandfather gone, the winds of power are shifting. Mark my words.'

Lysander watched him walk away; he knew if he moved he would throw himself at this man.

'Farewell, Lysander,' said Tellios. 'And remember our discussion from earlier. If I hear even a rumour that you've been opening your mouth about Vaumisa, it won't only be you who suffers.'

The Ephor walked through the gate and up along the track back towards the road. The soldiers followed, three red cloaks in convoy.

That man was Sarpedon's trusted comrade, Lysander thought bitterly. *How wrong could my grandfather have been?*

He turned back to the house, where he found Kassandra leaning on the couch. Her face was calm, her eyes dry.

'Curse Tellios,' he said. 'I could have taken one of those spears and driven it through his chest —'

'Oh, stop!' snapped Kassandra. She stood up and faced him, her eyes blazing. 'All you men ever talk about is fighting! Grandfather is dead — have you forgotten that?'

'Of course not,' said Lysander. 'I'm just tired of this Council of Elders which decides when we wake, when we eat, who we must obey . . . that Helots must die and even fellow Spartans be ground under foot.'

'No, you're not,' said Kassandra. 'You're angry because you've been passed over. You're angry because I've been given the estate.'

Lysander couldn't believe what his cousin was saying. He'd tried to defend her inheritance — for this? 'Don't be such a little fool,' he spat back. Instantly, he wanted to take the words back, but it was too late now.

Kassandra's face coloured. 'Get out of my house!' she said. 'Get out now! Hylas! Phrixus!'

From the kitchen came the rattle of utensils and

footsteps pattered down the hall.

'Fine,' said Lysander. 'I'm going. You can fight your own battles, *cousin.*' He swung his foot at one of the small plant vases that stood in the corner of the courtyard. It shattered into pieces, and clods of soil spattered Kassandra's tunic. Hylas and a larger man, whom Lysander guessed was Phrixus, hurried into the room, both wearing expressions of alarm.

'Just leave,' she sobbed, brushing the dirt from her skirts.

Before the servants could get near him, Lysander slipped out of the door that led into the courtyard.

He didn't look back.

The sound of grunts and the clash of wooden blades rang out as Lysander returned to the barracks. Had training begun again, so soon? Good. He entered by the front gate and went straight into the central yard.

The sun was dipping towards the horizon, but most of the yard was still bathed in light. The courtyard was filled with boys training, but there were fewer than before the battle. Some would be in the sanatorium in the village, but how many had died? Lysander's eyes darted around the courtyard as he counted. Ariston, Meleager, Hilarion, Cretheus, Euryalon . . . none of them had reached more than fourteen years.

He saw his friend Leonidas at one side of the arena, driving a spear into a bale of hay. The muscles on his arms bulged as he repeated the thrust again and again.

But another face caught his eye – an unfamiliar one. A man stood at the rear of the training ground, out of the sun against the dining hall wall. *He must be the new tutor*, thought Lysander. In the shade, his red cloak was dark. He was a little taller than Lysander, with hair the colour of sand, and a beard, almost white, thick but well trimmed. He was watching a row of four boys advance in a shield wall, lifting their shields in unison to thrust with their swords. The nearest to him was Drako, the biggest boy in Lysander's barracks, who Demaratos said was fathered by a Titan, one of the giants who ruled the Earth before the Gods of Mount Olympus.

As Drako came close, the instructor swept his leg out, toppling him into the dust of the courtyard. He fell badly and Lysander noticed bright red blood where he had cut his lip.

Drako looked up accusingly, but didn't say anything.

'It's no use having a strong shield arm, if you've no balance,' said the instructor. 'A soldier gets his strength from the ground up. Don't forget it.'

He caught sight of Lysander and shouted across the yard.

'Get over here!' Lysander approached, stepping past where Leonidas and Phemus had begun wrestling. He stopped ten paces from the stranger, who still hadn't stepped out into the sunlight. 'And who excused you from training?'

'I hadn't realised we'd been assigned a new instructor,' said Lysander.

'So you thought you'd leave the barracks without permission?'

'I've been at River's Rush,' said Lysander.

The Spartan burst out laughing, and stepped into the light, a hand shielding his eyes against the sun. Now Lysander could see that his hair wasn't sandy; it was white as snow. The tutor's skin was pale as well, as if covered in quarry dust.

'Did they need someone to clean their tables?' the tutor asked, looking Lysander over from head to foot.

Lysander forced himself to stay calm. 'I was invited to the feast,' he explained. 'My name is Lysander.'

A slight crease appeared in the Spartan's brow. 'The son of Thorakis?'

Lysander nodded.

'Well, well – the hero from the plains. Is it true that you killed the Persian general?'

Tellios' words rang through Lysander's head: *You never laid eyes on the general, Vaumisa.*

'It's exaggerated,' he said. 'We won the battle – that's all that matters.'

'A modest Spartan – your old tutor taught you well. My name is Aristodermus. The rest of you, take a break, drink some water.'

The boys congregated around the water bowls.

'Diokles never allowed us to drink during training,' said Lysander.

Aristodermus laughed. *Diokles didn't do much of that either*, thought Lysander.

'Forget Diokles,' he said. 'There's more than one way to train. Won't you take a drink?' asked Aristodermus.

'I have no need,' said Lysander.

'A child in the mould of Lykurgos . . .' said the tutor with a nod. 'They say as a baby he went without his mother's milk for three full days.'

'I'd rather train,' Lysander explained. There was so much to think about – too much. He'd prefer to lose all thoughts in the trials of physical training.

'Very well – why don't you show me what you're made of?' Aristodermus pointed into the centre of the yard, at an abandoned cart axle. The students used it for weightlifting. 'Start with that, let's see how many squats you can do.' He turned to the other boys. 'What's the record in the barracks?'

'Seventy-three,' called Tyro. 'Drako set the record, but he twisted his back so badly he was in bed for two days.'

'You couldn't manage twenty,' Drako sneered at the smaller boy.

'Seventy-four is the aim then,' said Aristodermus. 'If you fail the rest of the barracks will go without their meal.' A groan went round the courtyard. 'Is that *Spartan* enough for you, hero of the plains?'

Lysander walked to the axle. The wheels had been removed and large rocks tied on to each end with leather straps, where they swung loose. The exercise involved laying the bar over the shoulders and steadying it either side with a firm grip. If the squat was done properly, bending at the knees, the rocks should almost touch the ground on either side.

Lysander crouched and laid both hands on the axle, then hoisted it over his head, resting the worn wood across the back of his neck.

'Tyro,' said Aristodermus, 'you count.'

Lysander bent his knees and performed the first squat.

'One!' said Tyro.

Lysander repeated the action, allowing his breathing to guide the rhythm of the lifts. *Breathe in on the squat, out on the lift.*

'Two.'

In, out.

'Three.'

In, out.

By thirty, Lysander was starting to ache badly. At the bottom of each squat, his thighs burned, and he felt a twinge in his lower back with each rise.

'Halfway there,' said Aristodermus, as Tyro counted thirty-seven.

Lysander tried to shut out his voice and concentrate on the action. *Come on*, he told himself. *Do this!* He realised his hands were gripping the bar tightly, wasting energy, and he loosened them. He slackened his jaw as well, breathing in through his nose and out through his mouth.

'Fifty!' shouted Tyro. Lysander stopped at the top of a lift, and sucked in a deep breath then let it out again. He could feel his heart hammering in his chest, like a potter's foot on the wheel.

'Had enough?' said Aristodermus. Lysander arched his neck.

'I'm just . . . warming up,' he panted, managing a grin that turned into a grimace.

He lowered again. It felt like someone was driving red-hot pokers into his legs, and prising his knee caps with a chisel.

'Come on, Lysander!' said a couple of boys.

'You can do it!' said Phemus. 'Think of my dinner.'

Up again.

'Fifty-one!' The boys cheered.

Lysander took the lifts slowly, taking an extra breath each time he was upright. Nausea coiled in his belly, and he felt the sweat pouring down his face and back, tasted the salt on his lips. At sixty, his vision started to blur, and he clamped his eyes closed. His legs were trembling perilously at the bottom of every squat, and even upright he felt them shaking.

'Come on, Lysander!' shouted a voice he recognised. He opened his eyes. Leonidas! *Thank you*, Lysander mouthed to him.

'Sixty-eight!'

He could hear himself grunting in time with his squats. Deep, guttural, desperate sounds.

Lysander stumbled backwards on the lift, but he

steadied himself and straightened. Aristodermus grinned.

I'll show him.

'Sixty-nine!'

Lysander imagined he was back in the phalanx on the plains – imagined that each time he pushed, he was driving his spear into the shields of the Persian line.

'Seventy-one! . . . Seventy-two!'

'He's going to do it,' someone shouted. 'He's going to beat the record!'

'Seventy-three.'

Lysander dropped for the final squat. He couldn't feel his legs – it was just a leaden pain, like all his bones were being crushed. He tightened his grip on the bar, and imagined he was back on the prow of Vaumisa's ship, watching his grandfather plunge his sword into his own chest. He remembered Tellios calling his grand-father a coward and anger blazed through his limbs.

'Seventy-four!'

Lysander tipped sideways, and the axle slid helplessly from his sweat-soaked hands, crashing to the ground. Lysander fell to his knees, then forward on to his front. With his cheek in the earth, his broken nose throbbed as blood thundered through him.

The dinner bell rang.

'Clean yourself up,' said Aristodermus. Lysander watched the boys hurrying to the meal hall, each one clapping him on the shoulder as he went.

'Well done, Lysander.'

'Thanks, comrade.'

Leonidas slipped a hand under Lysander's armpit and helped him halfway up. Lysander waited for his head to stop spinning.

'Leave him be,' said Aristodermus. 'He asked for this treatment; let him deal with it alone.'

Perhaps this new tutor wasn't so different from Diokles.

Leonidas released Lysander's arm and, with a sympathetic look, followed the others inside.

Lysander staggered over to the well. With arms trembling, he pulled up a bucket and poured the ice-cold water over himself, relishing the sensation of the soothing water on his aching muscles. But his heart was still in turmoil. He allowed the bucket to clatter to the ground and turned round to survey the courtyard, leaning back against the well. *I've lost everything*, he told himself, thinking back to his argument with Kassandra. *Everything! The barracks will be my only home now until I'm thirty years old*. The years stretched ahead of him, seasons of relentless hardship and cruelty. What sort of man would he be when he finally left the barracks?

He felt a wave of sudden dizziness, and his skin turned cold. Fear gripped his throat like an invisible hand, choking him. He turned and rested his elbows against the rim of the well, staring into the blackness to prevent his head spinning. What was happening to him? He felt out of control, like a stone dropped into the abyss. He shut his eyes.

'I never asked for any of this,' he muttered to himself.

A sound rang out behind him.

Lysander turned. He saw a stocky boy, stumbling slowly towards him wearing a short tunic and immaculate red cloak. He leant heavily on a gnarled crutch, but when he looked up, Lysander recognised the face at once.

'Orpheus!'

He ran forward to support his friend. Orpheus was sweating from the effort of staying upright. In his other hand he was holding one of the wooden practice swords. Lysander's eyes fell to the wooden leg that emerged beneath his tunic. Orpheus' leg had been taken off below the knee by a Persian axe.

'Patched me up well, didn't they?' said Orpheus, knocking his sword against the false limb.

Lysander embraced his friend. 'I can't believe you're out of the infirmary already.'

'There are so many casualties,' said Orpheus, his face white and drawn. 'Only the most serious are kept in.'

'How did they . . . ?' Lysander looked down at the place where Orpheus's limb had once been.

Orpheus gave a shudder and looked away. 'You don't want to know,' he said eventually. 'I passed out with the pain. But they tell me I'm lucky to be alive. I'm back, now, for training.'

Lysander smiled and tried to ignore the prickles of doubt that crept through his body. Would the new tutor allow Orpheus to continue training with them? 'It's good to see you again,' he said, clapping his friend on the back.

Orpheus peered into the well.

'You look troubled, Lysander. What were you looking for down there – an oracle?'

Lysander laughed. 'Something like that,' he said. 'Answers, I suppose.'

'Well, the philosopher Thales thought that everything comes from water. But when Spartans want answers, they go to Delphi.'

'Of course!' said Lysander. He gazed up into the mountains. This was the inspiration he'd been looking for. The Delphic Oracle would be able to help him put to rest the demons tormenting his soul.

'Are you all right?'

'I am now,' said Lysander, pushing himself off the well. 'Let's get to dinner – there'll be nothing left but scraps.'

Orpheus shook his head and grinned, but Lysander's mind was racing.

That was it.

Delphi!

CHAPTER 5

'Someone needs to tell those Helots to use less vinegar,' said Prokles, pulling a face.

Lysander dunked his bread into the thick dark broth. It was made from pig's blood, but there was precious little meat in it. It was mostly plumped barley and a few figs. After the battle with the Persians, supplies in Sparta were running short.

'Apparently,' said a boy called Pelias, 'there was once a visitor from Athens. When he tasted the black broth, he said, "Now I know why you Spartans are willing to give your lives so easily on the battlefield – you won't have to eat this again."'

Laughter erupted along the table. Lysander smiled, but he didn't mind the taste. His thoughts were on the Oracle.

'Are you really going to ask?' said Orpheus. Lysander had whispered his plans to his friend between mouthfuls of food; the loud shouts and calls that rang around the dining hall meant they were in no danger of being overheard.

'I have to,' said Lysander. He glanced over at Aristodermus. He looked even more ghostly indoors, and his skin was pale as alabaster.

Will he let me leave the barracks? Lysander wondered. *Diokles would have said 'No' in an instant.*

'Good luck,' said Orpheus.

Leonidas leant over the table. 'What are you two whispering about?'

'I want to visit the Delphic Oracle,' said Lysander.

Leonidas raised his eyebrows in surprise. 'You'll need money,' he said.

'But it's a religious place, isn't it?' said Lysander.

Leonidas smiled. 'Even the Gods have palms that must be crossed.'

After the bowls had been cleared away and the rest of the boys had retired to the dormitory to polish their shields, Lysander went to Aristodermus' chamber. It had always been off-limits when Diokles inhabited it, but Lysander felt emboldened. If he didn't ask now, in private, the others were sure to find out. As he approached he heard words from within. Did Aristodermus have another visitor?

'Then said Achilles in his great grief:
I would die here and now,
for I could not save my comrade.'

Aristodermus' voice rose, and Lysander realised he was reciting poetry. The door was open a crack, and he peered inside. The tutor was sat at a table, lit by the

59

glow of a candle. His round shield lay face up, and Aristodermus was rubbing a pumice stone across its surface to remove scratches. It was a slave's work; why was he lowering himself to this task? Aristodermus continued.

'He has fallen far from home,
and in his hour of need I was not there.
What is there for me?
Return to my own land I shall not,
for I offered help not to Patroklus.'

Lysander knocked quietly.

'Enter,' said Aristodermus.

Lysander pushed open the door and walked inside. He was surprised that the room was much like where he slept in the dormitory. Sparsely furnished, with an oak chest, and a bed of blankets over dried rushes from the river. A collection of small statuettes stood around a wine bowl, with some pieces of pottery carved with symbols representing the Gods.

'Why aren't you tending your arms with the others?'

'I am seeking permission to speak with you,' said Lysander. 'About . . .' He searched for the words and cursed himself. *You should have rehearsed this, you fool.*

'Close the door behind you.'

Lysander did as he was asked, then stood awkwardly. How could he explain his reasoning? Would Aristodermus think less of him?

'You must have heard me speaking Homer's verses.' The words weren't a question.

'I heard something.'

'They are about the great warrior Achilles, son of the Goddess Thetis. Did you know, he didn't fight at all for the first nine years of the war? Refused to, and sat in his tent.'

'Was he a coward?' Lysander asked. *Why is he telling me this?* he wondered.

Aristodermus chuckled. 'No, he had an argument with the Greek commander – about a girl, can you believe? His pride prevented him fighting. But not for ever.'

'What happened?' asked Lysander.

'His friend, Patroklus, was killed. He knew then it was time to put his stubbornness aside and take to the battlefield. What brings you here?'

'I'd like to visit the Oracle at Delphi,' Lysander blurted out.

To his surprise, Aristodermus didn't laugh, or tell him to get out, but gestured with his hand to sit on a stool.

'Take a seat, Lysander. Explain yourself.'

Lysander's heart was thumping under his ribs. He sat opposite the tutor, but couldn't look him in the eye. What was he thinking? A boy asking to be excused from training to consult with the Gods! Who did he think he was? His cheeks felt like they were aflame.

'I . . . I . . .' The pressure inside his head was building and the sense of panic from earlier returned. He had to get out! Lysander tried to stand, but a wave of dizziness made him fall sideways, and he staggered against the wall of the chamber.

'What's the matter?' came Aristodermus' voice. 'Are you injured?'

Lysander shook his head. His vision blurred in and out of focus. He felt an arm guiding him back to his seat. 'Sit down. Drink some water. Take your time.'

A cup was placed in his hand, and Lysander swallowed a long draught.

While he waited for his breathing to return to normal, Aristodermus took a cloth and began polishing the dull surface of the shield.

Without looking up, Aristodermus began to talk. 'Tell me,' he said. 'Does this illness have something to do with your wish to visit the Oracle?'

'Ever since the battle . . . Since my grandfather . . .' Lysander began to reply.

'I know of Sarpedon's death,' said Aristodermus. 'He is a loss to Sparta.'

'I don't know my place any more. It feels like the world is dark, that I'm alone . . . I feel myself panicking, and suddenly I can't breathe. I've searched my heart, but can't find the answers there. The Oracle is my last hope.'

Aristodermus watched his face intently, then gave a small nod. 'It sounds as though you know what must be done.'

'So I may go?'

'You may leave at dawn,' said Aristodermus. 'I hope the Pythia gives you the answers you're looking for.'

Aristodermus' skin looked pale as the moon in the black sky. The flickering candle flame caught a pink tinge in his eyes. Lysander had never seen a man like him.

'You're wondering how I've survived, aren't you?' said the tutor. 'Looking like this.'

Lysander nodded.

'I was almost abandoned as a baby,' said Aristodermus. 'My mother thought I was cursed. But my father had waited so long for a boy child, he trained me himself within the walls of the house – made sure I was strong before I entered the agoge. I was bullied by the others, but I let it fuel my training. It's a case of adapting. My skin burns easily in the sunlight, so I train at dawn and at night. I keep in the shade when I can, and rarely remove my cloak in the day. You'd do well to remember the same, Lysander. Rest when you can. Fight when you have to. The Gods will take you when they want.'

Lysander smiled. 'It wasn't like that under Diokles. He used to say there was time to rest when you're dead.'

Aristodermus snorted. 'And do you believe that?'

'But that's all we've been taught to do,' said Lysander. 'The Spartan system relies on it.'

'Times change, Lysander. Despite what the old men would have you believe, nothing stays the same for ever. It's all very well following the strictures of Lykurgos, but our population is shrinking. One day we'll have to let the free-dwellers fight alongside us. Perhaps even the Helots . . .'

Lysander gasped.

'Just remember, I know what it's like to be different. Now, go.'

Lysander lay down on his bed. Some of the other boys were already asleep, but Leonidas called over quietly.

'What did he say?'

'He said I could go.'

Leonidas let out a low whistle. 'Do you know the way?'

Lysander shook his head.

'It's easy enough. Follow the northern road through Argos, and on to Corinth. Then take the road to Delphi along the northern shore of the Gulf. It's a long way, four or five days on foot.'

'I'm in no hurry,' said Lysander. 'I need to be away from Sparta for a while. I feel . . . suffocated here.'

Leonidas reached into the chest next to his bed.

'Remember, Lysander. At Delphi the Gods don't talk straight.' He threw something that landed with a clang of metal on Lysander's bed. It was a small bag tied with a leather cord.

'What's this?' he whispered, weighing it in his hand. 'Iron?'

'Better,' said Leonidas. 'Money — *drachma*.'

Lysander tipped the rough discs of metal into his hands. He'd never seen coins before — what use were they in Sparta, where iron bars were currency? But he'd heard the boys talk about them. In the dim light, he inspected one. A picture of an owl had been hammered into the surface. The other side showed a woman wearing a helmet.

'Where are they from?'

'Don't worry about that,' said Leonidas.

Lysander slipped the coins back into the pouch and placed them under his blanket. Leonidas's father was a king, so perhaps these were from the treasury.

'Thanks,' said Lysander, but Leonidas was already asleep – his breathing had become shallow and measured.

Lysander woke early, and fastened his travelling cloak – a brown one – in the darkness of the dormitory. He took his sack, and stuffed the blanket inside. Something glinted in the darkness by his folded clothes. The gold ring enclosing the lock of his father's hair. Lysander snatched it up and placed it into his sack as well. He'd need all the good omens he could get.

Pausing at the barracks door, he looked back over the bodies of his sleeping comrades. Would he ever really be one of them? Did any of them suffer the same doubts he did? Perhaps the Oracle could tell him.

Outside, he made his way quickly through the town, only stopping to buy a loaf. He descended into the centre of Limnae, where he saw the occasional Helot trudging between errands. He fought the urge to tear off chunks of warm bread; he'd need to ration himself. For a moment, he considered taking the road up to Kassandra's villa. He could see now how foolish their argument had been. Their grief, and Tellios' power games, had sown the seeds of doubt in their minds, turned them against one another. But what if she was still angry with him? She'd be asleep at this hour, surely.

He took the left fork northwards along the banks of the Eurotas. The water was deep here, and swept along quickly. On the far bank, a heron stood sentinel, still as a statue.

The cold air was refreshing in Lysander's lungs, and he walked quickly around the northern edge of Pitane, leaving the low rise of the acropolis behind him. Soon the morning sun rose above the mountains, and warmed his right side. He chewed on the bread, and swallowed some water from his flask.

Gradually the houses gave way to the farmlands north of Sparta. Huge fields stretched out either side of the river, with only the occasional stone equipment store, or shepherd's hut to break the expanse. Beyond the fields, mountains rose up, cupping the wide valley. Lysander knew from his Ordeal with Demaratos how wild and inhospitable those lands could be. It was no wonder foreign invaders had not encroached their territory for hundreds of years. The hills enclosed Sparta on three sides. The fourth edge of their territory bordered the sea. Only an audacious, and cleverly planned assault, would stand a chance.

But that was what Vaumisa had done, and it had taken the lives of thousands to drive him back. Sarpedon was not the only man who had died.

It must have been between dawn and midday when the first people crossed his path. It was a band of Helots being led by an overseer. From his own days working on the land, Lysander knew that the winter months were quiet, but hard. With little to do other than prune the fruit trees, harvest the crops of winter vegetables and repair equipment, everything fitted easily into the meagre daylight hours. But it was back-breaking work, bending and lifting, and many times he had gone to bed aching. Firewood was always a luxury, and he remembered seeing his mother's lips turn blue with cold in their ramshackle hut.

The grey-faced Helots trudged past him in two columns. Lysander passed the overseer at the rear of the group. He carried no whip on his belt, as Lysander's former gang boss had done, but the long staff in his hand had most likely landed across the backs, or the legs, of his charges in the past.

'May the Twin Gods be with you,' the overseer grumbled in greeting without breaking his stride.

Lysander couldn't help his darkening mood. Tellios' words had left no doubt that the Helots in his charge would suffer. Mistreatment – beatings, starvation, cold – would be commonplace. And there was nothing he could do.

★　★　★

Lysander walked late into the night, chasing fatigue in order to banish those images that still haunted him: Timeon's pale body under his shroud, his mother Athenasia being lowered into her grave, Sarpedon's twisted features as he drove a sword into his own chest.

Ghosts of the past, thought Lysander, as he marched along the track. *Will I ever be free?*

He slept in a pine forest on a soft cushion of fallen needles. In the stillness every sound seemed swallowed by the spaces between the conifers. Using the sun as his guide at dawn he continued north, following the river's course along the valley, and passing by several small settlements, though none were as extensive as the five villages of Sparta.

The land rose, and eventually he left the river along one of the tributaries. He began to see more people on the paths, other travellers like himself. Many eyed him with suspicion, no doubt fearful of thieves in the wild places, but Lysander was happy to run past them. He found the only way he could clear his mind was to push his body as hard as he could. Blisters stung his feet, but soon that discomfort died. Lysander took off his sandals, and marched barefoot across the rocky path, relishing the pain. As the night drew in, he walked on through the cold until his sinews burned, then collapsed by the track, exhausted.

On the third morning, he woke to dew on his face. He tried to eat some bread, but it had turned almost solid. He washed down a few mouthfuls with rank-tasting water, and continued on his way. Soon after dawn, he came upon a merchant guiding a low wagon, drawn by a single mule. Lysander had no intention of stopping to speak, but as he tried to pass by, rounding the wagon above the path, he tripped and fell, scraping his arms as he put out his hands to break his fall.

'Curse Hades!' he said.

'Whoa!' said the merchant, bringing his mule to a halt with a tug on the long reins.

Lysander dusted down his tunic.

'Are you hurt?' asked the merchant.

'I'm fine,' said Lysander, reaching to pick up his sack.

'Where are you in such a rush to get to?'

'Delphi.'

The merchant looked puzzled. 'Then you're going the wrong way, my boy,' he said.

Lysander frowned. 'But I was told that Corinth was the quickest route.'

'Not in these times. The Nemeans and the Athenians are warring again.'

'Then which way?' asked Lysander.

'My advice is to stay north-west,' said the man. 'Take the mountain tracks through Arcadia, across the Ceryneian plains, and into Achaea, then on to Agion. You can catch a boat across the water there. It'll be no slower, though you'll need money for the ferrymen.'

'Thank you,' said Lysander.

'Why not hop on board the wagon? I'm only going as far as the junction to Elis, but you can ride until

69

then,' said the stranger. Lysander looked at his dirt-stained clothes, and the new scrapes down his arms. He didn't deserve help.

'I prefer to make my own way,' he said.

'With an attitude like that, you belong at Sparta.' The merchant chuckled to himself and, with a crack of his whip, the wagon pulled away, leaving Lysander alone once more.

He passed a junction, at the lower end of a rocky gorge. A small shrine to Zeus, no more than a cairn of rocks marked with the God's name, stood at the cross-roads. Shards of pottery painted with votive messages stood around the base, and Lysander inspected one. 'Kamelos, son of Korinth, prays for the Thunder-God's Blessings in the javelin at Olympia.'

This must be the route to Elis, Lysander realised. The Olympic Games were held every four years in that region. He wondered if Kamelos' prayers had been answered. He had always doubted the Gods, despite his mother's warnings. What had they ever done for her, or him? She had died young from the coughing sickness, brought on by long hours tending the Spartans' crops. Lysander swallowed back the sorrow that tightened in his throat. No, now he had to trust the Gods; there was no one else left to turn to.

Lysander placed the tablet back carefully. But as he straightened up he felt the hairs stiffen on the back of his neck as a scream sliced through the air.

CHAPTER 6

Breaking into a run, Lysander darted off the path and climbed, hand over hand, up the ravine. He had to get to a higher vantage point.

He didn't have to go far. Below, some two hundred paces distant, were three men. One was seated on a horse, and the other two were rifling through a leather bag.

But his eye was drawn by the young woman who stood between the men, loosely holding the reins of her horse. She must have been sixteen or seventeen, with red hair. Lysander had never seen anyone with such flaming locks before. She screamed again.

'Get away from me, sons of Dis,' she shouted.

Lysander edged along the top of the ridge in a crouch, keeping out of sight. One of the men, small and wiry with a narrow face like a weasel, approached the girl and said something. She slapped him across the face. The sound echoed off the rocks like a whipcrack. The man staggered backwards, but his long-haired friend shoved the woman.

She fell to the ground. 'Cowards!' she spat, as she pushed her hair back out of her face.

The man who'd pushed her jumped into her horse's saddle, and tightened the reins.

Lysander reached for his sling. He was directly above now, maybe fifty paces away. Too far to hit a man accurately, and besides, there were three of them, all armed with daggers and maybe worse.

But perhaps I don't need to fight them all.

The third man, wearing a thick leather belt, climbed off his horse and stood over the girl.

Lysander slipped a sizeable pebble into the pouch of his sling, and began to swing it above his head.

Weasel-face grabbed the girl's legs, holding them together while the man on the girl's horse looped a rope. She struggled, beating her attackers with her fists, but they laughed as her hands bounced uselessly off their bodies.

Lysander released the sling and the pebble shot out. It fizzed through the air and smacked into the rump of the girl's horse. It gave a terrified whinny and reared, kicking the man wearing the belt in the neck. The rider cried out as he was hurled off the horse's back, landing heavily among the rocks. Weasel-face received a kick in the jaw and stumbled to one side. The robbers' abandoned horse gave a whicker of fear and cantered off down the dusty path.

Lysander dumped his sack and scrambled down the

slope. He grabbed a rock and charged forward. The fallen rider was back on his feet and spun round at the sound of Lysander's approach.

'Get away from her!' Lysander shouted, smashing the rock into the man's temple. He watched the man crumple at his feet. The young woman was trying to untie the ropes at her feet, and staring at Lysander in astonishment. Her horse was still bucking wildly and whinnying in pain.

The rope snapped in the girl's hands and she ducked under the horse's thrashing hooves to seize the reins. Weasel-face took one look at his fallen accomplices, turned on his heel and ran.

'Watch my horse!' the girl said, thrusting the reins into Lysander's grasp. She rescued a discarded dagger from the ground.

'Where are you going?' said Lysander.

But she was already sprinting after the bandit.

By the Gods, she's fast, thought Lysander.

The girl seemed to glide fluidly over the path. Lysander doubted whether he'd have been able to keep up. She caught the man after about seventy paces and heaved the dagger down between his shoulder blades. He careered into the ground, and she leapt on his back. Lysander saw her hand rise and fall a couple of times, then she wiped the blade clean and walked casually back. A thin streak of blood stained her cheek.

'You were quick as a fox,' said Lysander.

'Never seen a girl who can run?' she said, stroking

the horse's nose. 'There, there, Hector,' she soothed. 'What made you start?'

'I'm afraid that may have been my fault,' admitted Lysander, holding up his sling.

'Do you make a habit of attacking defenceless animals?' she asked, her eyes sparking. Her hair, up close, was like burnished bronze.

'I thought . . .'

'Don't worry,' she said. 'We've all had enough upset for one day. He's a tough old thing, aren't you, Hector? I'm Chilonis. Thanks for your help. I couldn't have fought them off alone.' Lysander could see that the girl was more upset than she wanted to admit.

Lysander peered down at the man who'd taken a hoof to the neck. He was unmoving, his head twisted at an unnatural angle.

'I'm Lysander,' he said. 'I think you probably could have defended yourself without my help, if you'd had to. But thank the Gods, I happened to be passing.'

'No. Thank *you*, Lysander. They were trying to rob me of my horse. Where are you heading?'

'To Delphi.'

'The Oracle?'

'Yes.' *Please don't ask me why*, he prayed.

'Me too,' she said. 'Where are you from?'

'Sparta.'

Her eyes widened, then narrowed with suspicion. 'You look like you make a habit of fighting – is your nose broken?'

Lysander smiled and nodded. 'It was an accident. I ran into someone on the street.' He had no wish to burden this stranger with his tales of the Krypteia.

'From the way you handled that sling, I wouldn't have taken you for the clumsy sort,' his new friend said.

Lysander laughed. 'What about you?'

'Argos,' she said. 'We should travel the rest of the way together. I hear there's a boat from Agion.'

Lysander had never met a girl like Chilonis before. She was so forthright, it was hard to disagree with her.

'Come on,' she said. 'If we hurry we'll make it before nightfall.'

Leaving the bodies of the bandits where they lay, Chilonis took hold of her horse's reins, and she and Lysander walked side by side along the path. The rocky gorge descended into a wide plain of rich farmland.

'The plains of Ceryneia,' Chilonis commented. After a moment's silence, she glanced over at Lysander. 'Why are you travelling on your own?' she asked, leading Hector through a shallow ford. 'Where's your father?'

'He died before I was born,' said Lysander, splashing beside her.

'I'm sorry,' said Chilonis. 'What about your mother?'

Hector had dipped his head to drink midstream.

'She's dead too — half a year ago.'

'I should stop asking questions,' she said. 'I don't seem to be doing very well.'

They continued along the path, which had turned

muddy where a minor tributary had overflowed its banks. Hundreds of footsteps marked the way – it was a popular route.

'Don't worry. What about you?'

Chilonis sighed. 'I ran away.'

'Why?'

'I fell out with my father. He's stubborn as an ass. He gets angry because I want to do things my own way.'

Lysander had to turn away so she wouldn't see his smile. *Stubbornness must run in her family*, he thought.

'Like what?'

'I want to be an athlete – to compete in the women's Games at Olympia.'

'*Women's* Games?' Lysander had thought the Games, held every four years, were only for men.

'Yes,' said Chilonis. 'The Elian Council have voted to allow the festival of Hera to fall in the period of the Olympic Truce.'

'You're certainly faster than any girl I've ever seen,' said Lysander. 'Faster than most boys too.'

'That's what I told my father,' she said. 'But he says running is not for women. He doesn't want his daughter growing up to be a "Spartan thigh-flasher".'

Lysander laughed. It was true that many Spartan women trained like men, and wore tunics with slits up the side for ease of movement.

'So why are you going to the Oracle?' he asked.

'My aunt suggested it,' she replied. 'She said the Oracle would be able to advise me on the correct course to take. But my father said the Oracle was a waste of time – "prophecy at a price", he calls it. So I packed some things, took Hector from the stable, and came anyway.'

They walked in silence for some way.

'Will your father be angry?' Lysander asked eventually.

'For a while, I suppose. But he'll forgive me in the end. Anyway, what about you?'

Lysander shrugged. There was something so open about Chilonis that he didn't feel the need to hide anything from her.

'I don't really know,' he said. 'I suppose I want to find out what I should do next.'

'Isn't there anyone you could talk to in your home-land? Who do you most admire?'

'My grandfather,' said Lysander, without thinking. 'He was the bravest man I ever knew. If I could be half the man he was . . .'

'Is he dead too?' asked Chilonis.

'We burned his body a few days ago.'

'I'm sorry for your loss,' she said, reaching out to rest a hand on his arm.

'Don't be,' said Lysander. 'It's my fault he's gone.'

They reached a spring, gurgling up from the mossy ground at the edge of the path. Chilonis reached down to fill her flask.

'I remember when my great-grandmother died,' she said. 'She was old – in her seventies. She was known all over the city for her knowledge of herbs and medicines, and for helping bring forth children. Even the rich men would come to our father's house when their daughters were with child. But even with my grandmother's skill, there would be complications from time to time. She always said the worst was when the mother died during the birth. She'd leave the birthing hut, and pass the screaming newborn to its expectant father. Often he could tell from her eyes that his wife was dead, but she always used the same words of comfort: "Honour the dead by caring for the living".'

'She sounds like a good woman,' said Lysander as they set off again. He couldn't be sure, but he felt that Chilonis had tried to help his tortured heart in the only small way she could. By sharing experiences.

They reached Agion late in the afternoon. It was little more than a collection of fishing boats and small houses clustered by the water. The sun, dipping to the west, cast a trail of golden fire over the water. One man was unpacking the tackle from his boat on a narrow jetty.

'We need to get over to Delphi,' said Chilonis. 'Can you take us?'

'Not I,' said the man. 'It's late for setting out now. You'd be best to wait for morning.'

'Is there no one who might cross this evening?' Lysander pressed. Now he was so close, he didn't want to wait to speak to the Oracle.

The man stroked his beard. 'There's old Ankises,' he said. 'He knows these waters well. Lives in a hut four or five stadia up the shore. Try there.'

Chilonis thanked the man and they followed his directions.

'Slow down,' said Chilonis, as Lysander marched off along the shoreline path. 'If he's in, he's not going anywhere.'

Ankises' cottage came into sight. Lysander ran up to the door and pounded it with his fist. There was no sound of movement within. Lysander hammered again, and the door creaked open to reveal a tall, lean man who looked older than anyone Lysander had ever seen. Deep wrinkles were carved into his cheeks and forehead, and his big hands were knotted like the roots of a tree.

'Yes?' he said.

'We were told you might be able to take us across to Delphi,' said Lysander. 'Tonight.'

'Tonight's a night for staying indoors by the fire,' said Ankises.

'We have money,' said Lysander, pulling his coins from the pouch.

The door shut in his face.

'Charming,' said Chilonis. 'Come on, let's head back to Agion.' They turned to leave.

'Where are you going?' asked a voice. Lysander glanced over his shoulder. The old man was stood beside the hut, dressed in a hooded cloak. 'You can tie your horse up behind the house. I'll feed him on my return.'

Lysander smiled at Chilonis, who led Hector to the rear of Ankises' hut.

They followed the old man down to the water, where a small rowing boat was moored. Ankises climbed in, surprisingly agile for such an elderly man.

'Come on then,' he muttered. 'The sooner you get there, the sooner the Oracle can give you a confusing and costly answer.' He laughed.

Chilonis climbed aboard, and Lysander unlooped the boat's tether from its post on the shore. As he settled beside her on the wooden plank that served as a seat, he began to doubt his mission. If the Oracle didn't give him an answer he could understand, would he ever find peace within himself? Hadn't that been his mistake before? He'd blindly trusted the prophecy on the Fire of Ares, and so far it had brought only hardship and suffering to those he loved most dearly.

Ankises pushed the boat off with one of the oars, then pulled in long strokes away from the shore.

It was the middle of the night when they reached the far shore, and Lysander paid Ankises his fee. As they stepped off the boat, the old man began rowing back towards his home.

'Don't you need to rest?' called out Chilonis.

Ankises laughed. 'I'm eighty-eight years old. Soon I'll have a very long rest indeed.'

Lysander watched as the oarsman was swallowed up by the darkness. Then he turned inland.

Is this where I'll find my life again? he wondered. *If the Gods are here, will they guide me?*

Most of the small hamlet was asleep. The only sound above the lapping of the waves on the shore was the whirr of the cicadas, trilling out their midnight song.

'Dawn won't be long coming. We may as well sleep on the shore,' said Lysander.

'You can,' said Chilonis. 'But I'm going there.' She pointed to a house where a light still glowed. A sign was painted over the door. 'It says they have rooms to let.'

Lysander tried to work out how the letters fitted together, but his brain was tired.

The innkeeper asked no questions when Chilonis said they were brother and sister. Lysander was too tired to say a word. She showed them to a bed of straw in the stables and gave them some stale bread and cold stew. After they'd eaten, Lysander lay back in the straw and listened to the scurry of mice.

He longed for sleep to overcome him. Finally, out of the darkness, Chilonis spoke.

'Lysander, about your grandfather. I'm sure you aren't truly to blame.'

Lysander fought against the images that came into his mind – Sarpedon, plunging the sword into his own chest. Lying pale-faced on the deck of Vaumisa's ship. His body on the pyre.

'You don't know what happened.'

'My great-grandmother always said that the Fates take you when it's your time. They spin your life on a thread and snip it when the Gods command. Your heart stops when the scissors close.'

Lysander fought against tears in the gloom.

'I think they might already have come for me,' he said. 'There's nothing left in my heart.'

Chilonis edged closer to him, and he felt her warm palm rest over his chest, where the Fire of Ares used to lie.

'You still have a heart, Lysander. Don't wait for the Fates to decide your future, seek it out for yourself. What's past has gone. Your grandfather wouldn't want you to stop living just because he has.'

Lysander was grateful for Chilonis' words, but he couldn't help pushing her hand away and rolling over on to his side. He stared out into the darkness. Beyond the walls of the stable lay the hills where he would find the Oracle and beg for help. *No, not beg*, he thought to himself. *I'll have to pay her*. Was the boatman right? Was he being a fool, looking for consolation amongst the hills? Lysander had no way of knowing. All he knew and felt was the ache in his heart that had not gone away since the death of his grandfather.

I have to do something, he thought, as he closed his eyes. *I have to hope.*

Right now, hope was all he had left.

CHAPTER 7

'Get in line!' shouted the attendant priest. To Lysander he looked more like a soldier, with broad shoulders and arms thick as saplings. 'Your time with the Oracle will come soon enough. Form a queue.'

'What a thug,' said Chilonis.

A chill wind rustled the leaves of the trees as they joined the line of supplicants. Evidently, Lysander and his new friend weren't the only people keen to see the Oracle. Despite their boat ride through the night, crowds had already been thronging the hills when they'd arrived. Now, the colours of the morning were muted, as though Aphrodite, Goddess of Love, had left a veil draped over the mountainside. In front of Lysander was an elderly couple – from their rough sheepskin shawls, Lysander guessed they were farmers, shepherds perhaps. They stood in silence, leaning on each other like the collapsed columns of a ruined temple.

'Don't worry,' whispered the woman. 'We'll find the

answers we're looking for.'

He wondered what they needed to see the Oracle for. Had they lost something precious? Had their meagre crops failed, leaving them starving and without hope?

Bleating cut through the silence, and Lysander turned to see another attendant dragging a black ram on a thin cord. The animal's hooves skittered on the rocky path and it strained against the tether, eyes rolling back in its head.

'Perhaps it knows what's coming,' whispered Chilonis.

The attendant stopped by the spring pool and was joined by his companion. Together they manhandled the ram on to a flat rock by the water's edge. The crowd watched with morbid interest. From a wicker scabbard, the attendant drew a slightly curved knife with a handle that glinted with polished bronze. He held it on his extended palms and lifted his face up to the mountain.

'Apollo, Bow–Bearer, Bringer of the Sun, bless those mortals in your service and bestow the gift of Fore-sight. Be true in your guidance.'

The attendant's voice was monotone, as though he'd performed the rites on countless mornings such as this. While his companion sat astride the ram and held its head steady, the attendant slipped the knife beneath the creature's throat and gave an upwards sawing motion. The ram struggled, but was trapped firmly in position. Blood spattered out on to the rocks and into the water below, tingeing the spring pink. The crowd watched in silence, some nodding their approval of the sacrifice, as though it were proof of the God's blessing. As the ram's shudders grew weaker, the attendant loosed his grip and let the dying animal collapse on its side, forelegs quivering. The last trickles of blood pooled in the water, and the eyes stopped moving in the head. Lysander turned away, bile rising up into his mouth.

'Are you all right?' asked Chilonis.

Lysander nodded. *What's wrong with me*, he thought, *I've seen death countless times.*

'The sacrifice is complete,' said the attendant, climbing to his feet. He wiped a blood-smeared hand across his shabby robe. He pointed to the first person in the queue, a pregnant young woman. 'You,' he said. 'You may go up.'

Accompanied by the attendant, and clutching her rounded belly, the woman set off up the roughly cut rocky steps. Lysander watched as she disappeared around the edge of a bush. The sky above had turned the colour of lead.

The elderly couple, tired of standing, were sitting down by the time the young lady returned. She smiled briefly as she passed Lysander, but he couldn't tell whether the look was one of happiness or sadness. The old man helped his wife to her feet, and together they ventured up the path. Chilonis leant against the trunk of an olive tree, but Lysander was so full of nerves, he couldn't rest.

What did the Oracle hold? What if his questions weren't answered?

'I wish they'd hurry up,' he said.

'I'd come under here, if I were you,' she said. 'It's sure to rain soon.'

She was eating some cheese and dried figs she'd bought from a vendor back in the hamlet. 'Do you want some of these?' she asked.

Lysander shook his head, staring up the path. 'What's taking so long?' he said. The clouds had thickened more, and were turning black like a bruise.

'The Gods don't keep time the same way as us,' laughed Chilonis.

When his turn finally came, Lysander followed the attendant up the winding track. Fat drops of rain splashed on his face and on the path, but he hardly noticed them. This was it – the time had come. He calculated that they must have climbed another five hundred feet, along a tree-lined path. No wonder the attendant had such sturdy legs – when Lysander emerged from the trees, his calves were burning and his chest rose and fell sharply. The wind was whistling at this height, and snatched at his damp cloak.

'Mind your step,' advised the man, as the path levelled off. Lysander's breath caught in his throat as he peered down the mountain. The path skirted the hillside and the drop beyond was sheer – bare rock giving way to trees and then finally fields. The gulf water lay beyond, black and still in the cold day. A fine curtain of rain misted the sky. Lysander felt his head swim, and backed away from the edge.

The attendant stopped ahead, and turned to face Lysander.

'We're here,' he said, holding out his palm. He gazed expectantly. When Lysander didn't do anything, he took a menacing step forwards, forcing Lysander close to the cliff edge.

Understanding dawned. He pulled out a coin from his pouch, and dropped it into the man's hand. He fixed Lysander with a stare.

'You insult Apollo?'

Lysander handed over another coin.

The man's face didn't shift, so he paid a third coin. 'Is that enough?'

The attendant grinned. 'Most generous, boy. I'm sure the Gods will be the same.'

Lysander felt his doubts grow again. If prophecies were for sale to the highest bidder, could he even trust what he was told? He'd have to hope that the Oracle itself wasn't as corrupt as those that served it.

'This way,' said his guide, with an elaborate sweep of the hand. Lysander saw only a wall of solid rock.

'Where to?'

But as he took a few more steps, he saw an opening in the rock face, a cave gaping black like a missing tooth in some Titan's head. A dim light flickered within.

'Go on, then,' said the voice behind him, and

Lysander felt a hand prod him in the back. He stooped under the overhang and stepped inside.

It took a few moments for his eyes to adjust to the darkness, but eventually he could make out a tripod stood over a small fire. Balanced over the flames was a round-bottomed cauldron billowing smoke. The cave smelled of burnt laurel wood and perfumed incense.

Two attendants with shaven heads, and wearing ghostly white robes, stood beside the fire. In the recesses of the lair, something moved, detaching itself from the wall. It was a woman, tall and thin like the twisted trunk of an olive tree. The Pythia – named after a beast the God Apollo was supposed to have wrestled in this very spot. With rasping breaths, she took her place on a tall three-legged stool in front of the fire. Her hair was dark as a raven's wing. With a movement like a willow in the breeze, she lifted a bony hand and pushed the locks from her face. Lysander noticed the dirt beneath her nails. He shivered as her eyes bored into him.

'Kneel before the Pythia,' said one of the attendants.

Lysander sank to the floor, and listened as her breath became less laboured. The wind whistled outside the cave. One of the attendants stepped into a recess in the shadows and came forward with some more firewood. He dropped it under the cauldron and a shower of sparks burst upwards, spinning into the darkness.

'What would you ask the God?' said the woman, in a cracked, quiet voice.

What *did* he want to know? He suddenly felt

foolish. He wasn't here like the others: he didn't need to ensure his child grew up healthy, or ask what crops to plant that year. He wanted the answer to his whole life; why he, a Helot in the fields, had been chosen by the Fates to become something he hated — an oppressor, a soldier, a Spartan.

'There are others waiting,' said one of the attendants. 'Apollo cannot read your thoughts.'

Lysander remembered his Ordeal in the mountains, and the night he'd lost all hope buried under the freezing snow, waiting for death to draw her hand over his eyes. That night he had seen his father's face in the stars; he'd awoken the next day feeling a new power lodged in his chest.

'I'm lost,' he said, his voice breaking. 'I want to speak with my father.'

He allowed his chin to drop to his chest as he felt his cheeks burn red with the humiliation of admitting what had been going on inside his head and his heart. After long moments, he dared to look back up at the priestess. She was nodding slowly, understanding lighting up her eyes.

'He is here,' she said.

Lysander felt the hairs on the back of his neck stand up.

'You have something that belongs to him,' said the priestess.

Lysander opened his bag and took out the roll of leather secured with the golden ring. One of the attendants came forward and held out his hand.

He handed over the leather. The attendant slid off the ring, and unrolled the material. The lock of hair from Lysander's father tipped into his palm. He handed back the ring and the leather.

'The God has no need of mortal riches.'

He handed the lock of hair to the priestess, and reassumed his position by a stone shaped like a large egg. The priestess rolled the hairs between her fingers, closing her eyes in concentration.

'He was a brave man,' she said eventually, 'and his spirit remains close to you.'

Lysander felt a prickle again. Was she really in touch with his father?

The priestess's head dropped to her chest, as if in a dead faint. At the same time, the wind outside stilled.

It was as if Apollo himself had suddenly laid a calming hand upon the earth. Lysander felt his mouth go dry and his eyes were drawn into the depths of the flames beneath the cauldron.

A strange rattling sound began to emerge from the Pythia's throat – it was like the choking sound of a dying man on the battlefield. Her body rocked back and forth as though buffeted by an invisible gale. Suddenly, her back locked straight and her chin jerked upwards. Lysander looked into her eyes; they shone like polished onyx. Her arm shot out, throwing the lock of hair into the fire, where it sizzled and burned. She pointed towards Lysander, her fingers trembling.

'Are you ready to hear?' asked one of the attendants. Lysander scrambled across the cave floor and snatched his father's charred lock of hair out of the fire. He looked back up into the face of the priestess, as she stared at him, her hand still outstretched. Her lips moved as she murmured to herself, struggling to contain the words that filled her mouth.

Lysander nodded.

CHAPTER 8

'You are a leader, but not so,' she shrieked. 'You are a slave, but to yourself. You must free yourself, child of two worlds.'

She gasped.

'The shackles that bind you are of your own making,' she continued. 'Fear not, your destiny is branded on your heart.'

Her head dropped back to her chest, and her body sagged lifelessly. She did not move from her chair, her hands hanging by her sides and her hair drooping over her face. The howl of the wind resumed outside the cave. One of the attendants jerked his head towards the cave entrance. His audience was over.

Outside the sky had darkened. Though it was still early in the morning, it seemed like dusk. The rain was pouring down as Lysander left the cave, and the air smelled fresh as spring.

'Apollo must be grumpy,' said the attendant, who was waiting at the cave entrance.

Lysander was light-headed. He thought it must be the effects of the incense, but something told him that it was more than that. The Oracle's words had been vague, yet precise. Had she really known about the lock of hair he carried with him, or simply guessed?

Child of two worlds – had she seen his mixed parentage?

He lifted his head, and tasted the rain. How could his destiny be written on his heart?

The attendant picked his way carefully down the path, which was churning with mud. Lysander set off at a jog, splashing through the puddles that had already gathered. As he reached the bottom, he saw the queue of waiting supplicants had grown. Chilonis was next in line. Her red hair was drenched and hung over her shoulders, and her clothes were sodden, but she smiled as she saw Lysander approach.

'What happened? What is she like?' she asked.

Lysander shrugged as he sought to find the right words. It had certainly been mysterious, a little frightening even. *Should I tell her that?* Lysander thought to himself. He saw the fire of excitement lighting up his new friend's eyes, and didn't have the heart to tell her that she might come away nothing more than . . . confused.

He smiled and placed a hand on her shoulder.

'You'll see,' he said. 'I bet she tells you you'll be the best athlete ever.'

'What will you do now?' she asked.

'I have to return to Sparta,' he said. 'The new barracks commander I told you about seems more patient than the old one, but I'd rather not test him . . .'

Chilonis surprised him by leaning forward and kissing his cheek. 'Thank you again, Lysander, for coming to my rescue.'

The sky flashed with lightning, and a great peal of thunder ricocheted off the mountainside.

'It looks like I'm in for a soaking,' he said, and Chilonis smiled.

'So the God wishes. Goodbye, Lysander. Perhaps we'll meet again one day.'

'I hope so.'

Lysander ran down the mountain. He took a steep short cut, hopping from rock to rock and skidding around bushes. He didn't understand the Oracle's words, but they had helped him nonetheless. His destiny was in his own grasp, written on his heart. All he needed to do was seize it.

The downpour chilled his skin, but after the days of hiking to the Oracle, it was welcome. All the dirt of his travels was washed away. No, more than that. It felt like the rain was scouring his spirit as well, cleansing the misery and pain that had gathered over the previous months.

By the time he reached the jetty, his clothes were plastered to his skin and his fingers were blue with cold.

'What do you have to grin about?' the ferryman

grumbled when Lysander climbed on board. He hadn't realised that he was smiling.

'I don't know,' he answered. As the boat pushed off into the gulf, and the driving rain pricked the water's surface in a million places, Lysander felt renewed.

He was ready to return to the barracks.

The journey back to Sparta seemed quicker than the trek to visit the Oracle. When Lysander reached the outskirts of Spartan territory, he paused in the road. It was good to be back in his homeland, and he longed to tell Leonidas and the others about his experiences with the Oracle. On the other hand, he'd enjoyed the freedom and anonymity of the previous days. The red cloak would bring back responsibility.

Lysander's fingers stroked the sling in his pocket. It had been his only weapon on this journey, and he'd needed to use it just once against the bandits attacking Chilonis.

Come on, Lysander, he told himself. *It's time to feel that shield on your arm again.*

As he walked through the streets of Sparta, the only signs that the city had recently been at war were the sounds of hammers ringing against iron in every black-smith's shop and yard. The whole city was working to replenish and repair the weaponry lost in the fight against the Persians. Everything else seemed back to normal. The Helots in the fields, the Spartans training at their barracks. Lysander saw them practising manoeuvres by the river. He heard the distant cries of orders being bellowed by a commander. He wondered how Kassandra was feeling. How foolish their argument had been! He promised himself that he would send a message with Idas the following day.

It was nightfall when he reached his own barracks, and a dog barked at him from the darkness. He sneaked into the kitchen and found the leftovers from dinner – some cold broth and hard cheese.

Back in his barracks, he sat on a bench and rested his head against the wall, feeling six days of weariness overcome him. His eyelids, heavy with sleep, closed.

'The traveller returns!' said a voice. 'And oversleeps. He's taken on the slack ways of the north.'

Lysander opened his eyes to see Aristodermus standing over him, with a Helot at his side. Lysander realised he had slept through the night, leaning awkwardly against the wall. He sat bolt upright.

'I'm sorry, sir,' he muttered. 'I got back late, and must have . . .'

Aristodermus frowned. 'Get yourself cleaned up,' he said. 'You smell like a Thracian.'

Lysander stumbled outside, washed by the well, then went to his dormitory. Dressed in a fresh tunic, he joined the other boys at the breakfast table. Orpheus looked shocked to see him.

'You're back!' he said. 'What happened?'

Lysander sat beside his friend, and noticed that

several of the other boys had stopped eating and were listening to their conversation. He took his time tearing off some bread and helping himself to a cup of goat's milk.

He gave a short version of his trip, keeping things light-hearted; he didn't want to share any of the important details, like meeting Chilonis or his conversation with the priestess.

'I was lucky enough to spend one night in an inn. Before that I slept out in the open, and found an abandoned shepherd's hut to shelter in another evening. Well, I thought it was abandoned until a family of foxes appeared before dawn. Scared me stiff like Medusa's stare when one of them licked my foot . . .'

Everyone laughed. Almost everyone.

'How exciting for you,' said a lone sarcastic voice. It was Prokles. 'The rest of us were training while you were off having fun.'

Demaratos put his hand on his friend's arm, but didn't say anything, and Prokles returned to eating. Ever since Lysander had put aside his differences with Demaratos, Prokles' hatred seemed to have grown.

Aristodermus came into the room, and flashed them all a look. His eyes lingered on Lysander, and he gave a nod, almost imperceptible, in his direction.

'We'll have marching practice today,' he said. 'Three times around the old walls, first at half pace, second at double pace, and again at half.'

The boys at the table let out a groan.

'Enough!' said the tutor. 'An army that can't get to the battlefield is as useless as a wine sack with a hole in the bottom. Finish your food and gather . . .'

The door burst open and Demaratos's Helot, a boy called Boas, fell into the room.

'Sirs . . .' he said. 'Masters . . .'

'What is it?' said Aristodermus.

'There's a stranger, master, by the well . . .'

'A stranger?'

'Yes, sir,' said Boas. 'He wouldn't say who he was.'

Aristodermus' hand fell to the sword at his side as he scanned the faces at the table.

'Lysander, Leonidas, come with me. The rest of you, stay here!' He strode out of the room.

Lysander stood up with Leonidas and they rushed out after their tutor.

'Get spears and shields,' Aristodermus said.

In the arms room, Lysander grabbed two shields and threw one to Leonidas, who caught and shouldered it deftly. He handed Lysander an eight-foot spear without a word, and they walked back out past the dining hall. *Greetings can wait*, thought Lysander. He heard the scuffle of feet as the other boys came to the entranceway to see what was happening.

Outside, Lysander watched Aristodermus walk purposefully over towards the well with his sword drawn. They ran to his side.

'Don't do anything without my order,' he warned.

There was a man drinking straight from the bucket

at the well's edge. The water splashed over his torn clothing – he wore no cloak, and one of his feet was bare and filthy.

'Face me!' shouted Aristodermus.

The man turned slowly around and placed the bucket on the lip of the well. His eyes took in the sword in Aristodermus' hand, but he didn't seem afraid. Lysander and Leonidas stood with their spears at the ready.

'Greetings, comrade,' said the man, without a trace of fear.

'I'm no comrade of yours,' said Aristodermus. 'Explain this trespass, or I'll send you straight to the fires of Hades with this iron in your belly. Where are you from?'

The man wiped his dripping chin with his sleeve. 'I'm a Spartan, comrade.'

'Which barracks?' asked Aristodermus.

'I don't belong to any barracks,' said the stranger.

'Then you're no Spartan.'

There was a supreme confidence in the man's eyes, and it unnerved Lysander. Was he carrying a concealed weapon? Lysander's grip tightened around the shaft of the spear.

'I'm from Taras,' said the man. 'My name is Lernos.'

'*Taras?*' repeated Aristodermus in disbelief, as though the man had just said he was from Poseidon's kingdom beneath the sea. 'The colony?'

'You know of another?' said the man. 'Put down

your sword, teacher. I'm a Phylarch.'

Lysander knew the name was that of a Spartan army commander, but he'd never heard of Taras. Aristodermus lowered his sword, but he didn't sheathe it.

'I've come to speak with the Council,' said Lernos.

'Then why are you here?' said Aristodermus.

'I was thirsty,' said Lernos, 'and this was the first barracks I reached. Another hour won't make any difference.'

'Any difference to what? Speak openly, or I shall lose patience.'

'Calm yourself, comrade. I've come to tell the Council that the colony is under attack. We're overrun.'

In Aristodermus' chamber, Lernos sat at the table cramming wine-soaked bread into his mouth. Their tutor had sent the other boys back into their dormitories, allowing only Lysander and Leonidas access to the stranger. 'I want to find out if he's genuine before taking him before the Council,' he had whispered.

'I've had nothing but wild roots for two days,' said Lernos. 'I tried to steal a chicken from a farm inland, but the farmer set his dogs on me.' He swallowed and took a gulp of water. Now he was sitting down, Lysander had a chance to look more closely at him. His hair was cut short, and his features wiry, but the taut muscles of his arms suggested he was strong and his face carried a fierce wildness, like a wolf. A short untidy beard matted his cheeks, and his eyes looked hollow, but alert. A nasty gash extended from his eyebrow, across his temple and into his hairline. It was scabbed and black now.

'What of Taras?' said Aristodermus. He was standing back against the door, as if afraid the new arrival might try to escape.

'The city has fallen,' said Lernos. 'It started when we raised taxes – we needed to. We don't have slaves – not like the Helots anyway, so there's always tension between us and the natives. They must have been plotting with the leaders of Messapia – the next city along the coast. The attack came out of the blue – our Council of Elders was holding a meeting at the old theatre, when a group of locals fell upon them, armed by the Messapian leader Viromanus.' He wiped his mouth with the back of his wrist. 'The Elders were slaughtered like chickens when a fox finds their coop. Next they set fire to our stores and armoury in the night, and attacked us like cowards while we were still in our nightclothes. We fled with our families. We didn't stand a chance.'

'Animals,' said Aristodermus, thumping the door. 'No Greek would fight so dishonourably.'

'It was clear we couldn't win,' said Lernos, 'but we fought anyway, with whatever was at hand. Pots and pans from the kitchen, wooden furniture, but it was hopeless. They seemed to come from everywhere, and cut us down. Some of my comrades fled out of town to the hills with the women and children. Others ran for their lives and left the rest of us – may the Gods curse their cowardice. I was with a group of fifty or so men who were pushed out towards the port, fighting all the way. Soon we were up to our ankles in the water, but the enemy kept on at us. Men fought until they could no longer stand, then drowned in the shallows. None perished with wounds to their back.'

Lysander's anger at the story was mingled with sorrow. He'd seen brave Spartans fight on against all odds when they did battle with the Persians. These comrades of Lernos had died on foreign shores, but he felt their loss as if they were from his own barracks.

'And what happened to you?' asked Aristodermus with a toss of the head.

Lernos lowered his eyes.

'I took a blow to my temple with the back of a meat cleaver,' he said. 'When I woke up, I was floating in the water – they'd left me for dead. I couldn't go back on shore – I was weak as a newborn and they'd have executed me on the spot. I found the body of one of my dead comrades, and used it as a float. By Zeus the water was cold, but I had the strength to swim away from the shore, until I was picked up by a spice ship coming from Sicily to southern Greece.'

'And then you came here?'

'That's right,' said Lernos, tipping the remains of the wine down his throat. 'Taras may be across the sea, but it's still Sparta. I persuaded the captain of the spice vessel to land at Gytheion. Then I dragged myself through the night to get here. The Council must send reinforcements.'

Aristodermus' face had turned serious. 'I will accompany you to the acropolis. Leonidas! Go ahead and have the Council summon its members. Lysander, come with me. We'll not let these Messapians spit in the faces of Kastor and Polydeukes.'

The names of the twin gods most dear to Sparta made the blood course stronger through Lysander's veins. As he left the barracks, Lysander wondered if this was what the Oracle had described; a chance to throw off the shackles that bound him?

My destiny is there for me to take. It's branded on my heart.

His hand went to his chest, but of course there was nothing there. Demaratos still wore the amulet.

I'll do whatever it takes, he promised himself. *Then I'll have earned the right to wear the Fire of Ares again.*

CHAPTER 9

'And why,' boomed Tellios, 'should we believe this man? He comes to us with stories of battle and miraculous escape.' He sneered. 'Truly he is blessed by the Gods.'

Lysander stood on the floor of the Council chamber, and gazed up at the semicircle of seats, where the Elders sat. Normally there'd be thirty of them, but as yet his grandfather Sarpedon had not been replaced as Ephor of Amikles. Twenty-three normal Elders, four other Ephors, and the two Kings. Lysander recognised King Cleomenes sitting beside another man. *That must be King Demaratos*, thought Lysander, *Leonidas's father*. They shared the same fair hair and grey eyes.

The Kings were dressed no differently to the others – all wore identical red cloaks – but they were younger. The minimum age for serving on the Council was sixty years. Lysander and Leonidas had only been allowed to attend as Lernos' guards. The stranger knelt on the floor, and Lysander and his friend stood either side with their spears at the ready. Aristodermus was kneeling in front of the Elders in the centre of the floor, and hadn't moved since he had related Lernos' story.

'What would you have us do?' said the Ephor Myron, standing by his seat in the front row. 'If we do not heed his warnings, and they are true, think of the damage to our reputation. Soon the word will be abroad that the Spartans cannot even defend themselves against a band of upstart brigands.'

'Myron is right,' said Cleomenes, pacing across the floor. 'Our enemies will seize upon this and it will drive them to similar measures. Indeed, even if it is not true, how can we trust other cities to separate fact from fiction? Think of the Helots as well. If they get wind of this attack, it may inspire them to look above their station once again.'

'So you propose to send an army of men across the sea to face a danger that is possibly all in this man's imagination?' said Tellios, pointing at Lernos. Lysander saw the man from Taras flinch, but he was wise enough not to protest.

Tellios stepped down from his seat in the third row, and walked slowly towards them. He gazed at Lysander for a moment, then spun round to face the other Ephors.

'The army is weakened as it is,' he continued. 'We need time to regroup and tend to our wounds after the struggles against the Persians. Another fight this soon would leave us vulnerable. With that there can be no argument.'

Lysander saw a number of the Council nodding, and a murmur of approval travelled along the lines.

'But these men are our allies,' said Myron. 'Spartan men, women and children. To leave them in their time of greatest need is an offence to our Gods.'

'Myron,' said Tellios, 'you are noble, but do not pretend the same can be said for the people of Taras.' He pointed at Lernos. 'They are not true Spartans.'

More muttering, louder this time, broke out.

'Silence!' said King Demaratos. 'The Council must decide on the motion. Should we send soldiers to Taras? All in favour, stand.'

Lysander watched as Myron took to his feet, and several of the men who sat near him did the same. Still, there were only nine men standing.

'It is decided, then,' said Demaratos. 'Give this man lodging in a barracks for a month, then send him back to wherever he came. The session is ended.'

As the Council members began to leave their seats, Lysander saw Lernos stiffen.

'Wait!' he shouted. 'They set fire to the shrine of Zeus Lakedaimon. They trampled our Gods!'

The Elders paused at the doorways and glanced at each other. The atmosphere shifted immediately.

'The vote is taken,' said Tellios. 'The case is settled.'

'But this is a new charge,' said Myron. 'Sacrilege.'

Tellios looked angry, but then his eyes settled on Lysander, and he smiled. 'Very well,' he said. 'I have an amendment to suggest.'

The Elders, walking stiffly, returned to their seats.

'Speak,' said King Cleomenes.

Tellios opened his arms. 'Let us send help to the poor citizens of Taras, but let us not jeopardise our own safety. Send those young men who acquitted themselves so honourably on the plains of the Eurotas against Vaumisa's hordes. Send the fortune-favoured grandson of Sarpedon and his barracks. About eighty Spartan boys, well drilled by Diokles, should be able to take back the town.'

Was Tellios serious? Lysander and his comrades go to Taras!

Aristodermus looked up from his kneeling position, and the Ephors on their benches shared nervous glances.

Lysander felt a crackle in the air, as before a thunderstorm. A mission to Taras could be his opportunity to prove himself again.

'We'll need more men,' said Lernos.

'You'll manage with whatever we bestow,' snapped Tellios. 'And if you speak again in this chamber, we'll have you thrown into the sea with rocks fastened to your neck.' He looked around, challenging anyone to disagree. 'I move to vote then.'

'Very well,' said King Demaratos, getting to his feet. Lysander could see he shared the same straight-backed posture as his son. 'All those in favour of sending the barracks of Aristodermus, stand.'

Myron remained seated this time, but one by one,

the others in the chamber rose to their feet. Lysander counted frantically: *twelve, thirteen, fourteen, fifteen.* Half were standing. Without another, the motion could not carry. Both Kings were seated.

Come on, Lysander willed them. *Let me go!* Lysander knew little about the men, other than they were of two families who famously disagreed. The eyes of the chamber were on them, and each King looked at the other. Slowly, Cleomenes stood.

'The boys' barracks will march,' said Cleomenes.

Lysander had been handed the opportunity to prove to himself that he was still a warrior.

But will we ever come back alive? he thought.

The boys in the barracks were wrestling outside when Lysander and his companions returned.

'Quit your games,' bellowed Aristodermus. 'We're shipping out! Gather your cloaks and weapons. The baggage carts will be here before dusk, and we march tonight.'

Orpheus hobbled alongside Lysander.

'Where are we going?'

Lysander explained the extraordinary debate in the Council chamber.

'Taras is at least three days away by boat,' calculated Orpheus. 'By now the Messapians will have consolidated their positions. We have to hope that some of the Spartans there will have survived and be in a good enough condition to fight.'

'We?' said Lysander. 'Surely you're not coming? You need more time for your injury to heal.'

'I don't think my leg's going to grow back, Lysander,' he laughed. 'You'll need all the men you can get.' Orpheus sat heavily on his bed, and unrolled his cloak.

'Why did Tellios say that the Tarantians weren't true Spartans?' asked Lysander. He fastened his marching sandals on to his feet.

'People don't talk about it often, and I only heard because we had a slave from Taras when I was young. The colony was founded about two hundred years ago, in Lykurgos' time,' said Orpheus, 'but not by pure-blooded Spartans. They say that during the long wars against your people, the Messenians, the Spartan leaders allowed Spartan women to bear children with free-dwellers, and Spartan men to father children with non-Spartan women. The idea was to give their offspring full citizenship – to let them wear the red cloak and grow the fighting population. But after the conflict ended, and Messenia was subdued, their citizenship was withdrawn. They had a choice: stay in Sparta and be no better than a free-dweller, or travel overseas and found their own city. They chose to leave.'

'So they're mothakes?' said Lysander.

'I suppose so,' said Orpheus. 'Taras is an important trading port as well.'

As Lysander gathered together his blanket and armour, he dwelled on Orpheus's words. He wasn't interested in the economics, but these people were outcasts, on the blurred edge of Spartan citizenship, just like him. Perhaps this was where the Oracle had foreseen his destiny, among his own sort. There he would no longer be tainted as the Spartan who was once a slave.

In Taras he would be normal.

'You look thoughtful,' said Demaratos. In his arms was a shield, and piled inside the bowl were pieces of armour – bronze coated with tangled leather straps. Lysander thought he could still smell the blood from the battlefield.

'I'm fine,' said Lysander. 'Ready to go?'

'Almost,' said Demaratos. He placed the shield on the ground. 'But, first, I think you should take this back.' He took the Fire of Ares from around his neck, and offered it to Lysander. The red stone glimmered with promise in the centre of the amulet. He reached out. As the jewel touched his skin, he expected to feel his old strength flood through his limbs, but nothing happened. He may as well have been holding a pebble from the training ground.

I'm not ready.

He hung the pendant back over Demaratos's neck.

'No,' he said. 'Not yet.'

'Whatever you say,' said Demaratos. 'I'll keep it safe until you're ready.' He picked up his equipment once more. 'Should we let Kassandra know? I haven't seen her since the victory celebrations.'

'Idas,' Lysander called to his Helot. 'Come here.'

The slave-boy hurried over. 'Yes, Master Lysander?' he said.

'Go to the house of the deceased Ephor Sarpedon. Tell Lady Kassandra, daughter of Demokrates, that Demaratos and I are going to Italy.'

'Yes, master,' said Idas. 'Is that all?'

'Yes,' said Lysander, then, 'No.' He reached into his bag and took out the singed lock of hair. If he died in Taras, he didn't want the only remnant of his father to be left there. 'Give her this.'

The Helot took the leather roll, throwing Lysander a curious glance, and quit the dormitory.

'Come on,' Lysander said to Demaratos.

An uncovered baggage cart was waiting outside the barracks, and Lysander was surprised to see a crowd had gathered – it was mostly women, and young children. Word must have spread about the mission to Taras – these were the boys' mothers. One or two came forward and hugged their sons, but most kept a reserved distance. It was nothing like the send-off when they had marched out to face the Persians. There were no songs now nor fanfares, no citizens crying out encouragement. The atmosphere was subdued.

Aristodermus stood waiting for them, beside a cart loaded with shields, spears and supplies. Lernos stood at his side and Orpheus came behind him.

'Even the cripple's lining up,' sniped Lernos.

'This cripple lost his leg for Sparta,' said Lysander. 'Which is more than you ever gave.'

'You little . . .' said Lernos, coming at Lysander.

Aristodermus stepped between them, and pushed Lernos backwards against the cart. 'Enough squabbling. Orpheus, you're barely out of the infirmary. I admire your courage, but this is no place for you.'

'I can march,' said Orpheus.

'He'll slow us down,' said Lernos.

'No, I won't,' said Orpheus. 'Look.' He threw down his crutch and hobbled quickly in a circle. Aristodermus sighed.

'I'll vouch for him,' said Lysander. 'I'll make sure he doesn't fall behind.'

'Very well. We march tonight for Thalamae. A rider has gone ahead to secure a ship, and it will be there tomorrow, but no later.' He pointed at Orpheus. 'If you don't make the pace, we leave you behind. Understood?'

'Understood,' said Orpheus.

While Aristodermus assembled the rest of the boys, Tyro emerged from the barracks leading four Helots.

'Are they coming with us?' Lysander asked him.

'As far as the sea,' said Tyro. 'Aristodermus said the Council didn't want to waste a good mule.'

The four Helots took hold of the ropes fastened to the cart and looped them over their shoulders.

Lysander didn't have any doubts who'd ordered that particular humiliation. Tellios.

'Get in line,' shouted Aristodermus. Lysander joined one of the two columns that had formed in front of the cart. 'Move out!' yelled their tutor.

As they marched, Lysander heard a few of the mothers shout out words to their sons.

'Come back with your shield, or on it,' said one.

'Your father died for Sparta,' said another. 'Make him proud with your death.'

A shiver went down Lysander's back. He couldn't ever have imagined his own mother saying such cold words of encouragement, but such was the Spartan custom. Death was something to be wished for, defeat and cowardice the ultimate failure.

What would my mother think of me now? he asked himself. *Would she even recognise me?*

As they left the river and rounded the fortification south of the village of Kynosaura, the column suddenly faltered to a standstill. Lysander stood on the heel of Kantor, in front of him.

'Watch it, you clumsy oaf.'

'I'm sorry,' he said. 'I didn't . . .' Then he saw her.

Kassandra.

She was wearing a long mauve wrap-around tunic. She was speaking to someone in the line. *It must be Demaratos.*

'Keep moving,' shouted Aristodermus. The column set off again, and Kassandra stepped back from the path.

How has she taken the news, he wondered. *Does she even care?*

But as he approached, his cousin turned her back and walked away.

Lysander tried to calm his anger. He watched her hair blowing in the breeze, and hoped she'd turn, just so she could see the hatred in his eyes. But she didn't.

Aristodermus led them out of Sparta to the west, as the sky turned dark blue, then black.

'It's like a funeral,' said Leonidas.

'That's because they don't expect us to come back,' said Demaratos.

Lysander had no idea if he would meet death in Taras. *But I'll find out what I'm made of,* he thought, as he marched. He was ready for the ultimate test – to face up to his demons, and defeat them.

CHAPTER 10

They marched out of Sparta and into the night. For some time, they followed the wide track that Lysander and Demaratos had used to get to the mountains for their Ordeal, but as the silhouettes of the peaks loomed above them, Aristodermus directed them on a left fork and the column faced south-west. The track became narrower, wide enough just for the single cart. Its rickety wheels trundled through the worn grooves made by countless others. The Helots sucked in huge breaths as they heaved it onwards.

It looked as though they'd have to climb high into the mountains, but as they passed the end of a ridge that ran east to west, he saw that the ground rose gently up into a wide valley, at the head of which was a pass, silhouetted against the dark sky.

'That's where we're going,' said Aristodermus. 'It's the lowest pass in the Taygetos Mountains, and a route through to Thalamae.'

They hiked up towards the pass, and when they were

a hundred feet below it, Aristodermus stopped them.

'We'll make camp here,' he said. 'The far side is steeper, and sometimes treacherous. Much easier to cope with it in the morning.'

Lysander could have slept were he stood, but Aristodermus pointed to him, his pale eyes flashing in the moonlight.

'You, Lysander and Leonidas, take the skins and get down to the river. Bring enough water for making a stew. The rest of you, set yourselves around the baggage cart, and get a fire started. Send the Helots to gather wood. We'll eat before we sleep.'

There was groaning all round.

'Can't we sleep?' said Demaratos in the gloom.

'Sleep if you like,' said Aristodermus. 'But if it snows tonight, you'll be fighting frostbite in the morning.'

Orpheus was already unhooking the straps that kept his fake leg attached.

Lysander wandered with Leonidas to the cart to get the empty skins, then descended the short walk to the river below. The water in the narrow stream was icy, and by the time the containers were filled, Lysander's hands were numb claws. As they climbed back to the camp, Leonidas spoke.

'Is Orpheus all right?'

Lysander shook his head. 'He barely spoke for the last few stadia. I offered him help on a steep section, but he refused.'

'Maybe a good night's rest will help,' said Leonidas,

but Lysander could hear the doubt in his voice.

By the time they returned, their fellow trainees had four small fires going, and were adding more wood to each. Some were already asleep, leaning back against the rocks and wrapped in their blankets, but Lysander forced himself to remain awake while the Helots prepared a vegetable stew in large pots over each of the fires.

'What's cooking?' said Demaratos, waking from his doze.

With his warm bowl cupped in his hands, Lysander ate with the other boys. It was good to feel the hot food in his belly. The Helots waited at the edge of the fire – they'd get the leftovers. He noticed that Lernos was sitting amongst the boys in the darkness, listening to their conversations.

'By the Gods, it's freezing,' said Drako. 'I thought the barracks were bad.'

After Lysander's Ordeal in the mountains, he knew he'd be able to cope.

'Get some more wood on that fire,' said Prokles to one of the Helots.

As the flames leapt higher, a boy called Endymion warmed his hands over them.

'What do you think of this new tutor then, Lysander? Better than Diokles, don't you think?'

'He's different,' said Lysander.

'He's lenient, if you want my opinion,' piped up Sophilus. 'He's only flogged one person since he arrived.'

'And that was unjustified,' muttered Drako drowsily.

'You cursed the name of Lykurgos,' laughed Keos. 'Diokles would have chopped you into pieces.'

The jokes passed over the campfire, but Lysander's mind was elsewhere. Could they really be going over the sea? He was the only boy in their barracks, other than Demaratos, who had stepped foot on a ship.

'What's Taras like?' Leonidas asked Lernos.

'It's a beautiful place,' the Spartan replied proudly. 'The harbour is wide, and shaped like a horseshoe. To the western end are sandy beaches, which often bear the brunt of sea storms. The eastern side is cliffs, rising sheer out of the waters, formed, they say, when the Gods of Olympus warred with the Titans and great boulders were hurled between the earth and the heavens. On calm days, the sea is emerald clear in the shallows, and the depths a blue the richness of which you've never known. Seabirds flock around the harbour, chasing the fishing boats, and many times a day larger ships dock to drop off cargo bound for destinations along the coast or further afield.'

'What sort of cargo?' asked Orpheus.

'All kinds,' said Lernos. 'Spices. Grain from the African coast, gold and silver sometimes. There's a mint at Taras, where coins are stamped, and there was a treasury too. No doubt the Messapians have ransacked it now.'

'And how will we land the ship?' said Lysander. 'Surely the Messapians will have planted a garrison near the shore to prevent any reinforcements landing.'

'That's a good question,' said Lernos. 'You've a soldier's brain, boy.' He tipped the last of his stew into his mouth. 'The harbour isn't the only way into Taras. You remember the cliffs I mentioned? Well, they're not all sheer. About twenty stadia from Taras is a small cove. It doesn't look like much from the sea, and it seems at first sight surrounded by insurmountable cliffs, but once on that strip of sand, there's a way to get inland properly.'

'How?' asked Lysander.

Lernos tapped his temple. 'A series of tunnels, bored long ago through the sandstone rocks by an ancient river. They're only as tall as a man for most of the way, but one leads right into the rolling fields above the city.'

'And don't the Messapians know of this route?' asked Orpheus.

'I think not,' said Lernos. 'It's east of Taras, and the land there is useless for farming because of the thin soil. We only found it by accident when a fishing boat was driven ashore in strong winds. The rocks lie just beneath the water at the entrance to the cove, so it's a perilous place to land.'

'Great!' said Prokles. 'So we'll be drowned at sea before we even have to fight in the city?'

'I know the way,' said Lernos. 'You'll have to trust me.'

'And what about the town itself?' asked Leonidas. 'Is it fortified?'

'In a way, yes,' said Lernos. 'The sea protects it on the south side, and though the first settlers tried to build a great sea wall, it's fallen into disrepair. The city is built up around a large central square on the quay, and rises gently in all directions. There are two smaller squares inland, two stadia from the main one and forming a triangle with it. Our barracks block was by the western one – it's probably ash by now – but many of the men lived with their families in houses further up the slope.'

'With their families?' said Demaratos, almost losing his mouthful of bread. 'The men didn't live together?'

'In the early days of the colony, yes, but over time men drifted away. We still train together every so often, and share communal meals at certain times of the year,' he grinned, 'but not as strictly as Lykurgos would have wished.'

Lysander was beginning to see why the Spartans of Taras were overcome so easily. Where was their discipline?

If Lernos was aware of the bemused stares of Lysander and the other trainees, he didn't show it.

'There's a theatre on the hillside to the east, which is passed if one approaches via the secret tunnels, but it's not used much except for public gatherings. The west, where the Messapians came from, is farmland as far as the river, then forest thereafter rising to a low ridge. We keep sentries out that way, but they must have been overpowered by traitors from within. Their eyes are always westward facing.'

Lernos paused and from the set of his jaw, Lysander guessed he was thinking of his fallen comrades. Shortly, he continued.

'The mint and the treasury are centred on the square furthest from the sea – the one we call Croesus Square. Nearest the sea is the fresh food market, where the day's catch is brought in, and in the other square, Daedalus, is the artisan quarter – the pottery ware is particularly fine, and fetches a good price at markets in Sicily and in the islands.'

'Don't worry,' said Lysander. 'We'll soon take back what is rightfully ours.'

Aristodermus called over. 'Lernos, we must talk.'

Lernos stood up, and left the fireside. The boys had settled into their cloaks and blankets. The sounds of light snoring came from around the fire.

'You sound more like Lykurgos by the day, Lysander,' said Prokles. 'Taras is days from anywhere. A whole ocean separates us from Italy. Yet you speak as though they're on the very doorstep. This isn't our fight. We've only been sent to buy the Council time to properly reinforce after the Persian attack. If they lose a few boys, plenty more can be trained.'

'What do you know of politics?' said Lysander, raising his voice. Some of the others sat up.

'Enough to see when we're being used,' replied Prokles. 'I, for one, plan to keep my head down behind my shield and not take any silly risks.' He looked hard at Lysander. 'I'd advise you to do the same, half-breed.'

'Better a mothax than a coward,' said Lysander.

As the words left his mouth, Lysander heard the other boys gasp.

'Mind your tongue,' said Prokles, 'or I'll tear it out of your head.'

But Lysander had taken enough of Prokles' criticisms.

'I only hope I won't be by your side when we go into battle,' said Lysander. 'I'd rather have someone who I'm sure won't run away . . .'

Prokles was up quick as a hare, throwing his blanket aside, and launching himself at Lysander. As his knee landed on Lysander's chest, Lysander jammed up his arms to prevent the force breaking his breastbone.

'Stop them,' shouted Leonidas.

They rolled down the path, and Lysander was aware of the other boys scrambling out of the way. 'Watch it!' grumbled Drako. 'I'm trying to sleep.'

Lysander ended up on top of Prokles, but the other boy's hands were clutching at his throat. Lysander smashed his fists into the crooks of Prokles' elbows, breaking the stranglehold, then swung his fists repeatedly into Prokles' face. The other boy managed to block some of the shots, but one got through with a satisfying crunch against Prokles' jaw. Prokles grunted, then spat a mouthful of blood and a tooth into Lysander's face. Lysander jerked back and Prokles had enough time to swing the back of his hand into Lysander's ear. The blow made Lysander's head ring and he fell to the side as Prokles squirmed out from underneath him. When he tried to get up his legs were unsteady, and he could do nothing as Prokles aimed a vicious kick into his ribs. Another knocked the wind out of him.

The other boys formed a circle around them.

'Knock him dead, Prokles,' said Sophilus.

'Watch his feet,' called Kantor.

Lysander looked up to see Prokles' face, lit by the flickering flames. 'Had enough?' he said through bloodied teeth.

'Go to Hades,' said Lysander.

Prokles aimed another kick but this time Lysander was ready and rolled his shoulder into the oncoming leg while grabbing his attacker's foot in both hands. He pushed off from the ground, and twisted Prokles' foot. Lysander lunged and Prokles cried out as he spun through the air and crashed into the edge of the fire, scattering sparks.

He howled in panic, and rolled over, trying to quench the flames, then scrambled to his feet. Lysander clenched his fists and readied himself, but as he stepped forward a foot tripped him. He slammed into the path, and felt a hand yank him around on to his back. Lysander raised his fists to face whoever was helping Prokles.

A drawn sword pointed at Lysander's face.

'What in the name of all the Gods do you think you're doing?' said Aristodermus.

123

CHAPTER 11

Lysander's chest heaved, and the blood pulsed in his head.

'Well!' said his tutor. 'What's going on?'

'Nothing,' he said, sprawled on his back in the dirt. Suddenly he felt young and foolish.

Aristodermus sheathed his sword, then jerked his head at Prokles.

'You. Anything to say?'

Prokles wiped the blood from his mouth, and shook his head.

'It was only a disagreement,' said Lysander, climbing stiffly to his feet. 'We've discussed it.'

'Discussed?' said Aristodermus. 'You both would do well to learn who the enemy really is. They're waiting, over the sea, with weapons sharpened to cut a band of Spartan novices into pieces. I won't have my reputation tarnished by indiscipline. Do you understand?'

'Yes, sir,' said Prokles.

Lysander nodded.

Aristodermus punched him in the side of the head.

'Answer me, boy!'

'Yes, sir.' He forced the words out.

'You can both sleep away from the fire as punishment,' said Aristodermus. 'Follow the trail back down for a hundred paces, and make your beds there. Don't come up till dawn.'

Lysander didn't wait for another blow. He wanted to be away from all the staring faces of his comrades. He gathered his blanket, and set off with Prokles on his heels.

He found a space at the bottom of a rocky outcrop, where at least they'd be out of the wind. The ground was lumpy, and it was impossible to get comfortable.

This is all I deserve, thought Lysander. He'd been a fool to lose his temper with such an unsuitable enemy. Prokles was nothing but a spineless bully; beneath Lysander's contempt.

'I'm not a coward,' said Prokles, as if reading his thoughts.

Lysander shifted and looked over at the other boy. 'Then why are you so keen to stay out of trouble? If you had your way, we'd never have left the barracks.'

'You don't understand . . .' Prokles tailed off. Lysander watched him struggle to get comfortable on the hard-packed ground.

Settling down in his own blanket, he stared at his hands. His knuckles were bloodied and swollen, but the pain he felt was deep within. He knew he'd goaded

Prokles, and given him no choice but to fight, but why should he take any boy's insults?

He looked up at the stars, and imagined Sarpedon watching him. He had always been patient with Lysander, as he tried to mould him into a Spartan warrior. Was this the way he paid his grandfather back, by fighting among his comrades?

A comet streaked across the heavens.

'Goodnight, Grandfather,' Lysander whispered. Then he closed his eyes.

'Get up down there!' shouted Demaratos.

Lysander woke as the sky was beginning to change from black to milky grey. He nudged Prokles.

'Come on,' he said.

Prokles stirred, and Lysander felt a flash of guilt. The other boy's lip was cut, and a patch of dry blood stained his cheek.

Together they trudged back up the slope and found the others gathering their possessions and piling their blankets in the cart.

'Has a night in the cold settled your differences?' asked Aristodermus.

Prokles looked at Lysander. Lysander nodded, and slapped Prokles on the shoulder. 'We're fine.'

'Good,' said their tutor. 'Get back in line.'

Lysander took his place beside Orpheus, who looked pale and exhausted, with sunken eyes.

'Sleep badly?' he asked.

126

'My leg,' said Orpheus. 'I don't think it's healing properly. It kept cramping in the night.'

'Don't worry,' said Lysander. 'I'll stick by your side.'

'Listen, Spartans,' yelled Aristodermus. 'Today we march quickly. Thalamae is over the pass, and a day's march beyond. We can't afford to stop for meals, or arguments. Right, march on!'

They climbed the remaining height to the pass. Orpheus's face dripped with sweat, and every few steps Lysander heard him let out a small whimper of pain. *He must be in agony.*

The land was more rugged on the far side of the pass, heavily forested, and in the distance the sea shimmered in the morning air. A rutted track zigzagged down from the pass, and there was still a little snow, packed hard into the crevices where the setting sun never reached. An icy wind gusted around them. Lysander's ears were frozen, and he couldn't feel his feet in his sandals. This was the main route into Messenia, the land of Lysander's forefathers, but now it was all under the Spartan yoke. When he was younger, Lysander had dreamt of crossing these mountains, and entering his ancestors' homeland a free man. He never would have believed he'd come this way wearing the red cloak of his oppressors.

'Halt!' called out Aristodermus.

Lysander drew up, and looked back. The baggage cart, containing their weapons and food supplies, was having trouble negotiating a bend, and one of its wheels had become lodged in a ditch. As the four-strong Helot team released their ropes from the cart, Demaratos took a draught from his water flask.

'Where are we heading?' he asked.

Aristodermus pointed down over the forest.

'You see those two low hills? They're called Helen and Penelope. A river runs between them, which we follow to the port at Thalamae. There should be a boat there for us.'

With a huge heave, the Helots managed to right the cart. 'Ready?' asked Aristodermus. The lead Helot, a sharp-featured man whose skin was brown as old leather, nodded.

'Keep marching!' bellowed Aristodermus.

The steep ground levelled off as they came out of the heights. The few patches of snow disappeared and were replaced by the rich greens of sheep pasture. Lysander's feet warmed up and his legs felt light. After the Ordeal he and Demaratos had faced in the mountains, fighting both wolves and their psychopathic leader, Agesilaus, the high ground felt like familiar territory. But at his side, Orpheus seemed to be getting worse. He was walking more awkwardly, and his mouth curled with each step. Lysander saw fresh blood streaking down the carved wooden stump.

'Rest on my arm,' said Lysander.

This time Orpheus didn't refuse the offer. He placed his hand around Lysander's elbow, and they descended together.

They reached the forest. The trunks were densely packed scaly salt cedars that came only a few feet higher than Lysander's head. There were several tracks winding through the vegetation, mostly made by animals, but they kept to the main one. Lysander noticed Aristodermus ahead looking anxiously up at the sun, which was already past its zenith and sinking towards the west. *We're falling behind*, he realised.

Rabbits darted in among the twisted roots, always staying at a safe distance. Lysander considered using his sling, but Aristodermus showed no interest in slowing down.

Soon he heard the sound of water, and they fell in beside a stream in a glade dappled with sunlight and shade.

'Fill your flasks,' Aristodermus ordered. 'But be quick about it.'

Lysander sucked in deep gulps of water and dampened the back of his neck. He was replacing the stopper in his flask, when he saw that Leonidas was helping Orpheus up from the water's edge. His face twisted in agony as he climbed to his feet.

Below the forest, the river fell in a series of little waterfalls between the two hills, which were actually the ends of long ridges extending down to the farmland plains near the coast. Lysander had been watching Orpheus out of the corner of his eye for the past few stadia, and his difficulties were obvious. Each step brought a wince, and more than once he'd had to stop.

Aristodermus was growing impatient.

'We have to make port by nightfall,' he said. 'Otherwise, the boat won't wait.'

'He's going as quickly as he can,' said Leonidas.

Aristodermus gave Orpheus a long, assessing look.

'I took a chance allowing you to come with us,' he said. 'Don't let me down.'

Orpheus flushed. 'I let down no Spartan,' he said, his voice trembling with anger.

Aristodermus looked pointedly at Orpheus's stump. Then he turned and led the way onwards.

The river became wider and faster as other small streams joined it. They crossed and recrossed it several times over bridges made from logs, but the cart had to be led down to the water and walked through at shallow points. After the second such crossing, as they were regaining the path, Orpheus tripped and fell awkwardly.

'He should have stayed behind,' mumbled Prokles. 'For his own sake.'

Leonidas crouched beside his friend and Lysander rushed over too. Orpheus lay on his back at the side of the path. A trickle of blood swelled out from his stump and Lysander could see the veins standing out under the cracked skin and yellow pus.

'Can you go on?' Lysander asked.

'Enough!' said Aristodermus. 'We have to go now.'

'And what about Orpheus?' asked Lysander.

'He'll have to remain here. Leave him some food and

he can make his own way back to the barracks.'

Lysander looked at Orpheus on the path. His friend needed rest and shelter, not another night exposed to the elements. He stood up and took Aristodermus' arm. He never would have done the same with Diokles.

'If we leave him here, he'll die,' he hissed.

Aristodermus shook his arm off. 'If we don't complete our mission, the Council will have us *all* executed.'

'I'll make sure he keeps up,' said Lysander.

Aristodermus spoke loudly enough for everyone to hear. 'Very well, but he's your responsibility now.'

The column moved off, and Lysander took Orpheus's arm over his shoulder and lifted him to his feet. Leonidas took the other arm, and supporting their friend, they stumbled along behind the rest of the boys.

'You shouldn't have,' said Orpheus. 'I've been left before, remember? I survived then too.'

Lysander laughed, but didn't break his stride. It was true, Orpheus had been abandoned as a baby because of his crippled leg – Spartans considered such weaknesses unacceptable. But that time a pack of wolves had found him and reared him as their own.

'If a wolf found you now, they'd not be so kind,' he said.

At first, carrying his friend was easy, but after some time an ache set in at the base of Lysander's spine. His breathing became heavy, though he tried not to show it, but from the sweat that coursed down Leonidas's face, he knew they couldn't make it all the way to Thalamae like this.

The column was walking past fields where two free-dweller farm labourers were digging a ditch, when Lysander spotted a horse in the adjoining field. It was no racing breed, but old and sturdy, with shaggy black hair: perfect for pulling a plough.

Or carrying a passenger.

Both the farmhands looked up from their work to watch the Spartan troop pass by.

Once the path dropped down out of sight, Lysander let Orpheus sit on the bank of the track.

'Wait,' Lysander called ahead, causing the column to stop.

'What is it now?' said Aristodermus. 'More delays?'

'I have an idea,' he said, and outlined his plan.

'You expect me to help you steal a horse?' asked Aristodermus.

'Diokles taught us stealing was the Spartan way.'

Aristodermus raised his eyebrows.

'If you can get it, so be it, but don't ask me to help.'

Lysander crept up the bank to the edge of the field, and hid behind a copse of trees. The labourers had returned to their work, and he could hear their grunts of exertion as they sank their shovels into the earth. The field offered little cover, other than the flimsy fence that lay along one side. The furrows of the tilled earth would offer some protection, but Lysander would have to stay low if he was to remain out of sight.

He threw off his cloak and made his way, weaving between the trunks of the trees, to the end of the fence. He looked back to see the other boys had ascended the bank also and were watching through the branches.

Don't let them be seen! he prayed.

On his belly, Lysander wriggled along the line of the fence, clawing with his hands and knees, his breath coming hot and laboured. He dare not lift his head, in case one or both of the labourers happened to be looking in his direction.

Finally he reached the far end of the fence, where a group of four olive trees stood, their gnarled and twisted branches clutching at the sky. Behind one of the trunks, Lysander stood in a crouch and checked his position. The farmhands were both facing away from him now, oblivious to the intruder who had just slithered within thirty paces of them. The horse was in the next field, and from the way its head was lifted and its ears pricked, Lysander guessed that the animal had spotted him. After the experience with Chilonis' mare, he knew the dangers of a startled horse, and so approached slowly, still bent over.

'There, there, boy,' he clucked, holding out one hand to seize the harness. 'I don't mean any harm.'

The horse tossed its head, and moved its jaws in a lazy chewing motion, but its eyes were wide and wary.

133

'That's good,' said Lysander. 'No need to panic.'

'Hey! What are you doing?'

Lysander turned to see the farmhands running towards the fence, both gripping their shovels in their hands.

'Stop, thief!'

There was no time to think. Lysander closed his hand around the reins and threw his leg over the back of the horse. It let out a brisk whinny, and immediately Lysander felt its rear legs leap into the air. He wrapped his arms around its neck and dug his heels into its flanks. Each spasm of the horse's back threatened to shake the teeth from his head, and the horse twisted and turned, trying to cast him off.

Lysander saw in blurred images the farmhands coming near, the look of murderous outrage on their faces. He yanked the horse's mane desperately and kicked its sides. The angry creature galloped across the field towards the fence. It was quicker than it looked, and soon the farmhands, and their wild cries, were left behind.

Lysander steered the horse through a gate and back towards the track, where he pulled his steed to a halt. Moments later, Aristodermus and the others appeared around the path at a light jog, and Lysander slid off the animal. He was covered in mud from crawling through the field and it was mixed with the sweat from trying to control the horse.

'Good work, Lysander,' said Kantor, slapping the horse's rump.

'Not bad,' said Aristodermus. 'But let us waste no more time.'

Lysander nodded and led the horse over to Orpheus, who grinned.

'I can't go on it all the way,' he said. 'We'll take turns.'

'Very well,' said Lysander. 'Do you need a hand getting up?'

Orpheus took hold of the horse's mane, and easily pulled himself into position. Despite his withered leg, his upper body was powerful. Lysander had done his duty by his friend; for now, Orpheus was safe again.

'March on!' ordered Aristodermus impatiently.

CHAPTER 12

It was dusk when they reached the outskirts of Thalamae, and again the clear skies had given way to black, rolling storm clouds. Aristodermus called them to a halt as they passed the first few farm buildings and ordered them to fetch their shields and spears from the baggage cart.

'We don't want every farmer in the region to know what's going on,' said Aristodermus, 'so we'll pretend we're on exercises. Look like Spartans, boys!'

Lysander was weary from walking, but once he had his shield on his arm and his spear in his hand, he felt fresh vigour gather in his limbs. They marched across muddy fields, with the Helots pulling the cart along.

'Where are we meeting the boat?' Lysander asked the tutor.

'South of the town,' said Aristodermus. 'Thalamae is a popular port. There will be spies there. If we moor a warship, news will be in Athens before the next full moon. We're heading to a small bay they call the Sickle.'

'What are the Council so ashamed of?' Tellios' face flashed into Lysander's mind.

'If this mission is a failure,' said Aristodermus, 'Sparta will deny all knowledge. Better that than lose face.'

'But it won't be a failure, will it?' asked Demaratos.

Aristodermus grinned. 'It depends on how you define failure. If my body is taken back to Sparta with wounds on my front, I've done my duty. That's all you should be thinking about.' Then he spotted something further back in the line and darted over, shouting, 'Nereus, don't drag your spear across the ground like an old man.'

With Aristodermus gone, Demaratos turned to Lysander.

'This sounds like a suicide mission.'

'What more could a Spartan ask for?' said Lysander automatically, recalling when a Spartan soldier had used the same words on the eve of the battle with the Persians.

Demaratos rolled his eyes. 'Lykurgos would be proud.'

A fresh breeze was blowing inland and Lysander smelled the sea before he saw it. A fine rain was falling when they finally reached the shoreline, and the wind created shifting patterns in the curtains of drizzle.

They were high up on a cliff top, and Lysander could see nothing through the gathering mist but the dim outline of the coast.

'Stay away from the edge,' said Aristodermus. 'This

area suffers from landslides.'

The path picked its way along the top of the cliff, through scrubby gorse bushes, some twenty paces inland. Orpheus climbed off the horse and it was tethered to the side of the baggage cart. The combination of the rain and the wind chilled Lysander to the core, and he flexed his fists and toes to keep the warm blood flowing. The path's unevenness meant marching in order was impossible, and gradually the line became ragged. Lysander dropped in beside Leonidas, who was marching towards the rear of the group.

'Look at that!' said one of the students from ahead. A low chatter passed among the column and Lysander stared at where several boys were pointing out to sea. He could see nothing through the fog.

'What is it?'

A gap in the mist appeared, and he made out a ship anchored off the shore. The Sickle was smaller than he expected, less than a stadion across, and a squat boat was moored on the grey-green sea, bobbing gently as the choppy sea rolled beneath it. It looked like a sturdy vessel, and Lysander could see a single set of oar-holes along one side. The single central mast held a furled sail.

'It's hardly much of a warship,' said Prokles. 'I was expecting a bireme at least.'

Aristodermus, Lysander noticed, was frowning, but he hid the expression when he turned to face them. 'It will suffice.'

There was a round of grumbling and Lysander heard

Prokles whisper something about 'wanting us to fail'.

Lightning forked across the sky, so close he was blinded. Lysander heard the horse whinny in panic, and the hurried voices of the Helots.

'Look out!' said a voice. Lysander spun around, and saw the horse galloping towards him, the small baggage cart bouncing along behind, clattering on the track. He leapt out of the way, as the horse tore past him, and landed in a spiky gorse bush. There was a splintering sound as one of the narrow cartwheels sheared away, and it listed to one side.

The horse careered towards the cliff, dragging the cart behind it.

Lysander was first to move, and scrambled after the bolting horse. Blood streaked his hand from the thorns, but he ignored the stinging pain.

'Stay away from the edge!' yelled Aristodermus. But Lysander couldn't stop; Orpheus might need that horse's help again.

Lysander splashed through puddles after the terrified animal. The horse reared up and wheeled round, but thunder cracked across the sky with another flash of lightning and the horse broke into another canter. Lysander drew his sword and sliced through the rope that harnessed the horse to the cart, but he could do nothing as the maddened creature disappeared over the edge of the cliff.

'Is it dead?' said Endymion, his eyes wide with shock.

Lysander looked over the edge of the cliff, and a few of the others gathered at his side. The horse's carcass lay still on the rocks below, lashed by the rain.

'It was only a horse,' shouted Aristodermus. 'Find some shelter.'

'Phemus!' someone shouted. 'Help him.'

Lysander turned and saw that one of the boys was lying on the ground, with smoke rising from his cloak.

'The lightning must have hit him,' said Leonidas.

Lysander ran to Phemus' side, as did Demaratos. The edge of his tunic was completely burned, and beneath it the skin was stripped away in a pattern like a fern-leaf. His head lolled to one side but he opened his eyes. He was alive.

'Now we have two invalids!' said Lernos.

Lysander's anger flared, but this was not the time to pick another fight.

'There's a cave further along,' said one of the Helots.

'Pick him up,' barked Aristodermus. 'Get him out of the rain.'

Lysander and Demaratos lifted Phemus, taking an arm each, and marched him towards where the Helot was signalling. It was barely a cave – more a natural shelter under an overhang, but it was better than nothing. With the help of the band of Helots, some of the boys dragged the cart into the entranceway, blocking the worst of the driving rain.

From the cave mouth, where he huddled alongside the others, Lysander could see the huge breakers smashing themselves against the rocks below. The ship rolled back and forth on the waves a little further out.

One of the Helots brought some linen bandages from the cart. Tyro and Demaratos stripped Phemus' charred clothing away, and applied a flaxseed poultice to the worst of the burns along his neck and shoulder. Phemus was beginning to come round, and mumbled, 'What happened?'

'You were hit by lightning,' said Demaratos. 'You're lucky not to be walking with the shades.'

As they bandaged the wounds and retied his clothes, Lysander saw what looked like the small figure of a man appear on the deck of the ship with two lanterns. Narrowing his eyes, Lysander peered through the rain to watch the sailor swing the lamps back and forth.

'We must leave now,' said Aristodermus, holding up a hand to his face to gaze in the same direction.

'But there's a storm raging!' said a boy called Spiros.

'That's why we have to leave,' said Aristodermus. 'We need to get the boat away from the rocks, or it will be smashed to pieces by dawn. The marine is signalling to us. Take a shield and spear, and get out to the ship at once.'

Lysander led the way down to the shingle beach, picking a careful path over the jagged rocks, with his shield strapped over his back, steadying himself with his spear. Demaratos and Tyro supported Phemus, whose legs were still not strong enough to carry him. Orpheus clattered down on his wooden leg.

Once they'd all reached the bottom, the spears were lashed together with cord. Phemus managed to cling to the middle, and the two strongest swimmers, Leonidas and Aristodermus, swam out using them as a float. One by one, the boys threw themselves into the surf, powering out towards the ship. Lysander looked for Orpheus, but saw his friend was already ploughing through the surf.

Lysander made sure his shield was secure, and walked straight out towards the waves. The water churned over the pebbles towards him, and swamped his feet and ankles.

The man from the ship's deck was shouting, but the gales whipped his words away. Lysander was knee-deep when he looked back and saw that Kantor was still standing on the beach, looking nervously into the water.

'What's wrong?' he yelled.

'I don't . . . I . . . I can't swim!'

Lysander came back to Kantor's side, the water dragging at his heels.

'Come with me,' he said. 'I'll get you there. It's easy.'

Kantor, lips blue with cold, nodded.

Lysander pushed out against the surf, pulling the boy with him. The waves broke against his torso. Saltwater sprayed his face. Kantor was coughing beside him, screwing up his eyes against the onslaught. When the water reached his chest, Lysander swam, attacking the barrage of water.

Kantor gripped his tunic belt, and the extra weight threatened to pull Lysander under.

His chest heaved as he sucked in massive gasps of air.

A quick look up revealed he'd barely swum ten paces – the ship was still another twenty out to sea. Lysander pressed on, pulling against the water with everything he had. The waves rolled over his head, sucking him back towards the shore. His eyes stung with the saltwater, and his arms felt like rocks.

He had no spare energy to turn and check Kantor. The fingers that gripped his waist were enough for Lysander to know he hadn't drowned.

Ten paces to go.

On the deck lanterns rocked, blurring through the piercing rain. Men were gathered, black shapes folding and unfolding under the ink-black sky. He saw his comrades being pulled up on to the deck like giant fish.

Lysander couldn't feel his arms any more, but he knew they were moving because of the pain in his shoulders. His shield was heavy on his back, pressing him into the water. A wave swept over his head, and Lysander was completely submerged. His world flipped over, and suddenly he was lost in an underwater abyss. The sensation of Kantor's grip melted away. As the last of the air tried to push out of his lungs, Lysander's chest felt scorched and raw. His eyes searched the water for the other boy – nothing. He didn't even know which way was up.

Water flooded his mouth.

He never thought he'd die this way.

CHAPTER 13

Something tugged at his armpit, and Lysander choked in a breath as his head broke the water's surface.

'Hold on!' said a voice.

Lysander slipped under. He was so weak.

Again something pulled him up.

'Get another hook on him.'

Something nudged his shoulder, then slid under his other arm. He was lifted out of the water. He banged against the side of the ship, felt hands seizing his tunic and cloak. Then he was lying on something hard.

'Is he alive?' said Kantor's voice. 'Tell me he's alive.'

Lysander managed a smile. At least he was safe. He opened his eyes to see Aristodermus and Kantor standing over him. Coughing racked his chest, and he vomited up a mouthful of sea water.

'On your feet, Lysander,' said his tutor. 'Get down below with the rest of the boys.'

Lysander half sat up, and looked about. He was on the deck of the ship.

Two men in Spartan cloaks were winding up the anchor, and another two were tethering boathooks to the inside of the deck-rail. Presumably the ones used to heave him out. The same men then started dragging at ropes over the side, drawing up the fenders.

'Down below!' barked Aristodermus. 'We have to get ourselves away from the shore.'

Lysander stood up and fell sideways with dizziness, landing against the deck-rail. Kantor disappeared through a hatch in the middle of the deck, which emitted a pale glow. Lysander stumbled over. Six steep steps, almost a ladder, descended into the belly of the ship. He half fell, half climbed down, and found himself on the oar-deck. The faces of his comrades stared back at him, illuminated by two oil lanterns swinging back and forth from the ceiling. They were lined up on benches either side of the ship with an aisle in between. There were about twenty benches on either side, each carrying two boys. Long oars rested over their laps. Kantor had already taken a place behind Drako.

'Good of you to join us,' said a grizzled, red-faced sailor. 'Take a seat.'

Lysander looked across the benches. Demaratos sat beside Prokles. Leonidas was with Orpheus. All the boys were paired up.

'Where should I go?' he asked.

The marine pointed to an empty bench. 'You'll have to pull an oar on your own.'

'No, he won't.'

Aristodermus climbed down the ladder, and sat on the bench. Lysander took a seat beside him. His teeth were chattering with cold.

'Ready?' asked Aristodermus.

Lysander nodded and took hold of the oar. His knuckles were purple.

'Listen,' said the man at the front. As the lanterns swung his face was in turns illuminated and in shadow. Two thick scars were etched from his mouth back to his ear as though his cheek had been torn open at some point in the past. 'My name is Moskos and I am the captain of this vessel. That means you do as I say, without question. You,' he said, pointing to Lysander's side, 'are port. You,' he pointed to the other side, 'are starboard. Two sides, simple. When I say "One", you extend the oars straight out from the side of the vessel. Do not let them touch the water. When I say "Two" you lean forward, pushing back the oar. "Three" is let the oar drop into the water. "Four" is the most important part. It means you pull with all the strength the Gods have given you.' He accompanied each instruction with an action. '"One" is lift out again. Understood?'

'Yes, sir!' they shouted.

'Good, let's try and straighten her up. Port. One!' Lysander and Aristodermus pushed their oar out over the water. It slid easily through the hole pins that kept the oar in place. The moonlight caught the crests of the silver waves. 'Two!' They leant forward on the bench.

147

'Three!' The oar dipped. 'Four!' Lysander pulled, feeling the oar glide through the water. The boat turned a few degrees, creaking as it went.

'And again,' shouted Moskos. 'One . . . Two . . . Three . . . Four . . . Starboard as well. One . . . Two . . . Three . . . Four . . .'

He continued to count and Lysander and his comrades moved in unison, dipping their oars and propelling the boat through the dark water.

One of the other marine soldiers came down, and took up the count on a small drum. There was no need for the numbers once they were into their rhythm, and the boat rose and fell over the swell.

'Keep pulling,' said Moskos. 'We'll be clear of land soon enough.'

'The spirit of Diokles lives,' muttered Drako.

Through the hole pins, Lysander could see the black sea rolling. The motion churned in Lysander's stomach. He concentrated on keeping in time and found his nausea was quelled if he kept his eyes fixed on the marine at the front.

Others weren't so lucky, and Lysander heard his comrades retching. Vomit spattered his ankles as Drako leant over his oar and emptied the contents of his stomach.

'Sorry,' he said, sheepishly.

Moskos laughed. 'Looks like we've got some fresh ones here, Sirkon. Slow down the count.'

The marine with the drum laughed as well, and left

a little more time between each strike. Moskos walked down the aisle, tapping each of the central rowers on the shoulder, numbering each row off as he went. Lysander was number eight.

'Odds, rest on one,' he shouted, 'and draw in your oars.'

Half the oars lifted from the water, and the vessel slowed down. Lysander and his tutor continued to pull their strokes. Lysander counted them in his head. He lost count when he reached eight hundred and realised he was no longer cold. His fingers had regained their colour and his back was wet with sweat. His mouth was sore from the dried salt, and his tongue felt thick. Aristodermus rowed without complaint – the only clue to his weariness was the rasping breath forced out with every stroke. He was just another Spartan now, taking orders like the rest of them.

They continued to row through the night, taking turns on the oars. Between sessions, Lysander slept sitting up, leaning against the oar, rocked to sleep by the sea. He dreamt of the Oracle's words:

You are a leader, but not so.
You are a slave, but to yourself.
You must free yourself, child of two worlds.
The shackles that bind you are of your own making.
Fear not, your destiny is branded on your heart.

Sometimes he thought he was rowing asleep, and performed the practised motion with his eyes closed.

He lost track of time – there was only rowing, and

not rowing. In their breaks, water was passed around in a flask – just a swig each, and then on to the next boy.

'Make it last,' was Moskos' mantra. 'Make it last.'

Dawn came as a surprise, with light peeping through the oar-holes. They were all rowing in a daze, with great heaving breaths, heads lolling on their necks.

'All rest!' said Moskos.

As one, the crew drew up their oars, then fell across them with a mighty groan.

'That felt like the thirteenth labour of Herakles,' said Drako, gasping.

Lysander was too weak to laugh, but after resting for a few moments, he felt strong enough to stand. He joined the queue heading topside.

After the stench of sweat and vomit, the fresh air tasted divine, and Lysander went to the edge of the deck and sucked in deep lungfuls. The sea had calmed down, and the blue expanse spread all the way to the horizon. A steady wind was blowing, and one of Moskos' men was halfway up the mast, untying the sail. After it was unfurled, two marines pulled on ropes and it spread open like a seabird extending its wings. The ship lurched into motion.

'Eurus, God of the eastern winds, is with us,' cried Moskos.

Lysander looked at his palms. They were smeared with blood and the skin was broken. New blisters had formed beneath the ones that had burst.

'Get some saltwater on those,' said one of the marines, tying off the sail. 'You'll get used to it soon enough.'

Phemus hobbled out on to the deck, and Lysander joined the crowd of boys around him. Aside from his charred hair, he seemed in good spirits.

'You had us worried,' said Lysander. 'Not many live whom Zeus strikes with his bolt.'

'My family make their sacrifices regularly,' said Phemus. 'The King of the Gods should have nothing against me.'

Orpheus smiled. 'Did it hurt?'

'I don't remember anything about it. Just waking up on board this ship.' Phemus shifted slightly and grimaced. 'It hurts now though!'

'At least you're spared the rowing,' said Lysander.

'One of Moskos' marines is teaching me how to navigate,' said Phemus. 'It's all to do with the stars, and the sun.'

Bread was passed around — stale and rock hard — with dried fish that smelled worse than it tasted. Lysander had to moisten the bread with water before he could even swallow it.

'Come over here,' shouted Demaratos. 'Look at these!'

He was standing at the deck-rail, pointing at the ocean. Lysander rushed over, to see something smooth as polished metal break the surface of the water. An animal with a long nose. Lysander's heart jumped. He leant over as another split the water, easily keeping pace with the ship.

Other boys crowded around, as the creatures multiplied. There were five, ten, fifteen of them, cutting through the waves.

'What are they?' said Prokles. 'Are they nymphs?'

One of the marines bent over laughing.

'They're dolphins, you imbeciles! We seamen say they're a good omen for fair sailing.'

'They're beautiful,' said Orpheus, without shame. Lysander marvelled at the way their glistening bodies scythed the waves.

The dolphins stayed with them for much of the morning, then disappeared as quickly as they'd arrived, melting into the water. Lysander hoped that wasn't an omen too.

The wind stayed with them for most of the day and night, but for the next few days, Lysander was back beside Aristodermus on the bench. He was four hundred strokes through his second shift of the fourth night, when the cry came from above.

'All lights off! Black out! All lights out!'

Two marines scrambled down the steps, and extinguished the lanterns by capping them. The oar-deck was in darkness. The eyes of Lysander's comrades shone in the fine silver light from the stars.

'Are we here?' whispered Orpheus. His voice was slurred with fatigue.

Some of the boys had already ditched their oars and were climbing topside. Lysander was glad to release his grip and stand stiffly from the bench. Orpheus's face was ghostly white, and he leant across his oar halfway back on the Odds side. Careful not to trip in the gloom, Lysander went to him. A strange smell hung around his friend. Not sweat, or blood, but something sickly sweet. Even in the murk of the oar-deck, he could see the purple bruising around the top of Orpheus's stump, spreading up his thigh.

'The infection's getting worse,' said Lysander.

'There should be some dried sac fungi in the supplies,' said Orpheus. 'I'll take some when we land.'

'You need it now,' said Lysander, turning to go.

'No!' said Orpheus, seizing Lysander's arm. 'I won't slow us down. Promise me you'll wait.'

Lysander looked into his friend's eyes. 'Very well,' he said. 'As soon as we land.'

Lysander made his way to the upper deck. Here the air was still and cool, and the sweat dried on his back. The boys and the marines were all gathered along the starboard side of the vessel, peering over the rails.

'I can't see anything!' Spiros was saying, but Lysander knew that he was short-sighted; they always joked in training that he wouldn't see the enemy until the sword was in his belly. Lysander saw in the distance a few pricks of light, like distant stars on the horizon.

'Is that Taras?' he asked.

Lernos nodded. 'That's it,' he said. 'We need to keep

153

close to the coast, and we should get to the bay before dawn.'

Aristodermus turned to the boys. 'Back below!'

Lysander took up his position on the bench again beside his tutor; Orpheus seemed to have gathered his strength, and sat straight in his seat. They rowed at half pace. Through the oar-holes, Lysander saw Taras disappear out of sight, and the coastline approached. Moskos signalled with a lift of his upturned palm for Lysander's side to draw up their blades, and the other row to keep pulling. The ship turned level with the shore, and then Moskos raised his hands for Lysander and his crew to resume. Three days before, Lysander hadn't known how to hold an oar; now, they were a well-oiled team.

The only sounds above the steady breathing of the other boys were the thumping of the oars between their pins and the splashing of the blades in the water.

'Keep steady,' said Moskos, anxiously peering through the observation hatch. He turned to Lernos. 'You're sure you know the depth here?'

'I've sailed these waters all my life,' said Lernos, frowning.

Lysander concentrated on pulling in time with the others, and stared round at his comrades. Their faces were grimy with sweat and dust, their eyes dark hollows. Leonidas's jaw was set firm and the muscles on his arms stood out like cords as he pulled his oar. Demaratos was hunched awkwardly, and Lysander could tell each stroke brought him pain by the twitch in his cheek. Aristodermus' pale skin seemed to glow in the twilight beside him.

'We're almost in,' said Lernos. 'Steady now. The entrance to the beach is narrow. Let me take charge.'

'Very well,' said Moskos.

Lernos took his place at the head of the aisle, all the time flicking his head to look outside.

'You must listen carefully,' he said to them. 'The current here is strong, far too strong to swim, and rocks line the bay on either side. We have to turn and enter perfectly straight, or a boat this size will not make it. Do you understand?'

'Yes, sir,' Lysander said with the others.

'When I give the signal, we'll complete the turn, and then row hard into shore. Ready?'

'Ready.'

They rowed a few more strokes, then Lernos lifted his arms to signal oars up. The ship drifted onwards, but then was buffeted hard by a wave. 'Ignore it,' said Lernos. 'Port. One . . . Two . . . Three.'

Lysander and his side obeyed in unison. He leant forward and let his blade hover over the water. The boat turned.

'Starboard also. One . . . Two . . . Three . . .'

The other side dropped their oars into the water.

Lysander heaved in time to the Tarantian's voice, and the boat surged forward. It felt good. From the side, he could see the dark water, and the silhouette of the land rising up behind. The channel didn't look narrow, but perhaps the water was shallow.

Lysander tried to keep his oar in time. The sound of wood knocking on wood was quickly followed by a more terrifying crunch that seemed to shake the whole boat.

Lysander heard gushing water.

Suddenly, his feet were wet.

Lysander turned with the others. Water surged through a jagged gap in the timbers like some creature from the depths swamping the ship. It soaked the benches and lapped up against the side of the oar–deck. Flecks of foam showered Lysander's face, and he screwed his eyes against the spray. He tasted salt on his lips.

'The hull's breached,' shouted Lernos. 'Abandon ship!'

CHAPTER 14

The thunder of the water roared in Lysander's ears.

'Take in your oars!' said Moskos. 'Topside, all of you.'

Boys streamed past Lysander's bench, almost falling over each other to scramble away from the gaping hole. Leonidas was already standing at the bottom of the steps, ushering the others to safety.

'Come on,' said Aristodermus, taking Lysander's arm and pulling him toward the crowd heading up the steps.

The water in the hull was around Lysander's ankles now, and still rising. How long till the boat sank?

The bay was little more than a thin patch of sand a hundred paces away, backed by wave-swept rocks, enclosed by two headlands like a set of crab's pincers. Boys stood against the deck-rail, peering over the back of the ship where the water was coming in.

The ship lurched as the aft tore free from the submerged rocks. Lysander struggled to stay on his feet and slammed into Aristodermus, who steadied him.

'Salvage what you can of weapons and equipment,' he shouted, 'and get overboard.'

The ship was already sitting lower in the water. The sky was just giving way to grey but the sun was not yet up, and Lysander could see the dark shapes of the rocks just beneath the surface of the sea.

Another wave buffeted the vessel closer to the shore. 'What about the ship?'

'Forget the ship. It's useless now.'

Moskos was suddenly between them, stabbing Aristodermus with a finger, his weather-beaten face close.

'We take the ship in with us.'

Aristodermus' hand flashed upwards and seized Moskos either side of the jugular, pushing him backwards on to a pile of ropes. 'I won't send my boys back down there to row.'

Moskos choked out his words. 'You don't need to. We must drag her in. Get ropes tied to the aft, above the breach. My men can do the rest.'

Aristodermus stared at Moskos for a moment, then released him. He turned to Lysander.

'Get ropes secured firmly to the deck-rails, and anything that won't break off.'

Lysander found a crowd of boys and repeated Aristodermus' orders.

'But how will *we* get to shore?' said Phemus.

'Another swim,' said Lysander.

Phemus pointed into the water. 'We'll be torn to pieces on the rocks; you saw what happened to the ship.'

'We have our orders.'

Boys ran to the ropes and began tying off knots against the deck-rails. Others were busy fastening on their swords. Lysander was impressed with their quiet organisation.

Moskos and his small crew waited, and he was shaking his head impatiently. *To Hades with your ship!* thought Lysander. His comrades descended on the weapons store like bees to their nests, plucking shields and spears. Leonidas handed Lysander his.

'Are you ready?' shouted Aristodermus.

'Yes, sir!' they shouted back. All had their cloaks rolled up and fastened to their fronts.

The ship listed suddenly to port, sending two or three of the boys to the deck. Those who stayed on their feet, including Lysander, stumbled instinctively to the other side to try and steady the vessel. Lysander tripped over the ropes that lay tangled across the deck.

'We haven't got long,' said Moskos, looping a rope over one shoulder and under the opposite arm. Sirkon and the other crew did the same. 'If she takes in any more, we're going to lose her. Get your *army* in safely. We'll need them to drag the ship in.' He turned to the marines. 'Have you all made sacrifices to Poseidon? You're in his hands now.'

They nodded, then one by one climbed on to the deck-rail and slipped overboard. The ropes around their middles snaked over the rail and five sploshes sounded as they hit the water.

Lysander looked over the side. The marines were already making for shore. 'Forget Poseidon,' Lysander said. 'Trust in yourselves. Regroup on the sand, and good luck.'

Lysander saw the others hesitate, so decided to act first. He clambered over the deck-rail, and stood on the outer ledge. The waves slapped the side of the ship, and he could see the rocks more clearly beneath the surface now, with pale patches between them. The rest of the boys followed his example. He let his shield drop into the water below, then picked a safe-looking spot. He couldn't be sure, but there was no time to waste. He stepped off.

For a moment he thought his legs had struck something solid, but the water gave and he plunged downwards. His spear shot loose of his hand and burning saltwater filled his nostrils. Cold wrapped itself around him and squeezed.

His limbs were heavy from the days of rowing, and he clawed back to the surface, finding his shield and spear floating on the undulating waves. All around boys fell into the water like stones, surfacing with splutters and coughs. Lysander turned on to his back and began kicking towards the shore. The cold seemed to close on his heart like a fist.

Swimming with his cumbersome weapons was like dragging himself through thick honey, but Lysander sucked in deep lungfuls of air and willed himself on. The sky above was growing paler by the second, and the stars were vanishing one by one. Lysander fixed his eyes on the brightest and kicked on.

Something brushed his head, and he twisted in the water. A rope. His fingers gripped it. He saw the marines standing on the shore, beckoning them in. Lysander pulled himself along the lifeline, kicking at the same time, until finally a wave plucked him up and he floated in on its surge. His legs were wobbly as he felt the ocean floor, but he supported himself on his spear and managed to drag himself up the beach. His feet crunched and he saw that among the pebbles were littered the fragments of shells, big and small. Some, spiralled and luminescent in the pre-dawn light, were beautiful.

The others were finding their way ashore as well, heaving their soaked bodies on to dry land like strange creatures from the deep. Kantor was clinging to one of the stronger boys, who carried him on his shoulders as he swam. All Lysander wanted to do was lie down and rest, but a strong hand tugged him to his feet. It was Moskos.

'The job's only half done,' he said. 'Get on a rope.'

Lysander dropped his shield and spear, and stood behind Sirkon, who had planted his feet firmly in the pebbles. Leonidas rushed up behind Lysander, and the rest of the boys spread themselves along the five ropes, some right at the water's edge, others further up the beach. *Surely it was futile*, thought Lysander. *How could they drag a ship that size?*

'Heave on three,' yelled Moskos. 'One . . . Two . . . *Heave!*'

Lysander tightened his freezing fists around the ropes and pulled with everything he had. For a moment, it looked as though the ship was not going to move at all, but then the back, where the ropes were fastened, shifted towards them.

'We're doing it!' shouted Demaratos. 'It's moving.'

Lysander's legs and arms were racked with tremors, but he heaved until his eyes felt ready to burst. The aft swung around towards them, and the ship began to drift slowly in, as though propelled by a light breeze.

'Keep pulling!' ordered Moskos.

Lysander took a step backwards up the beach, then another, as the ship's pace increased. Then he was pulling hand over hand. With a grinding sound, the stricken vessel climbed out of the water, its keel pocked with barnacles. It scraped across the pebbles to a halt, and water began pouring out of the oar-holes at the bow end.

'Well done, men,' said Moskos, coming to Lysander's side.

'It will be fine there,' said Lernos. 'When the tide goes out, it will be completely on dry land.'

Up close Lysander could see the breach in the hull wasn't as big as he'd thought. It was a tear as wide as his arm was long, but only a plank in depth.

Lysander sank down again among the shields on the beach beside Leonidas and Orpheus. Leonidas plucked up a conch shell from the beach, just like the polished ones sold in the market in Amikles along with sea sponges. Inside, its horned exterior shone bright pink.

'They say Poseidon's son Triton carries one of these, and when he blows it, the sea turns wild.'

'Then it looks like Triton is against us,' said Lysander.

Orpheus patted his shoulder and gave a small chuckle. 'If the Gods were against us, we wouldn't be here now, would we?'

They rested on the beach as the sky gave way to grey, then blue. One of the marines ventured back on to the vessel and the boys took it in turns to form a chain in the water, along which to pass the remaining weapons, armour and supplies. Thankfully, the flasks of water had kept dry above deck, and Lysander swallowed a few mouthfuls of the brackish liquid. They all began to sort through their equipment, and helped each other fasten their armour. Lysander's leather breastplate chafed against his skin, but as soon as the arm and leg-guards were fitted as well, he felt his determination hardening.

'What's Lernos doing?' asked Orpheus.

Lysander saw the Spartan at the far end of the beach where the pebbles gave way to sand. He was crouching to examine the ground, then jumped up and came running back with a frown.

'Is something troubling you?' asked Aristodermus.

Lernos stroked his chin. 'Footprints. In the sand. Someone has been here recently.'

163

'You said smugglers used this cove.'

'Yes,' said Lernos. 'You're probably right. Are we ready to move?'

Aristodermus turned to face them. 'Take your weapons, boys.'

Lysander fastened on a still-wet cloak, along with his sword and helmet, then took a spear and shield from the pile in the sand.

Lernos addressed them, pointing back up the beach. 'The tunnels are reached up a narrow gully at that end. It's pitch black inside, so stay close to the man in front, and don't get lost. There are several other smaller passageways that lead off the main branch. It's like King Minos' Labyrinth down there.'

Lysander's mother used to tell him the stories of the maze built under the palace in the kingdom of Crete. A monster lurked down there, half man, half bull, and it feasted on human flesh. He'd stopped believing in such tales before his tenth year.

Aristodermus was speaking to Moskos in whispered tones.

Their tutor addressed them. 'The marines will stay here and try to repair the ship. We'll reconnoitre the city, then form a plan of attack. Are you ready, Spartans?'

'Ready!' Lysander shouted with the others.

They marched along the beach, with Lernos leading alongside Aristodermus. The sun was up now, behind thin hazy clouds, and it was beginning to warm

Lysander's back. It looked like they were heading straight towards a mound of boulders, but a sandy path, lined with long grasses, opened up leading upwards and inland. On one side a steep rocky wall rose up, with boulders strewn around its base. Lernos led them between the rocks until Lysander saw a dark opening. It was triangular, about as tall as him, and barely two paces wide at the base. It looked completely innocuous, and if Lernos hadn't said, Lysander would have assumed it was nothing more than a minor cleft, terminating quickly.

'Lysander, stay at the rear with Orpheus,' barked Aristodermus. 'Make sure he doesn't get left behind.'

Lysander stood outside the mouth of the cave with his friend, while the others filed through. When it finally came to his turn, he stooped under the lip of the tunnel mouth. Immediately, a cold draught enclosed his body.

'Keep your hand on my shoulder,' he said.

Orpheus did as he asked. For the first few paces, the other boys were like ghosts in the shadows, but then darkness set in, and Lysander strained his eyes in the pitch black.

'It's tall enough to stand upright,' Lernos' voice echoed along the line. 'Keep close to the boy in front, and everything will be fine.'

Lysander straightened up, and followed the sound of the shuffling feet ahead, dragging his fingers along the slimy wall. It reminded him of the blindfold exercises he used to do with his grandfather. *You have to trust yourself to the darkness*, Sarpedon had said.

Orpheus's hand fell off his shoulder, and Lysander turned.

'What's the matter?'

'I tripped over something. It's fine.'

Lysander reached out and found his friend's arm.

'Come on, we can't fall behind.'

Lysander thought he could hear the other boys ahead, and hurried along, keeping a firm grip on Orpheus's arm, using his other hand to feel ahead. He thought about calling out for them to wait, but the others would laugh at him if he did.

A dim light approached.

'It must be the way out,' said Orpheus hopefully.

But something about the flickering told Lysander it wasn't natural daylight. It wasn't the tunnel exit.

'Wait.'

They froze, with their backs against the cave wall, as the light grew stronger, illuminating the tunnel wall, which glistened with moisture.

'Where did they find a torch?' said Orpheus.

Lysander heard a noise to their side, and turned to see a stocky man carrying a flaming torch. He wasn't a Spartan.

'Who are you?' he said, reaching for his sword.

The man circled them, as two others approached from ahead, each carrying a torch as well, with unsheathed swords glinting gold in the flickering flames. Where was the rest of their squadron?

'Help!' Lysander cried. 'Back here!'

The man grunted a few words in a language Lysander didn't understand. The short man took a step in and Lysander saw him swing an arm. Lysander lifted his sword, but the blow was too strong. A club hit him on the side of his head.

'No!' he heard Orpheus cry out.

The ground rushed up to meet Lysander as he toppled forwards, pain tearing through his skull. He put his hands out to break his fall, but it was too late; his face smashed into the hard rock floor.

CHAPTER 15

'Wake!' said a voice in heavily accented Greek.

A hand slapped the side of his face, and the first thing Lysander saw was a blade. He tried to move away, but there was a great weight pinning him to the floor. One of the men swam into focus, kneeling on his chest. He had long dark hair hanging loose and his thin nose looked like the beak of an eagle.

Lysander felt for his short sword, but it was gone. They must have taken it.

The man cleared his throat and spat into Lysander's face. Despite the cold underground, Lysander felt sweat prickle over his body, as fear opened his pores.

'Orpheus?' Lysander said.

'I'm here,' replied his friend weakly. Lysander twisted his neck and saw that Orpheus was against the cavern wall. Two men held his shoulders and arms back, while another stood in front, holding a broad dagger in the flames of his torch. There was no sign of the other Spartans.

Four enemies.

Only two of them: unarmed.

'What do you want?' he said to the man, trying to keep the fear out of his voice.

The man nodded to his friends, and the one with the torch handed it down to Lysander's captor. The man played the flame back and forth over the length of his arm, close enough to be uncomfortable.

Lysander turned away, unable to watch as the man grinned and brought the torch closer. It felt like the flames were ants, burrowing into his flesh just above the armour that covered his forearm.

The smell of singed hair filled the tunnel, and Lysander's body shook with the effort of not crying out.

Only when the man handed the torch back did Lysander dare look. A patch of his skin was red and blistered, with clear fluid dripping from the skin.

If only he knew what these men wanted, perhaps he could bargain with them.

Orpheus cried out in agony, and Lysander smelled burnt flesh. The man with the torch was pressing the heated blade against his friend's upper thigh.

'Stop!' begged Lysander. 'Punish me instead.'

The man took the knife away, then held it over the flames again. Tears of pain streamed down Orpheus's face.

'Let them,' he said through his teeth. 'I'm no coward.'

The man with the blade looked at Lysander without pity, then placed the blade across Orpheus's other leg. His friend writhed against the hands holding him, but there was no way he could escape.

They don't want anything from us, Lysander realised. *They only want to hurt us.*

One of the men punched Orpheus in the stomach and he tumbled forward into a ball.

'Orpheus!' Lysander shouted, but his friend was gasping for breath. The men all laughed.

The man who had been torturing Orpheus knelt behind Lysander's head. He brought the knife close to Lysander's face, hovering with the point over his eyes. Lysander turned his head away and felt a searing pain as the blade was held against his earlobe. It felt like his whole ear was being slowly ripped off.

This time he did cry out, and without shame.

There must be a way out!

Brute force wouldn't work, but if he lay here, they'd surely torture both him and Orpheus, until they were no longer capable of fighting back.

What had Aristodermus said?

Rest when you can. Fight when you have to. Adapt.

The knife was lifted from his ear, and Lysander felt blood ooze along his neck. He let his head roll to the side, and played unconscious.

The men made grumbling noises at their fun being cut short. Lysander felt the pressure on his chest lessen a little.

This is my chance.

He jerked with his legs and bucked his hips upward, then used his arms to lever the man over his head and into his tormentor with the knife. He twisted on the floor, and kicked out at one of the standing men, sweeping his legs from underneath him. The torch fell to the ground and flared.

From the floor, Orpheus drove his elbow against the thigh of the other man who had been holding him. He dropped with a howl.

The scarred man and his stocky friend gathered themselves and ran at Lysander. He sidestepped to keep one blocking the other, and kicked the armpit of the man holding the dagger. The blade clattered to the ground and Lysander dived for it. As his hand closed around the hilt, someone stamped on his back. Lysander swung the blade, and drove it into the knee of his attacker, the man with the loose hair. He screamed and fell backwards, clutching his leg.

Lysander saw two others barrel into Orpheus, and then the flash of a blade as one of them stabbed Orpheus's breastplate. The world seemed to slow as the dagger pierced the metal. The armour was only good for deflecting glancing or weak blows, not a direct attack.

Orpheus let out a moan as blood gushed up around the hilt.

Lysander stumbled backwards.

'No! No! No!' he heard himself mumbling.

He ran towards the two men, but the other attacker scythed into his side, sending him crashing against the cave wall. He saw Orpheus sink to the ground, his hands fumbling at the wound to his chest.

Lysander swung a punch at his attacker, but it was poorly aimed, and had no power. The others joined in, kicking him in the ribs and stomach, and all he could do was cover up his head with his elbows. A blow caught him on his broken nose, and white pain exploded through his head.

He fell on to his back and clutched his face. The men all laughed.

Through his fingers Lysander saw the flash of a sword blade and there was a sickening crunch. The chuckling stopped dead, replaced with a scream. Something landed on Lysander's leg, and he looked through his blurred watering eyes. It was an arm – the fingers still gripping the hilt of a knife.

As the man stared in terror at his missing limb and the blood pumping from the wound, the other three were looking out into the cavern at the three entrances, gabbling to each other. One held a dagger, and the other two had Orpheus's and Lysander's swords. No one looked at Lysander.

The man with the missing arm moaned on the ground.

There was movement from one of the tunnels and a shield spun out, striking the lead Tarantian in the thigh, and doubling him over. A scarlet-cloaked figure charged in its wake from the darkness. For a moment, Lysander dared to believe that it was Orpheus. Was his friend alive?

But it was another face that came into the arc of torchlight.

Prokles.

He was carrying a sword that dripped black in the gloom, and he drove it upwards through the stomach of the distracted enemy, grunting with the effort. One of the other men swung his sword at Prokles, who deflected the blade with the guard on his arm, then punched the attacker in the face with the back of his fist. Lysander heard his jaw crunch. Prokles was wearing a wooden knuckle-duster.

Lysander sprang up, and tackled the legs of the other Tarantian. He felt an elbow dig into his back but ignored it, lifted the man off his feet and ran him into the opposite wall, driving his shoulder into the man's stomach. He collapsed at Lysander's feet.

Lysander put an arm around his neck from behind, seized his chin with the other hand, and yanked the head around as hard as he could. The neck snapped like a twig, and the man went limp.

Prokles had finished off the man with the broken jaw, and was pulling a sword from his chest. The scarred man was lying face down in a pool of blood. Only one was still alive, and he was crouched against the cave wall, clutching torn rags to the awful wound at his shoulder, his face bloodless and ghostly pale. His eyes flitted from one of them to the other.

'What shall we do with him?' said Prokles, picking up his shield.

Lysander was speechless. Orpheus was surely dead. But Prokles had saved him. The boy who had been his enemy since day one in the barracks. The boy he'd called a coward just a few nights before.

Prokles raised his sword over the cowering man.

'No!' shouted Lysander.

Prokles turned and gave a confused look. 'He'll tell others about us.'

'Take him back to Aristodermus. He might be useful.'

Prokles hesitated. 'You're right,' he said, after a moment. He jerked his sword in front of the bleeding enemy. 'On your feet.'

The man understood, and shuffled groggily to his feet. Lysander went to Orpheus's body. His friend's eyes were open, but lifeless, his lips slightly parted. Lysander felt as though his stomach was being turned inside out, and he lowered his forehead until his skin touched Orpheus's brow.

Orpheus was the first Spartan ever to have shown him kindness, a boy who knew how it felt to be an outsider. He had taken Lysander under his wing in the early days of the agoge, and protected him from the others. But what he'd shown Lysander more than anything was that the red cloak didn't have to mean cruelty; it could mean honour, and nobility.

'I'm to blame,' said Lysander. 'I said I'd look after him.'

'We have to go,' said Prokles. 'The others will be waiting.'

Lysander nodded slowly, then reached out with a hand and closed Orpheus's eyes.

The Fates had taken him. His life threads were cut.

'He was a good Spartan,' said Prokles. 'He died with a wound to his front.'

'He was my friend,' said Lysander.

They tied a tourniquet around the prisoner's arm using the belt of one of his dead companions. He winced as Lysander tightened it.

'You're fortunate to be alive,' hissed Prokles.

As they marched their captive through the twisting tunnel by torchlight, Prokles told Lysander how they'd come out the far end in a dry riverbed, and the count had showed two short. Lernos had wanted to leave Lysander and Orpheus behind, but Aristodermus had insisted someone go back.

'And you drew the short straw?' asked Lysander.

'Someone had to.'

'Well, thank you. You saved my life.'

Prokles shrugged. 'We need all the fighters we can get.'

Light began to infiltrate the tunnel, and the ground became littered with small rocks, and then larger boulders until Lysander caught sight of a patch of white light. They came out into a ravine between two shallow grassy banks. Aristodermus and the boys were sitting on rocks which must have been carried down when a river once flowed there. They jumped to attention when they saw Lysander.

'Who's this?' said Aristodermus. 'Why is he injured?'

'He and three others attacked Orpheus and me in the tunnels,' said Lysander.

Leonidas stepped up. 'Where is Orpheus?'

'I'm sorry,' said Lysander. 'I couldn't save him.'

Leonidas sat heavily on a rock and placed his head in his hands.

'He didn't deserve to die in the dark,' said Demaratos.

'He didn't deserve to die at all,' whispered Leonidas.

'And these other men?' said Aristodermus grimly. 'Where are they?'

'Dead. Prokles killed two, and I killed the other.'

'This one should die too,' said Demaratos from his place on a boulder. He drew his sword, and panic spread in the prisoner's eyes.

'Wait,' said Lernos. 'I know this man – he's a trader called Tullius. Let me question him.'

'Go ahead,' said Aristodermus.

Lernos spoke to Tullius in the native tongue and at first received only one word answers. But when he pointed around the Spartans and made a slashing motion across his throat, the prisoner became more talkative, pointing with his remaining arm into the tunnels and then over the ravine.

'He says that the four of them were a lookout, nothing more.'

'So no one else knows of our presence?' Aristodermus asked.

Lernos had a brief exchange with Tullius, who shook his head.

'Can this man be of any more use to us?' asked Lysander's tutor.

'It's doubtful. As soon as he gets a chance, he'll reveal our position.'

'No, he won't,' said Aristodermus. He turned his spear and slammed the point through Tullius' chest, knocking him to the ground. The Tarantian heaved a couple of times, then sank back among the rocks.

Lernos led them along the natural cleft carved out by the old river, and it wasn't until they emerged into a wider plain that Lysander got an idea of the landscape. Rolling hills spread into the distance, some covered in olive groves, but many seemingly deserted. A huge forest spread over several hills.

'The town is over that range,' said Lernos, pointing northwest, 'but if Tullius was speaking the truth, we should find Nikos and my comrades nearby.'

Leonidas had walked in silence until that point, but now he spoke to Lysander.

'Did he suffer?'

Lysander remembered the way Orpheus's face had

writhed in the torchlight, and the gurgling sound as the blood filled his throat. He couldn't tell that to Leonidas.

'No, it was quick. He died like a warrior.'

They reached the edge of a forest of fir trees, and skirted around the eastern side with the sun on their cheeks.

'I think he knew he was going to die,' said Lysander.

'What do you mean?' asked Leonidas.

'His leg was infected, and it was spreading. He could have stayed in Sparta, but he chose to come with us. He must have known he was too weak.'

'I should have made him stay at the barracks,' said Leonidas, his head lowered.

'You couldn't have,' said Lysander. 'Remember when he insisted on facing the Persians – he was as stubborn as a mule. No, he knew this would be his final mission.'

'I always thought he was blessed by the Gods,' said Leonidas, with a thin smile. 'Everyone did. His life seemed a miracle. Abandoned as a baby and kept alive by a she-wolf. It's the stuff of legend.'

Lernos entered the forest by a narrow track, and Lysander found himself treading more quietly as they walked through the eerie gloom between the trunks. His eyes were drawn into the dark centre, and his breath came more quickly.

There was movement to his left and something thumped into a tree. The whole column ducked in

178

unison and weapons were drawn. Lysander gripped the shaft of his spear. There was no person in sight, but there, buried in a trunk, was an arrow.

'Lower your weapons, or die,' boomed a voice.

CHAPTER 16

'Keep hold of your weapons,' shouted Aristodermus, 'or you will die at *my* hand.'

Another arrow fizzed through the air and landed in his shield. Aristodermus spun around. 'Show yourself, coward!'

From behind a tree, some fifty paces away, Lysander saw a man emerge. He wore only a short tunic, and carried a bow. His skin looked black in the distance.

Lernos pushed forward.

'Nikos?' he shouted. 'Is that you, comrade?'

'Lernos?' said the stranger.

'I bring reinforcements from Sparta.'

'By the Gods, let that be true.'

The two approached each other and embraced. Lysander saw that the man's face, arms and legs were smeared with dirt.

'Come out!' shouted Nikos. 'These men are our allies.'

Lysander gasped as shadows peeled away from the

trees around them. None of the men wore cloaks – all were camouflaged like their leader. The men appeared from every side, all carrying weapons, swords and curious short spears, only half the length of the eight-footer Lysander carried. Many looked gaunt with hunger, or carried roughly bandaged wounds.

Lernos took his friend by the elbow and threw a hand towards Lysander and the others.

'Nikos, this is Aristodermus and his troop. The High Council of Sparta sent them to our aid.'

Aristodermus held out his hand.

'You look unusual for a Spartan,' said Nikos, 'but it is not your fair hair we need you for; it's your sword arm.' Lysander noticed his accent was strange and the way he spoke was slightly old-fashioned. 'Tell me, Aristo-dermus, where are the rest of your men?'

Aristodermus pointed at the boys. 'This is all of us.'

Nikos chuckled. 'Then you must have Kastor and Polydeukes on your side.'

'This was all the Council could spare,' said Lernos.

Lysander noticed Nikos struggle to keep the disap-pointment out of his face. 'Listen well,' he said eventu-ally. 'The Messapians are a thousand strong. We have two hundred men here, perhaps another two hundred held prisoner in our former barracks in Taras. While we stay in the forest, we can keep our families safe. The environment evens out the numbers, but in the city itself, we would stand no chance. We'd be outnumbered five to one.'

'I can kill five men,' said Lysander.

Nikos laughed.

'Me too,' said Demaratos, joining his side.

'Your boys do not lack bravery,' said Nikos. 'Very well, you have pledged yourselves, and we are grateful. Now you must be hungry, so follow me.'

Nikos led them deeper into the forest.

They entered a clearing where tents were set up. Men milled around, sharpening weapons, gathering firewood and drying clothes. A few horses were tethered to a fallen tree. The smell of roasted meat filled the air.

'Aren't you worried the fires will attract the Messapians?' asked Lernos.

'They know we're here,' said Nikos. 'We have lookouts around the perimeter of the forest. We can move camp quicker than any scout can get word to a party of attackers. The forest is good for pheasants, deer and wild boar, and there's a good stream three stadia away.' He pointed to a central tent. 'Aristodermus, get your boys some food. They'll need their strength. Hunting is difficult whilst we hide, but we manage to kill just enough to fend off starvation.'

Lysander took his place in a line where the boys queued for food, and was handed a wooden platter with a slab of venison, cut from a spitted carcass. At a distance, a great crowd of women and children watched them warily with hollow eyes. A few looked elderly, and some carried babies on their hips. Their faces too were emaciated, and creased in desperation. They were Spartans, but they resembled an army of peasants.

They look like Helots, thought Lysander in astonishment.

The men began to make their final preparations, donning what scraps of armour they had, and fastening their grubby cloaks.

Nikos took his place on the fallen log where the horses were tethered, and addressed the gathered soldiers.

'Men of Taras, you know me for a man of few words, and I shall not disappoint you.' A cheer went up. 'Our land was taken from us unjustly. With the Gods' favour, it shall be returned.' Another cheer, as the men raised their arms. Nikos jumped down. 'Sulla, Cimon, Anaxander, Phlebas, gather round with your seconds. Aristodermus of Sparta, bring your lieutenant.' Aristodermus looked at Lysander, who felt the faces of the other boys turn towards him.

'You've been promoted,' whispered Demaratos.

While the others finalised their arms, Lysander joined Aristodermus and the other summoned men with Nikos. On a patch of bare soil, the commander took a stick and sketched a slightly curved line, then drew a cross halfway along. 'That marks Taras, the line the coast.' Inland, he drew a half circle. 'The ridge is above the city, almost enclosing it. Three roads lead into Taras, and we must split our forces along each. We pour men into the centre, clearing the enemy as we go, then gather in the central market square,' he said, drawing a large rectangle, 'that sits on the harbour front behind a wall. The key is surprise and speed. We kill anyone who stands in our way, Messapian or citizen. Both are our enemy now. Understand?'

Lysander noticed Aristodermus frown.

Is he thinking the same as me? There was a flaw in the plan. They couldn't possibly cover every route; some inhabitants of Taras would escape and regroup.

'How will the troops be split?' asked one of the men.

'Sulla will go with you, Phlebas, down the western road,' said Nikos. 'Cimon and Anaxander will take a hundred men along the east. I will march with Lernos, Aristodermus and his troop. We'll approach from the north. That way, if one lieutenant dies, there will still be another to lead.'

'And what of the prisoners?' said Lernos. 'If we can free them, we'll have perhaps two hundred more men.'

'The stables where they're held are towards the western edge of the town, and will be heavily guarded. It will hold up the advance if we reroute troops there.'

Lysander cleared his throat.

'If we don't tackle the Messapian soldiers who guard the prisoners on the way in, they'll be able to regroup behind us. Plus if we enter the town like you've suggested, we're sure to let several of the enemy slip away through the closing net. They'll be able to counter-attack.'

'If I wanted a child's opinion, I'd have asked for it,' said Nikos, his face colouring.

'Perhaps the boy's right,' said Lernos.

'Silence!' said Nikos, breaking the stick across his knee. 'We may not be in Sparta, but I'll still have you flogged if you question my orders again.'

Lernos bowed respectfully, but Aristodermus was not cowed.

'With respect, Commander. I see a way to rescue the prisoners.'

Nikos' expression calmed. 'Go on.'

'The Messapians will be expecting soldiers to storm the barracks on the edge of the town, but as you have said, we are not normal soldiers. There must be boys in Taras though. Normal boys who play in the streets and cause trouble. Grown men couldn't get near to the barracks, but boys stand a chance.'

Nikos raised his eyebrows and smiled. 'An ambush?'

'A distraction,' said Aristodermus. 'Just to give us the element of surprise.'

'An interesting proposal,' said Nikos. 'Let's do it. Choose ten of your best, and tell them to take off their armour and cloaks.' He turned to his man Phlebas. 'Do we still have the farmer's cart?'

'It needs repairs, but it should be fine.'

'Good,' said Nikos. 'Have it fixed immediately.'

Lysander and Aristodermus ran back to the main group.

'I need some volunteers,' said their tutor. 'Nine boys.'

185

'Nikos said ten,' said Lysander.

Aristodermus turned to him. 'I've chosen one already.'

Lysander smiled; he knew what an honour this was. His destiny lay in Taras, he was sure of it. This was his chance to break free from self-doubt. He'd give his life for Taras, if that's what was needed.

CHAPTER 17

'Ouch!' murmured Demaratos. 'Can't you get your elbow out of my side?'

'Keep the noise down,' came Lernos' voice. 'We'll enter the town soon.'

Lysander peeped out from under the cover that concealed them in the cart. Lernos was sitting astride a horse, wearing a brown cloak. Drako walked beside him, guiding the two horses that pulled the cart along the uneven path. Two other boys walked on the other side.

The sky was beautifully clear. Under the sackcloth though, it was stuffy, and his eyes watered because of all the straw. They went over another bump, and Lysander's sword dug into his ribs. He shuffled to get comfortable in the bed of straw and twigs, and Prokles cursed.

There had been no shortage of volunteers, and Lysander had been glad to see Leonidas and Demaratos step forward. Prokles had been more of a surprise, but he hadn't hesitated for a moment. *He's changed since we crossed the sea*, thought Lysander. *I was wrong to call him a coward.*

There were three others hidden in the cart as well. Lernos was there to lead the way, and to do any talking should they be stopped. Lysander wondered how the other forces were progressing. Aristodermus' eyes had gleamed at the prospect of the attack they were about to launch. 'See you in Taras,' he said as they departed. 'Or failing that, in the fields of Elysium.'

'Even if all the armies make it,' said Lysander, 'we still leave ourselves exposed.'

'What do you mean?' said Demaratos. 'We'll deal with the Messapians on the way in.'

'And what about the normal citizens who don't come out to fight; who stay in their houses?' said Lysander. 'If they had anything to do with the previous attack, they might not sit back and let Nikos retake the town.'

'If we stick together and follow orders, we'll stand a chance,' said Prokles.

The cart bounced along between low white-washed houses, and a couple of people called out greetings to Lernos in accented Greek. Then came a gruff voice.

'Halt! Who are you?'

Lysander held his breath.

'A simple tradesman,' said Lernos. 'These three are my sons.'

'What's your trade?'

'Courgettes and marrows, anything that grows this

188

time of year in my wretched soil,' Lernos laughed. Then he added, 'Take a look. If you wish.'

'What's he doing!' hissed Prokles.

Lysander gripped his sword and tried to remain still.

'I have no wish to, trader,' said the soldier. 'You're late for market. Be on your way.'

Lysander breathed again, despite the sweat running down his temples. They were safe. But as Lysander turned to smile in relief at his friends, he saw Prokles rubbing at his eyes. Lysander could see his nostrils flaring.

No, Lysander thought desperately. *Not now*. Clearly, he wasn't the only one suffering from the hay dust.

Prokles' body shook with the violence of a sneeze that he tried to bring under control. But the canvas covering them shifted as Prokles' shoulders jerked, and there was the unmistakable sound of a boy sneezing.

'What was that?' said the man.

'What?' said Lernos.

'Take off the cover,' he ordered.

A hand came under the cover. It grabbed one of the swords that was stashed in the cart. Lysander heard a blade slice into flesh, a scuffle. He dared to look out. Drako was holding a young soldier in distinctive black leather with a sword buried in his neck. The man's body spasmed then went slack.

'Get him off the road,' said Lernos. 'No one has seen.'

Drako dragged the body off the path by the feet,

leaving a long streak of blood, and threw it in a ditch. He scattered water from his flask and splashed the evidence away.

They continued as if nothing had happened, but Lysander's heart was pounding. They had so nearly been discovered. After a little while, the cart pulled up.

'The barracks are a stadion away,' said Lernos, 'on the outskirts of the town. It looks like all the stall doors have been sealed.'

Lysander looked out and saw a long low building a little like their barracks. A crowd of twenty soldiers, armed with swords, were standing in a group at the front. More were posted every ten paces along the outside of the building, and more still were pacing around the perimeter. Maybe fifty in all.

Lernos led the cart off the track.

'Out, all of you.'

Lysander threw off the cover, grateful for some fresh air. Lernos went over the plan a final time, until everyone was clear. They unhooked the horses, and took their spears, some of which had been cut down to half size. Demaratos struck a flint into the dry kindling that lined the cart. Flames crackled the air, and sent up a column of black smoke. The horses whinnied, but Drako calmed them.

'Let's hope they see the signal,' said Prokles, staring back up the ridge to where Sulla and Phlebas would be waiting.

Lysander, Demaratos and Leonidas threw the sack

back over the flames, and for a moment it looked like they might be extinguished. But almost straight away, a patch of black began to grow in the middle. They pushed the cart back out into the road, and aimed it down the hill towards the entrance to the barracks. A single column of smoke emerged through a hole in the sack.

'If the plan fails,' said Lernos, 'it was an honour.'

'For Sparta,' said Demaratos.

'For Sparta,' the others replied.

Flames took the sacking, and suddenly the heat in Lysander's face was intense.

'For Orpheus,' he said to himself.

Together, they set the blazing cart rolling down the road. It shot down towards the barracks, and the guards began to point and shout. For some it was too late, and it slammed into a group of five, throwing them aside or crushing them beneath the wheels, before overturning and skidding to a halt. The flames licked up the side of the barracks building.

Lernos charged after the cart, and Lysander and his comrades streaked down the hill in his wake. He was dimly aware of a hunting horn sounding in the background, followed by two other blasts.

The signal to advance!

The net was closing.

The soldiers were regrouping below. Lysander met the first before he even had time to draw his sword and ran him through with his short spear. He took the man's shield, a small but light circular one. Another soldier, fat and sweating, ran up to him, and Lysander smashed the shield into his chin, knocking him out cold.

A cry went up from massive Drako, and Lysander saw he had a man lifted above his head with both hands. He threw him against the flaming barracks door, smashing it open. Smoke billowed out. Messapians were closing in from all sides. They had no chance if they waited to be surrounded.

'Advance!' shouted Lysander, running out to meet the nearest attacker. He stooped and drove his spear up into the groin of a leather-clad giant, then sliced with his sword across the back of another man's knees. A sword blow glanced off his shield, and cut into his shoulder. He drew a breath through his teeth and head-butted his attacker.

Someone ploughed into his side, and landed on top of him. Lysander scrambled out, using the hilt of his sword to box the man's ears. He was nearly free when an almost naked figure appeared above him, holding a sword.

But the man didn't attack. Instead, he pulled away the body that was pinning Lysander. His ribs were pronounced above the scraps of tunic.

One of the prisoners!

'Nikos sent us,' said Lysander, getting up. 'They're retaking the town.'

Screams came from all around as the remaining

Messapians were overcome by unarmed men, emerging out of the prison like pale ants from their nest. They looked malnourished and desperate.

Lysander's rescuer took a sword from one of the dead guards and raised it above his head. 'Freedom!'

'Freedom!' came the shout.

He saw Demaratos tying a scrap of clothing around his forearm, using his teeth to pull the knot tight, over a blossoming patch of blood.

Looking about, it seemed no one else was hurt, apart from the Messapians. Their bodies lay all around, broken and battered.

A horn sounded from higher up the slope, close this time, and Lysander saw a sea of red swarm down the road. Four men wide, and twenty-five deep, the block of soldiers led by Phlebas and Sulla marched at double time. The ones at the front all had short spears, helmets and shields, but Lysander knew that further back they were less well equipped.

When they saw their freed countrymen, there was much shouting and embracing, but soon the ragged men had been absorbed into the corps.

Phlebas slapped Lernos on the back. 'Two hundred men freed by a handful of children. Perhaps the Council does like us after all. Now it's only two against one.'

They descended into the town. Taras was larger than any of the five Spartan villages, the white-washed houses tightly packed around narrow alleys. Sweat trickled down Lysander's back. The enemy could be just around the next bend, and he'd only know when they were upon them.

As the track widened, and the column fanned out to fill it, terrified inhabitants scurried across their path. Lysander saw them fleeing into their houses like rabbits bolting into their warrens. A few hovered by the edge of the homes, prostrating themselves on the ground to show they meant no harm. Ahead, he caught glimpses of the glittering sea, and the pediments of a temple.

'They kneel now,' said Phlebas. 'The same ones who were baying for our blood a month ago.'

But Lysander was worried. All the people he saw were women and children, or the elderly. He had hardly seen one able-bodied man.

'This doesn't feel right,' said Lysander.

They reached a storehouse surrounded by pottery wine jugs, when a shriek came from ahead. Suddenly, through a gate in a wall ahead burst a huge band of soldiers in brown leather uniforms and fat conical helmets strapped under their chins. Their shields were small and round.

Messapians!

The enemy soldiers ran in disarray towards Lysander's line, shouting in a foreign tongue.

'On my count!' barked Sulla. 'Left . . . Right . . . Left . . . Right.'

Lysander's lines moved forward in formation, gathering speed until they too were running.

'Cut them down!' shouted Phlebas.

Lysander saw there were perhaps three hundred Messapians, all armed. As he had been taught by his former tutor Diokles, he chose one, a strapping man whose chest hair seemed as thick as a dog's pelt, and ran at him.

Lysander parried the enemy's sword with his shield, and thrust down with his spear, but the force of the collision sent him cartwheeling through the air. He thumped into the midst of the Messapian line, scattering soldiers around him. But he had lost his spear. Up like lightning, Lysander backed away from a sword swipe, drew his own blade, and lunged. The man who faced him was cautious, and stayed out of reach, and their blows sailed harmlessly wide. Lysander saw a helmet on the ground. He placed his toe beneath it, then flicked the helmet into the air at his attacker. The man swung his sword to knock it away. Using the distraction, Lysander took two quick strides forward and sliced across the man's sword arm, drawing a high-pitched cry from his throat. He put all his weight behind the swing, cutting deep into the soldier's side.

A Messapian rolled over at Lysander's side, his face streaked with blood. As he tried to sit up, one of the unarmed Spartans drove his elbow into his face. The Messapian's head smashed on to the ground, and he didn't move again. The Spartan grabbed his shield and re-entered the fight. Lysander joined a group of three

Spartans who were surrounding a Messapian. He was swinging his sword wildly to force them back, but Lysander barrelled through their midst and caught him off balance. They slammed into the ground and the others piled on, pinning back the Messapian's arms while another punched his face again and again.

'Good work,' said the Spartan, as he stood over the body.

Two of the men shared the dead Messapian's weapons – a shield and short dagger, while the third stripped his stiffened leather armour.

Through the streets, the Messapians were overcome, and with each that fell, Lysander saw the Spartan force grow stronger. Suddenly, a shout passed along the Messapian line, and they turned their backs and fled. Lysander and the others swarmed after them. Lysander caught one and buried his sword to the hilt between his shoulders. He felt the blade burst through the other side and the man crumpled to the ground, lying face down in the road.

'That was for Orpheus,' Lysander said.

The Spartans coursed down the road, clambering over walls and through vegetable gardens, chasing down their foe. It was a surprise when the road suddenly opened up and Lysander reached the market square. It was larger than he had envisaged. A small temple of marble gleamed, and a statue stood on a plinth at the base of wide steps. The portico looked out towards the sea, and several other buildings looked administrative –

perhaps a law court and a counting house. On the far eastern side was a huge wooden hall, two storeys tall. A low wall, crumbling in places, separated the open space from the sea beyond. Two jetties, one a hundred paces long, and another much shorter, jutted out into the sea and were lined with boats. The square itself, which backed on to the sea on one side, was thronged with Messapian soldiers, all facing outwards to meet the oncoming attackers. They were trapped like sheep.

Lysander saw Nikos on a tall, chestnut horse, directing his men on the far side of the square, beside the market hall. Leonidas and Aristodermus stood side by side in the front line, with the rest of the boy's division ordered around them. The Spartan army waded among the enemy in tight formation, mowing them down with spear thrusts. They showed no mercy, but Lysander knew enough of his city's ways not to expect any.

A horn sounded as another gang of Spartans surged from behind the temple, led by Anaxander and Cimon. They joined the crush, and Lysander watched as the Messapians ran towards the sea. They sprinted along the long jetties, pushing each other into the water in a last hope of escape.

Lysander threw himself into pursuit, driven by a lust for revenge. His dead friend was worth a hundred of these men. He remembered Lernos' words – they'd killed the Elders of Taras like sheep. He leapt over the harbour wall, and on to the beach, then sprinted along the jetty after the fleeing enemy. They splashed in the water either side, struggling to keep themselves above the water in their armour.

They'd rather drown than face a Spartan, thought Lysander. *Well, let Poseidon have them.*

'We did it!' said Demaratos, appearing at his side. Lysander saw the Fire of Ares glint beneath his cloak. 'We freed the town. Come on. Let's regroup in the square.'

Lysander found himself alone on the jetty. As the bodies writhed in the water, he felt elated, but uneasy. *Can it be this easy?*

He spat into the water.

'Cowards!' he shouted. 'Ares turns his head from you in shame.'

One of the men in the water gripped the side of a rowing boat and stared at Lysander.

'Come on, Messapian!' yelled Lysander. 'Why do you cower like a crab where I can't get you?' A smile spread across the Messapian's lips, and Lysander felt uneasy. 'Come out and face me.'

The man stayed where he was, and Lysander looked back towards the square, a sea of red cloaks, where the Spartans who brought up the rear were finishing off the remaining Messapians who were trapped there. Leaving the man, he paced back along the jetty and climbed up on to the sea wall. *Something isn't right.*

He saw Demaratos further along the wall, and jogged over to his side. The square below was littered with dead Messapians.

Into the middle of the carnage came Nikos on his horse, looking every bit the victorious leader. His face was flushed with excitement but Lysander noticed that his sword was not even bloody.

'The battle for Taras is over!' shouted Nikos from horseback.

The Spartans lifted their weapons and cheered.

'From now on, the people of Taras will know who their true leaders are. This is a colony of Sparta!'

The men shouted again.

'Sir,' said Anaxander, running up to the horse's side, 'we have the Messapian leader — Viromanus.'

'Bring him out,' said Nikos.

The crowd parted and Lysander climbed on a jetty stone to look over the heads of the men. A ragged man, whose clothes were soaked in blood, was dragged along the ground by two Spartans and thrown at the feet of Nikos' horse. He stood up and faced Nikos. It was strange; despite his bloodied clothes, there was still the light of triumph in Viromanus' eyes.

Something caught Lysander's eyes behind the temple. A flicker of flame. *It must have been set by our men*, he thought. In fact, there were several small fires in the streets above the square, and trails of smoke spiralled into the sky.

'Nikos will kill him, for sure,' said Demaratos.

Lysander saw several young men scurry across the street up the hill from the square. They had no uniform or armour. Not Messapians. Citizens of Taras, surely. They made their way towards the fires, carrying something.

Putting out the fires?

Nikos dismounted and called for a spear. One of his men handed him an eight-footer. The crowd had backed away now, leaving a wide circle around Nikos and the Messapian leader.

Silence fell.

Lysander's eyes flitted back up the hill away from the spectacle. He could see more men now, perhaps twenty scattered among the houses around the fire. But they weren't making any effort to douse the flames. Then he recognised the objects in their hands. Bows.

'Look out!' Lysander shouted. All heads turned in his direction, and he pointed up the slope. 'They're getting ready to attack!'

A cry went up, and was answered across the breadth of the town. More men flooded out of buildings, dropped down from trees or emerged from empty barrels. They dipped their arrows into the flames, and rested them against their bowstrings. The yellow tips flickered, all pointing into the square.

He remembered the smile of the Messapian in the water. Now it made sense.

The men fleeing into the sea had been a trick; a distraction.

Now Lysander and his comrades were trapped.

CHAPTER 18

'Take cover!' shouted Lysander.

The air whooshed as arrows sailed from the bows.
Lysander leapt from his vantage point. Across the square,
men who had shields lifted them above their heads.

The deadly hail fell, thudding into the ground and
into men's bodies. Cries came from all over the square,
and a Spartan soldier collided with Lysander. They fell
together, and Lysander grunted as the man toppled on
to him. The air around was suddenly hot with fire.

He wriggled from underneath. The Spartan was a
dead weight. One arrow was lodged in the man's chest,
another had entered at the base of his neck. Lysander
gagged at the aroma of seared flesh, from the dying
flames of the arrows. Across the square, panic had set in.
Many had fallen, and were either lying still, or writhing
across the ground to find shelter. He saw Demaratos
breaking the arrows from the front of his shield. The
men on the slopes were lighting another volley of
arrows.

As the archers released, Lysander grabbed the dead man's body and pulled it on top of him just in time. Another two shafts buried themselves in the corpse.

'Spartans, rally!' shouted one of the leaders. 'Attack their positions.'

Lysander ran back into the middle of the square, and found the rest of the boys' division gathered around Aristodermus.

A group of Nikos' Spartans were streaming up the hill, roaring at the archers ahead. Lysander took a spear from the ground and headed after them.

'Stop, Lysander!' It was Aristodermus.

Lysander turned. 'We need to neutralise the archers, otherwise we're all dead.'

'Let Nikos' men handle it,' said his tutor. 'We must stay here to face any who attack from the flanks.'

The Tarantian Spartans were twenty paces from the archers. 'Take aim!' yelled a voice above the din. They brought their bows level, and fired into the oncoming wall of men. Lysander watched as several from the front Spartan rank collapsed, their places only to be filled with more red cloaks. They reached twenty paces, and the bowmen fired again at point blank range. They couldn't miss, and although most of the arrows slammed into their shields, soldiers collapsed as other shafts pierced their legs or slipped though the gaps. They were scythed down like fresh corn.

'Keep on them, men!' shouted Nikos from the base of the hill. It was suicide, but Lysander realised that without the attack there'd be nothing to stop the archers. The Spartan advance was slowed, but still they reformed and trudged on. The archers tried to reload, but there wasn't time. Lysander lost sight of them as the Spartan soldiers leapt the fires and overwhelmed them. The archers fell beneath their spears. Screams were cut short as the points drove through their flesh, or the heavy lizard-stickers smashed their brains from their skulls.

From his right came the rumble of feet, men running. A huge mob, many hundreds strong, careered down the western entrance to the square. Most wore simple tunics, and made no effort to stay in order. Lysander took his place beside Demaratos and Prokles in the front line.

Any remaining people of Taras had finally come out to fight.

'Fall back!' called Nikos. 'Back to the square.'

Where had these people been hiding? In cellars and attics, no doubt. Packed together in courtyards watching as the Spartans marched through their streets unchallenged.

From the smattering of matching leather jerkins, Lysander saw there were some remaining Messapian soldiers among the crowd, but most of the fighters looked like ordinary men. They marched to the edge of the square, then drew up, facing the Spartans.

Nikos' men descended the hill again, and quickly took up their positions behind the ranks of boys. Lysander felt better with them at his back. The phalanx was dense, but would it be enough?

This was happening just as he had said – a few of the enemy soldiers had slipped through their tightening grip, and had marshalled the angry populace.

For the first time since the battle against the Persians, Lysander felt the thud of true fear in his chest. His hands tightened into fists as he tried to control the emotions that whirled through him.

The men didn't hold ordinary weapons. A few carried axes for chopping wood. Some had rough pieces of timber jutting with rusty nails, or strapped with sharpened flints. One man, whose shoulders bulged with muscle was brandishing a blacksmith's mallet. They had no armour to speak of, and wore simple peasant clothes, but Lysander could tell from their eyes that they'd fight to the death.

'Let go your weapons!' said a Messapian from the front of the Tarantian force. 'And live.'

All eyes went to Nikos, but he looked around him with uncertainty. Lysander let his gaze travel over the men – there were maybe two hundred and fifty left. The Tarantians numbered twice that many, at least.

He can't surrender! thought Lysander. The shame would be too great to live with.

He looked backwards towards the eastern entrance to the square. They were hemmed in. To turn and flee that way would be futile.

Aristodermus jumped up on to the edge of a collapsed stall.

'If you want our weapons, Messapian, come and get them!'

Lysander cheered and the other Spartans joined in the shout of defiance. The lead Messapian turned to his men and raised his sword over his head. He gave a blood-curdling howl. The other men took up the cry and the square was filled with the sound of rage. The Messapian lowered his weapon and pointed. The desperate mob flooded into the square.

There was no chance to gather into formation, no time to assemble the phalanx. This was fighting beyond Lysander's training. He had a sword, a shield, and his courage. As the two armies clashed, Lysander picked a Messapian carrying a spear. The point thrust towards his head, an elementary mistake. *Always aim at the biggest target – the body*, Diokles had said. Lysander dodged and jumped forward, piling his knee into the soldier's stomach. As the man bent over, he adjusted his grip and rammed his sword downwards into the spinal column.

He was pulling out his sword when a blow caught him on the upper arm. As he spun around, a Tarantian bore down on him, swinging a poker. Lysander half ducked, half stumbled out of the way. The man's eyes were wild.

The Tarantian took a swing, and was momentarily off balance. Lysander stabbed and drew blood from his torso. When the man's glance dropped to his wound, Lysander finished the job, hacking down into the neck. The corpse sank at his feet, gurgling blood.

The square resounded with the thud of metal on wood, and the shouts of pain, fear and anger. Lysander found himself attacking anyone who wasn't in a red cloak. Someone crashed into his back and he spun round, sword raised. Prokles stood there, short spear poised and dripping with blood. For a heartbeat they stared at each other.

'Save some for me, comrade,' he said, then plunged back into the crowd.

A Spartan soldier tumbled like a felled tree in front of Lysander, dead before he hit the ground. The side of his head was brutally caved in. Lysander saw why. A man wearing the charred leather apron of a blacksmith held aloft a mallet.

'Are you ready to die, Spartan?' he shouted.

'A Spartan is always ready to die,' said Lysander.

The man growled and swung his mallet with ferocious speed. It connected in the centre of Lysander's breastplate. He flew backwards through the air, feeling every bone shake, and slammed into a market stall, jarring his back.

His ears and head rang, and his vision blurred double. He lay back on the wood, and tried to find his breath.

A shadow loomed above him, and the mallet arced towards his face, ready to crush his skull. Groggy, Lysander rolled sideways and heard the hammer crunch into the wood, showering his face with splinters. As the man struggled to free the head, Lysander sliced across the back of his legs, severing the tendons under his knees. The man gave a throaty groan like an ox being slaughtered, and smashed face first into the stall. The wooden structure fell in from above, burying him.

Lysander tried to stand, but his chest was in agony from the hammer blow, and he saw that the bronze of the chest plate was heavily dented. He managed to hobble towards the temple. Two men were struggling hand to hand at the base of the statue, and Lysander realised one of them was Aristodermus. He'd lost his helmet and his hair was as white as the marble of the temple. The man he was fighting had a short dagger in his hand, and Aristodermus was gripping his wrist. Aristodermus suddenly turned, and threw the man over his hip. With a clever twist of the wrist the knife was in his hand, and he slashed the inside of his enemy's arm, through the artery. The man screamed and gripped the wound, but the sound was cut short when Aristodermus stamped on his exposed throat.

Lysander swallowed a lungful of smoke and coughed. The fires had caught nearby, and black clouds were drifting across the square, temporarily obscuring the fighting men. They cleared for a moment, and Lysander saw Demaratos and Leonidas side by side, fighting with short spears and swords. They faced four locals, who were circling them. One carried a harpoon and a fishing net. Demaratos caught a blow with a club to the ear, which made Lysander flinch, and his friend fell out of sight. His attacker lifted the club high and for a terrible moment, Lysander thought Demaratos would be killed.

He jumped down from the steps and ran. As he approached, Leonidas caught one of the attackers in the belly with his spear and the man keeled backwards, screaming as he clutched his punctured bowels. But at the same time, the Tarantian with the net had entangled Leonidas's feet.

Lysander ran through the crowd as the man stabbed at Leonidas with the harpoon. His friend managed to block the movement with his hand, but the point tore his skin, and blood coursed along his arm. The man raised his weapon to stab again but Lysander buried his sword up to the hilt in the man's side. The point emerged on the other side, streaked with gore, and the blood rushed over Lysander's knuckles.

'Thanks, friend,' said the prince.

Lysander searched the ground.

'Where's Demaratos?'

'He was here a moment ago.'

With a great cry, another wave of Tarantians pushed into the square, this time from behind the temple where the archers had been hiding. The fires had taken hold of several buildings now, and the smoke stung Lysander's eyes. He searched around for Demaratos.

'Fall back!' came a Greek voice. 'Abandon the square!'

Lysander could see it was hopeless. They were outnumbered, and exhaustion was taking its toll. The corpses of both sides lay together all around the square, by the doors of buildings and on the temple steps. There was no sign of Nikos, but his horse was standing by a water trough.

The remaining Spartans were leaving their sporadic fights and gathering towards the eastern side of the square by the large hall, and Lysander sprinted behind Leonidas to join them, avoiding the missiles thrown by the locals.

Suddenly something swamped him from behind, and Lysander lost his footing. His sword clattered to the ground. Someone was on his back, and hands clawed at his face. He felt nails gouge his cheeks as the fingers searched out his eyes. With one hand trapped beneath him and holding his shield, he managed with the other to bat the hands away, but they closed again on his throat. He spluttered for breath, but the grip was strong.

Looking across the ground he caught sight of a rock. If only he could reach it.

The person strangling him let out a screech, and Lysander felt his strength waning. The tendons of his shoulder and elbow popped as he stretched for the rock.

His fingertips stroked the ground. *Just a fraction more.*

The world lost colour, and blood rushed up behind his eyes. He could feel the hot breath of his attacker on his neck.

With the last of his strength, Lysander jerked his hip

and managed to close his fingers around the rock. He threw it backwards and heard it connect. Suddenly, the pressure on his throat was gone. Twisting, he threw the person off, and scrambled to grab his sword. The attacker was clutching his face where the rock had struck him, and long hair trailed over his hands. Lysander drove his sword into the man's heart.

With a choked breath, the attacker fell backwards and the hands fell away from the bloody face. Smooth skin and dark features.

A woman.

Lysander's eyes fell over her slender, well-muscled arms. Her legs were strong and lithe.

An athlete, perhaps, thought Lysander. *Like Chilonis.* This is how desperate the fight had become; even the local women were joining the rebels to attack Spartans like Lysander. He felt a rush of emotion as he thought about Kassandra and Chilonis, his dead mother – the only females who had come close to touching his heart.

'I'm sorry,' he told the dead woman, closing her eyes.

'Lysander!' shouted a voice. 'Come on!'

He turned to see Prokles calling to him from the double gate of the two-storey market hall. That must be where the Spartans were going to regroup.

Lysander left the woman's body, and ran towards Prokles. Spartans were streaming in through the gates, while a small phalanx, four men deep, had linked shields to guard the entrance. He slipped inside.

'Fall in!' came the cry. The remaining soldiers drew up their shields and retreated inside. The last two dragged the doors shut behind them, and pulled down the heavy wooden beam into place.

The roars from outside became muted. They were safe for the moment. And trapped. Lysander looked around him at the groups of Spartans who were wiping blood from their swords and straightening their red cloaks.

Never before in my life have I retreated, Lysander thought to himself.

As soldiers, they had failed.

CHAPTER 19

The door thudded as Tarantians threw their weight against it, and the reverberations filled the vacant hall. Spartans arranged themselves in a row with their backs to the wooden door. It shook again.

'It won't hold for long,' said Cimon. 'We're finished.'

'We're not finished until our blood stains the earth,' said Aristodermus. 'Where's Nikos?'

'He lost his horse,' said Lysander.

'He's dead,' said Phlebas. 'Gutted like a fish and hung from the temple rafters.'

A gasp spread through the men. Desecrating a body was the ultimate offence.

'He was dragged from his horse, and stabbed to death.'

The hall was full of Spartans. Tables were being pushed back against the walls, and two chickens flapped among their feet, feathers flying. Half the hall was double height, built of solid logs, with small half-open shutters high up providing the only illumination. The far end had a second-storey platform reached by a ladder. A pulley was set up there, presumably for lifting heavy objects to the upper floor. The centre of the wide hall was supported by a row of wooden columns, hewn from full trunks.

In the meagre light Lysander inspected the weary faces of those around him. Streaked with blood and dust, many carrying wounds, the remains of the force looked defeated. Even Leonidas, who stood holding an axe in one hand and a Spartan shield in the other, looked full of fear. He saw at best fifty other boys from the barracks. But no Demaratos. There were twice as many of the native Spartans. Anyone else was already dead. Or left outside. Lysander shivered at the thought.

The thudding on the gate fell silent.

'What's happening?' said a Spartan. 'Why have they stopped?'

'We're at their mercy,' said Cimon, stepping forwards. 'Why rush?'

'We need to make a plan,' said Aristodermus. He climbed on to a table, and Lysander saw his hair was matted with blood. 'Gather round.'

'For what,' laughed Cimon. 'Death awaits all of us. You included. Prepare for it.'

A torch, flaming at one end, landed on the floor in the middle of the hall. A soldier ran over and stamped it out. Looking up, Lysander saw where it had come from – the open shutter.

Two more came through the windows on opposite sides.

'We have to close the windows,' said Aristodermus. 'Quickly!'

There was a long pole made of supple wood leaning against the wall by the nearest shutter, and Lysander used it to unhook the shutter. He did the same with the others, and soon the room was cast in near darkness besides the dying embers of the extinguished flames.

'That will only buy us a little time,' said Cimon.

'Share your weapons,' said Aristodermus. 'Make sure each man has at least a fighting chance.'

Lysander fell in at Leonidas's side.

'What happened to Demaratos? He disappeared.'

'Maybe he found somewhere to hide.'

'No,' said Lysander. 'I saw him knocked unconscious.'

'Then I pray the Gods spare him the same indignity Nikos suffered.'

'I have to go back for him.'

'Courage for the sake of hope is nothing but fool-hardiness,' said Leonidas. 'You go out there, you die.'

The smell of smoke was suddenly stronger in the air, and Lysander saw a carpet of fumes flowing under the doors, beneath the feet of the Spartans manning them. The grunts and shouts from the men outside diminished. Were they backing off?

'They're trying to smoke us out!'

'Or burn us alive,' said Prokles.

The Spartans on the door tore off their cloaks and

214

padded the base of the doors, covering their mouths as the smoke thickened.

Lysander walked up to Phlebas.

'There must be another way out.'

The lieutenant shook his head. 'This building is used to hold slaves and stores from trading ships before market. It's meant to be secure. There's no other way.'

Lysander looked around desperately, and his eyes fell on the low-beamed upper floor. The rafters were thatched. *If only we could get up there.*

'What about the roof?' he said.

'What about it? Are you Icarus, young man, with wings made of wax and feathers?'

Lysander ran to the ladder. Though his legs and arms were heavy with the day's fighting, he scaled it quickly, and climbed on to the upper floor. Standing on the pulley block, he felt along the inside of the roof between the rafters. The thatch boards were thick.

'Does anyone have an axe?' he called down.

The Spartans gathered below were like shadows through the smoke which continued to billow under the gate; they must have lit fires all around the front of the building. It wouldn't be long until the air became unbreathable. One of the Spartans stepped forward, coughing into his hand.

'I have this.' He was holding a mace – a wooden handle with a heavy ball of iron on the end.

'Throw it to me,' said Lysander.

The man drew his arm back and on the forward

underarm swing, let go of the mace. Lysander caught it, and almost overbalanced. It weighed as much as a fattened lamb. He took his position under the rafters. With all the force he could gather, he thrust upwards with the heavy end into the wood. It cracked along its length.

'What good will that do?' said Cimon.

'It will let the smoke out for a start,' said Lysander, coughing.

Three more strokes and he could see what remained of the daylight. Dusk was drawing in and the moon was already in the sky. Straight away, smoke began to funnel through the hole, to be whipped away by the breeze.

Lysander dropped the mace with a heavy clang and tugged at the jagged edges, ripping the tightly packed straw away. Leonidas joined him. The noise from the crowd outside reached his ears. They were shouting to each other.

'We'll roast them and feed them to the pigs!'

'They'll have to come out soon; watch the front doors, Plautus.'

But we're not going that way, Lysander said to himself.

Soon he had torn away enough of the roofing material to climb through, and Leonidas gave him a foot up on to the roof. Two gutters – dry now – ran the length of the building to carry away rainwater and the roof rose on each side meeting the vertical wall, so that

Lysander was shielded from the view of the people below. He climbed up on to the ledge and peered over. The vantage point afforded Lysander a view over the whole town.

Hundreds of bodies were strewn about, along the harbour wall, across the market square, and up the streets that led away from it. The sea was calm; corpses bobbed in the water like driftwood. The fires among the buildings up from the square had mostly been put out, but the glow of orange flame flickered at the far end of the building where the entrance was. Behind the town the ridge rose like a dark cloud.

What have we done?

Even if they drove the Messapians out, would there be any people left to live in Taras? How many of the houses would be empty, how many families decimated by their actions?

What glory is there in that?

'Kill them all!' shouted a voice below. 'Down with Sparta.'

The words shook Lysander to his senses. He was here because he had to be. It was his destiny. Why else had the Gods guided Lernos to his barracks? His father and grandfather had both given their lives to Sparta. Lysander would make the same sacrifice. He kept low, and made his way in a crouch across the roof to the rear of the hall – the eastern end – where he peeped out over the end into a deserted alley.

Another set of low buildings, workshops of the

artisan quarter if Lernos had spoken accurately, spread out, separated by a warren of narrow passageways. Was it possible they could make their escape that way?

Leonidas crawled alongside and inspected the drop. It was at least four times Lysander's height.

'We'll break our legs,' said Lysander.

'We could tie cloaks together, and climb down,' said Leonidas.

'We'd be lowering ourselves into a den of lions,' said Lysander. 'But if we could get on to the workshops,' he pointed across the gap, 'we could separate; more could escape.'

Leonidas inspected the gap. 'Even with a run up, it's a long way.'

He was right, but Lysander had another idea.

'When Timeon and I were younger, we used to cross a narrow point in the river to bring our mothers wild garlic from the far bank. We used to cross the river without getting our feet wet by using an old piece of fence post. You know, by vaulting.'

'We don't have a fencepost, and our spears aren't long enough.'

'We have the window pole.'

A grin broke out across Leonidas's face. 'It's ambitious, but it might work.'

Lysander clapped his friend on the back. 'Your father, the king, would be proud of you,' he said.

Leonidas smiled, as two red spots appeared on his cheeks. 'I've learnt a lot, fighting beside you.'

'Then let's put that learning to good use,' Lysander announced.

He climbed back into the upper floor – the men within were all lying close to the floor to avoid the worst of the smoke. Lysander descended the ladder and leapt the last few steps.

'We have to fight them,' said Sulla, shifting his shield further up on his arm. 'I'm not waiting here to suffocate.'

'No,' said Lysander, 'there's another way out.'

'You talk too much boy,' said Sulla. 'I've lived here all my life – there's no way out of this building but through that front gate.'

Lysander grabbed the long pole. 'We can get across to the workshops using this. The townspeople aren't watching the back of the building.'

A huge crash shook the door of the hall, and the Spartans guarding it were thrown clear. Immediately they hurled themselves back against it.

'It looks like their patience has run out,' said Aristodermus, with a wry smile. 'Let's see if Lysander is right. Head for the roof!'

The door shook again, and the sound of wood cracking split the smoky air.

'Go,' said Lysander, pushing his shoulder up against the door. 'We'll hold the door.'

The men coursed up the ladder close on each other's heels. The doors thudded, and this time the beam that locked them splintered a little. It wouldn't hold much longer.

The window pole was passed up and threaded through the hole in the roof to the men who had already got that high. Lysander could hear the growing shouts from the crowd outside.

'You'll be food for the dogs soon!' someone called out.

The last of the men were at the bottom of the ladder, and Prokles shouted back to Lysander.

'Come on, leave the doors!'

With a terrifying crunch, the wood split above the beam as the battering ram punctured the door. Lysander could see a smooth lock of hair chiselled into marble. They were using the statue!

'Sacrilege!' said one of the men. 'They defile Sparta.'

The ram withdrew, and the cries of the mob pierced the hall.

'Tear them apart!'

'Down with Sparta!'

Then the ram smashed again, sending splinters into the hall. Lysander caught a glimpse of something familiar.

It can't be!

'Take it from them!' Lysander said tersely. He had no idea commands would ever flow so easily from his mouth; he, who had once been a slave. Two Spartans pulled away from the door, and seized the head of the statue. Lysander looped his arm around the massive torso and heaved.

The marble cracked across the middle, and Lysander

and his comrades fell to the ground holding their fragment.

'Come on, this is a waste of time. We have to go – now!' said one of the Spartans. 'Let's join the others on the roof.'

Lysander was staring at the statue, heady with shock. It wasn't the familiar face that drew his attention. No, it was the familiar carved emblem resting on the statue's chest.

He ran his fingers over the outline of a jewel surrounded by ancient script.

The Fire of Ares shall inflame the righteous.

CHAPTER 20

The Fire of Ares!

The amulet had been passed down from father to son in his family for over seven hundred years. It could mean only one thing.

My ancestor. Here, in Taras.

The wooden beam buckled as the Tarantians hammered again with the remains of the statue.

'Come, Lysander. Run!' said Prokles. He was at the top of the ladder, calling down.

Lysander let go of the marble fragment and dashed to the ladder, scaling it like a lizard. The beam on the door split in two and the pieces dropped to the floor. Angry attackers streamed into the hall.

One of them shouted and pointed to the second-level platform, and they charged for the ladder. One, barely older than Lysander, reached the bottom and started placing hand over hand on the rungs.

Lysander tried to kick the top of the ladder away, but it was nailed to the platform. The boy reached the top, so he swung a foot into his face. With a cry, the attacker let go and tumbled backwards, taking another man with him. Lysander kicked ferociously at the ladder until the nails shook loose and it toppled backwards into the hall. Rocks and pieces of wood flew towards him, hurled by the people below, and Lysander shielded himself with his arm as he lumbered through the hole in the roof.

There were still five Spartans on top of the hall, including Aristodermus and Prokles, but others were already over the alleyway, and running across the roofs of the workshops. Leonidas was standing on the far side, catching those who swung across and throwing back the pole. Nikos' lieutenant, Sulla, went over. The pole came back.

'We have to hurry,' said Lysander. 'They'll work out soon enough what we're doing.'

'You go next,' said Aristodermus, pointing to the gap.

Lysander shook his head. 'I'll follow you. If this goes wrong, the others need their commander.'

Aristodermus gave a brisk nod. 'Death and honour, Spartan.'

'Death and honour,' Lysander replied.

Aristodermus ran to the edge, grasped the waiting pole, and vaulted smoothly across. As his feet hit the roof opposite, he rolled and righted himself. With a final look back, he made his escape across the roofs. Leonidas pushed back the pole. It was painfully slow, and Lysander could hear the confused shouts in the hall below. It wouldn't be much longer.

Kantor went next, sailing over.

Now up stepped one of Nikos' Spartans. The soldier ran to the edge, took the pole in both hands and took off.

Something went wrong.

The Spartan's hands must have been sweaty, or his arms not strong enough. He slipped down the pole and slammed into the opposite wall. He rebounded and landed on his back in the alleyway below. After that he didn't move.

The pole landed beside him.

Someone shouted. The cry came from the end of the alley. A band of five Tarantians, armed with Spartan short spears, had seen the fallen man.

'Leander, get up!' shouted Sulla from the far side. The fallen man stirred a little, reaching a hand to his head.

The Tarantians were on him like a pack of dogs, stabbing with their spears. Blood spattered their faces and clothes, spilling out into the road. Lysander thanked the Gods that Leander's death was quick.

Prokles pulled Lysander back from the edge.

'Stay down.'

It was just the two of them left on the roof now, and Leonidas who waited for them on the rooftop across the alley. The others had obviously made it to street level, pursued by the bloodthirsty cat-calls of the Tarantians.

Lysander signalled to Leonidas with his hand: *Go!*

Leonidas stepped to the edge of the workshop roof and looked into the alley beneath. Lysander could hear that it was thronged with angry townsfolk.

Leonidas looked back at Lysander and their eyes met across the empty space that separated them.

Go, friend, Lysander willed him. Leonidas lowered his gaze and turned, bounding across the roofs until he disappeared from sight.

Maybe it's our turn to die, Lysander thought.

'Over here!' hissed Prokles. He was by the northern side of the hall, where thick smoke billowed up the side of the building. He held his arm over his nose and mouth, and pointed down. 'Think we can make it?'

Lysander peered over the edge, and saw a stack of wooden cases in a yard, no doubt ready to be loaded on to a ship. There were pottery wine jugs too, some as tall as a man, others half and quarter size. Now the people of Taras were pursuing the fleeing Spartans, Lysander counted only three people about thirty paces away, but their attention was on stripping the armour from the dead bodies. The drop was about fifteen feet.

'What choice do we have?'

Prokles turned and lowered himself over the edge, extending his arms to get as near as possible to the ground. He let go, and hit the ground with a thump. Lysander heard him draw a sharp breath and grip his knee, but he managed not to cry out.

Lysander prepared himself to jump. As he tensed his

muscles, a band of four Messapians came around the corner. They were at ease, with loosened armour, big men, laughing to each other as a man tried on a Spartan helmet. Only one seemed to be carrying a weapon – a sword. Lysander lay flat on the roof to wait for them to pass.

But they didn't.

The men took their seats on the outlying crates, just a few paces from where Prokles was hidden below. Lysander saw the sheen of sweat on Prokles' brow. He looked up, and motioned for Lysander to jump.

'How can I?' he whispered. 'They'll see me.'

Prokles gazed back up at Lysander, a frown creasing his brow. Then Lysander saw the boy's face clear; it was as if he'd come to a decision. Prokles crept out from his hiding place behind the crates.

What's he doing?

Prokles shuffled around so that he was within spitting distance of the enemy, concealed only by a small stack of cargo. As Prokles put his hands against the top crate and began to push, Lysander realised his plan.

He's saving me!

Prokles lunged, and the crate toppled off the pile and smashed open on the floor in the middle of the group of men, making them stumble backwards. Bolts of linen spilled out over the ground, and Prokles made a dash for it, but he was hobbling from the fall. The startled Tarantians paused for a heartbeat, then started in pursuit, yelling at each other. They caught Prokles as he

226

tried to slip between two buildings, and tripped him. Immediately, they were kicking and clawing, and Prokles rolled into a ball to protect himself.

'I have to jump,' Lysander muttered. 'I can't let Prokles' sacrifice be wasted.'

Lysander took a few steps back up the roof, then ran at the edge and leapt off. His legs circled through the air, and he smashed on to a crate, splintering the wood, then rolled forward to break his fall. He jumped down to another crate and then to the ground. The man with the sword was telling the others to move aside so he could finish Prokles, and it was a Messapian at the back of the group who turned and saw Lysander coming towards him.

Lysander took hold of the ears of a small jug, and swung it around. The pottery exploded against the side of the man's face, showering red wine over the group. With the shard that remained in his hand, Lysander slashed across the throat of the man with the sword.

A fist hit him in the kidney, and Lysander buckled to one knee. As a second punch came towards his face, he blocked with his elbow and pulled the attacker over his shoulder. He stood, then brought his knee down on the shoulder and heard the joint break. The man scrambled away. Lysander turned to see Prokles grinding his foot into the other man's neck. The Messapian was trying to twist Prokles' ankle, but from his flailing hands Lysander could see his strength was waning.

'Go to Hades,' said Prokles, as the man's face turned purple.

Prokles' own face was covered in scratches and the split in his lip, from the fight with Lysander back in Sparta, had reopened.

'We'll be spotted like this,' said Prokles. 'Help me with these bodies.'

They dragged the corpses of two of the men into the path between the houses, and stripped the Messapian leather jerkins, replacing their own soiled cloaks.

'If we head roughly east, we should meet the road back to the ridge,' said Prokles.

They wasted no time, and slipped between houses. They went unchallenged, keeping their heads down. A few scattered bodies of the dead – Messapians and Spartans both – lay draining their blood into the narrow streets. Lysander didn't dwell on their lifeless faces, but furnished himself and Prokles with a short spear each, plucked from cold fingers. Soon the houses gave way to fields, with only the occasional farmhouse. As they passed what looked like an olive press, Lysander heard the gabble of voices from ahead. He seized Prokles' arm.

'Quick, hide,' he said, and they both ducked behind the wooden contraption used for crushing oil from the olives.

A band of Messapian soldiers and some local Tarantians came over the brow of the hill. All walked heavily, and were still sweating from the pursuit. Lysander wondered how many of the fleeing Spartans they'd managed to kill.

He waited for them to pass out of sight, and then set off again. They crossed the top of the hill, and saw the forest in the distance. There were bodies on the track, Spartans, by the colour of their cloaks.

They approached the low walls of a sheepfold on the left side of the path, and a voice called out in Italian. Two Messapians were behind the wall, stripping the breastplate of a dead Spartan.

Lysander and Prokles stopped dead and shared a look. One of the Messapians spoke to them again, obviously thinking they were on the same side. Lysander recognised the face of the corpse they were ransacking: Phlebas.

When they didn't reply, the faces of the Messapians showed confusion, and one of them stood up, and tried to draw his sword. It jammed in the scabbard. Lysander leapt into the sheepfold, and ran him through with his short spear. While his screams were still in the air, the remaining Messapian threw up his hands in surrender. Prokles didn't hesitate, stabbing first the stomach, and then the heart as the soldier fell.

Phlebas moved.

'He's alive!' gasped Prokles.

'Just,' whispered Phlebas, with barely moving lips. Blood had soaked his tunic and his face was white.

'We'll get you back to the forest,' said Lysander, taking his arm.

'No,' said Phlebas, 'I'm halfway to the Underworld already.'

'Your wounds can be tended,' said Lysander.

Phlebas opened his eyes a crack, and smiled. 'My wounds are beyond tending.' He frowned. 'You are the boy who dared to argue with Nikos.' He coughed, and blood spattered his lips. 'You were right. Our tactics were . . . flawed.'

'That's not important now,' said Lysander.

Phlebas' lips twisted and his back arched. He squeezed Lysander's arm, exhaled a long breath and sank back. His eyes closed.

'Come on,' said Prokles, turning to go.

Lysander lowered Phlebas' limp arm to his side, then looked back along the road. So many Spartans slaughtered. And for what? A piece of land in a foreign country.

CHAPTER 21

The light was fading as they entered the forest. Lysander had been worried they might not be able to find the camp again, but the way was clear from the churned footprints on the ground. The smell of woodsmoke drifted through the trees and soon they saw the orange glow of the Spartan campfires.

The camp had turned into an infirmary, and the sound of moaning mixed with the clanging of metal as weaponry was mended. The women and children were busy fetching water and looking after the injured soldiers. Lysander saw a man whose hand was hanging off. With a spit of wood between his teeth, the injured wrist was placed over a rock and a soldier sawed through the remaining tendons and bones with a short sword. The man writhed while three others held him down. Several men wore eyepatches or had bloody bandages on their heads.

'Lysander! Prokles!' Aristodermus approached through the crowds. He had no obvious injuries other than a thick swathe of linen wrapped around the top of his left arm. 'We thought you were dead.'

'How many are left?' said Lysander.

Aristodermus cast his eyes over the camp. 'We have around two hundred men able to fight, and forty-one from our barracks.'

'Only forty-one?'

Aristodermus looked to the ground. 'Twenty-seven are confirmed dead, and eleven more are unable to fight on. It is a heavy toll, but they died with honour.'

Twenty-seven from the barracks dead. Twenty-seven empty beds in the dormitory.

Lysander felt sick.

'Take some food,' said Aristodermus, 'and get some rest. We'll keep watches throughout the night. Tomorrow the Gods may favour us.'

'What happens tomorrow?' asked Prokles.

'We take back the town,' said Aristodermus grimly.

Prokles barked a laugh. 'With what? We've lost half our men already.'

'We still have half our men left,' said Aristodermus. 'The retreat was tactical.'

'We ran away,' said Lysander, suddenly angry. 'They defeated us.'

'The battle isn't over,' said Aristodermus. 'What did I tell you at the barracks? We *adapted*.'

Aristodermus' eyes gleamed as he spoke. Lysander didn't know what to believe. Since his earliest days in the agoge, he'd been told that retreat was not an

232

option, that a Spartan would rather die than turn his back on the enemy. He wasn't sure he wanted to be alive if it came at the cost of cowardice.

I won't ever retreat again, he promised himself.

Having eaten some cold roasted meat, Lysander borrowed a sewing kit from one of the women. The needle was made of a piece of carved bone. Prokles was already asleep by the fire when he found him, but he stirred his comrade.

'Go away, I need to sleep.'

'Let me look at your eye first,' said Lysander.

Reluctantly, Prokles sat up. The wound above his eyebrow was partially scabbed over, but Lysander could still see a patch of raw flesh beneath. Using a sponge, he dabbed lightly at the wound. Prokles' jaw flexed, but he didn't protest.

The air was full of snoring, and quiet mumblings as the soldiers spoke in their sleep, traumatised by the day's fighting.

'I don't understand,' said Lysander, cleaning the last of the dirt from the cut. 'You could have been killed distracting those Messapians by the crates.'

Prokles threw a piece of wood on to the fire, and stared into the flames.

'But I wasn't.'

'That's not the point,' said Lysander. 'We've never been good friends. You fought me back in the mountains.' He threaded the needle with black cord. 'Lie down.'

Prokles lay down on his back. 'You called me a coward.'

'I'm sorry for that – your courage speaks for itself. You put your life on the line for me. I'm grateful.' Lysander brought the two edges of the wound together with his finger and thumb.

'Do you know what you're doing?' asked Prokles.

'Of course.' He'd watched his mother stitch in their tiny hut in the Helot settlement. *How different can this be?*

Prokles shifted on the ground.

Lysander brought the tip of the needle to the bottom edge of the wound, and pressed it against Prokles' skin. 'Ready?'

Prokles grinned. Lysander pushed the tip into the flesh.

'By Kastor and Polydeukes!' hissed Prokles.

Lysander pushed further, through one side, and then the other, drawing the cord with the needle. Blood dribbled down Prokles' cheek, and he wiped it away with the sponge.

'Only seven more to go, I think,' said Lysander.

Prokles rolled his eyes. 'Make it quick.'

With a steady hand, Lysander completed the stitches. Fresh beads of sweat had formed across Prokles' forehead.

'How does it look?' he said.

Lysander wiped the remaining blood from the wound, and looked at the ragged stitches. 'It'll be a fine scar.'

Prokles laughed and took a swallow from a water flask. 'I should never have listened to that Helot of yours.'

'What do you mean?'

Prokles looked away. 'Nothing.'

'Tell me.'

Prokles sighed, and shrugged.

'I wasn't meant to tell you, but before we left Sparta your Helot – what's his name? – came to me and asked me to look out for you. He offered me money – gold.'

'Idas offered you gold?' said Lysander. 'Where from?'

Prokles shook his head. 'I don't know. He said someone important was looking out for you, and there'd be honour, as well as money, if I could keep you out of harm's way; get you back to Sparta in one piece.'

Someone wants to keep me safe? Who could it be?

'So that's why you risked death, for gold?' he said. 'I don't believe it.'

Prokles laughed a little and lay back again.

'I gave him the gold back. What does a soldier need with riches? It made me realise though, a Spartan is wealthy when he can rely on the man next to him in the phalanx. Sacrifice is the Spartan way. Nothing else matters.'

Lysander had never heard Prokles speak in such a way before, but it made him remember Demaratos. Despite the heavy weariness that seemed to hang from every limb, he dragged himself up, and picked his way over to the fire where Aristodermus lay. His tutor was easy to spot by his white shock of hair.

'What is it, Lysander? Sit down.'

Lysander crouched, and sat on a fallen log.

'It's Demaratos, sir.'

Aristodermus nodded. 'He was a brave soldier, and I know he was your friend. But his death will be remembered and his mother need fear no shame.'

'I think he might be alive,' said Lysander. 'I saw him dragged away in the fight.'

Aristodermus shook his head. 'He's probably suffered the same fate as Nikos, poor wretch.'

'Maybe,' said Lysander, pushing the image to the back of his mind. 'Or perhaps they've kept him alive for a reason.' Aristodermus didn't look convinced, so Lysander pressed on. 'What if they're torturing him for information, about our location, or the tunnels.'

'You think he would tell them?'

'Of course not,' said Lysander. 'He'd rather die first.'

'Then we don't have a problem.'

Lysander looked into Aristodermus' pale pink eyes. They betrayed no sign of emotion.

'We can't let him die.'

'There's nothing we can do now,' said Aristodermus. 'When we attack again in the morning, we'll look for him then.'

'It will be too late by then.'

'The men are tired now,' said Aristodermus. 'They can barely stand. We can't risk everyone for the sake of a boy who's probably already dead.'

Lysander walked back to his place at the fireside. He'd spent the Ordeal with Demaratos. Five days in the mountains, on the cusp of life and death. They'd fought, bonded, and learned to rely on one another, and Lysander knew he owed his life to his friend. He was sure Demaratos was still alive.

Prokles was already asleep, snoring on his back.

The Gods send help in the strangest of forms, thought Lysander, as he lay down beside the fire.

He didn't sleep well. It wasn't only the cold, or the fear of attack, or the grumbles of pain from around the camp. His mind kept shifting images around. He remembered his harsh words for Kassandra, and the broken vase.

I should have apologised. Why didn't I?

Stubbornness? Anger? Shame?

Orpheus was gone too. A Spartan unlike any other.

And what of the Helots on Kassandra's settlement? Lysander recalled dimly the cold winter days with his mother, when firewood and food were short. The slaves would find no help from Tellios.

Pick the battles you can win, his friend Timeon had always said.

So many gone: Timeon, Orpheus, his mother, his grandfather Sarpedon. All the victims of Sparta.

He wouldn't be a victim. Sparta wasn't a set of rules to be followed. There was nothing to be gained by following Lykurgos blindly. Were these the shackles the

Oracle had spoken of – the ones that bound him?

Being a Spartan was about honour, putting your comrades first. He wouldn't sit here, bound by orders, the chains of tradition. Not when one of his friends might be alive in Taras.

I have to act. I have to help my friend.

Nothing else mattered. He wouldn't wait like Achilles in his tent at the edge of the battlefield while Patroklus perished. He'd throw himself into the fray.

The Gods can do with me what they will.

He crouched in the darkness, and looked over towards Aristodermus. His tutor's chest rose and fell slowly. Should he take his sword? No, it would be better not to be recognised. He stripped off his cloak.

A simple boy from Taras – that's all I am.

Goose pimples stood up over his skin in the chill pre-dawn air, and his bones cracked as he made his way away from the dying fires. He stepped lightly between the sleeping men. If any saw him, they didn't speak. Soon he was among the trees again, heading for the forest edge.

He crossed the fields leading back to Taras, and met the track as dawn broke, the sky streaked with red like wine stains. On the road, ravens and crows were already alighting on the dead bodies, looking for soft tissues to scavenge: eyes, tongues, lips.

The first sounds he heard from the town were the dirges of mourning. High wails and low-pitched guttural sobs rang out. Everywhere smelled of charred wood, with a sickly scent lingering beneath. He heard people ahead, and peered around the edge of a potter's shed.

He saw dozens of red cloaks lining the ground. Spartan corpses.

A hole had been dug in the ground, and men, working in pairs, were lifting bodies by the shoulders and feet, and throwing them like sacks of grain into the burial pit. They wore cloths around their mouths and noses, and worked in silence. The smell reached Lysander in waves: stale blood, sweat and rottenness.

As he watched, another cart approached and tipped a pile of bodies by the hole. Two Spartans, a Messapian and several civilians. All equal in death.

Lysander took off the sash that girdled his tunic, and tied it over the lower part of his face, then stepped out from his hiding place and joined the queue of men. It was a risk, but he had to see if Demaratos was there. He shuffled forward until they reached the pile of corpses, then took the feet of a dead Tarantian while another lifted the head. They heaved the body over to the pit, and swung it in.

Lysander couldn't see Demaratos among the dead, but he saw several others from the barracks: Philo, Klemen, Dorixos. All boys he'd trained with, eaten with, slept alongside. Boys who'd faced the Persian hordes with him in the phalanx.

They were all dead for a piece of Sparta they would probably never have seen if it wasn't for Lernos arriving at their barracks.

He slipped away and rejoined the track towards the market square. As he left the residential buildings, the sound of wailing diminished.

In the square, blood stained the walls and left dark patches on the ground. The hall was blackened with soot around the lower parts of the walls, the door completely off its hinges and lying in pieces inside. The smashed statue of Lysander's ancestor was outside, and someone had scrawled writing across it.

Looking out towards the small harbour, a few corpses and bits of equipment were stranded on the narrow beach. The sea rolled and lapped at the shore.

Lysander didn't know where to start looking for Demaratos. He crept quickly around the precincts of the temple, looking for any sign of a red cloak, then paced up towards the stables where they had freed the prisoners the previous day. There were a few larger houses, presumably once belonging to wealthy Spartans, and Lysander searched through courtyards, not daring to enter the villas themselves. He walked back and forth among the narrow alleys separating the workshops, peering into the door of each.

He heard a muffled cry, and froze. The sound wasn't one of mourning, but of pain.

Rounding a row of stables, he listened for the sound again. The horses hung their heads in their stalls, and eyed him dispassionately.

Another shout of agony nearby.

Lysander picked up a horseshoe that was lying on the ground. It wasn't much of a weapon, but it was better than nothing.

At the far end of the line of stables was a building with a smoking chimney. Lysander heard the hiss of hot metal being plunged into water. A blacksmith's forge?

A spine-chilling scream pierced the air, and Lysander broke out into a run, reaching the door where the sounds came from. It was open a crack, and he put his eye to the gap.

The heat from the interior blasted his face, and his skin tightened.

The sight inside made his heart thud.

Demaratos was lying on a wide bench, his hands tied together and pulled taut by a cord attached to a ceiling hook. His feet were off the ground, tied together. His tunic had been pulled off his shoulders and was loose around his waist. Sweat dripped off his torso, and several deep red welts had been seared across his chest and abdomen.

Lysander ducked away slightly as a man came into view. It was the same Tarantian who must have spared Demaratos's life in the market square. He held a branding iron in his hands, glowing orange.

'No. Please,' pleaded his friend.

But the man didn't listen, and held the red-hot metal over his chest again. Then he let it wander upwards towards Demaratos's face. Lysander's friend twisted away, the tendons in his neck standing out.

'Don't!' he said. 'What have I done? Tell me what I've done wrong.'

Lysander kicked open the door. 'Don't touch him!'

CHAPTER 22

The man with the branding iron turned slowly, and looked Lysander up and down. Holding the horseshoe in his hand, Lysander suddenly felt ridiculous.

'Another Spartan boy?' said the man. 'When did the mother country stop sending real men?'

'You'll find out what this boy can do if you don't back away,' said Lysander. The heat from the forge was overwhelming, and Lysander's eyes stung with the smoke.

The man looked down casually at Demaratos. He still held the iron a few finger widths from his face.

'Put down that horseshoe, boy. You're in no position to make demands.'

Lysander gripped his only weapon even harder. His palm was already slippery with sweat.

A voice grunted behind him, and with it came the stink of stale wine. Lysander felt the tip of a blade against the back of his neck.

You idiot!

He dropped the horseshoe, and it thudded on the hard-packed floor of the blacksmith's chamber. A hand pushed Lysander to one side and he saw a small, older man with a face like a stray dog. A few whiskers of grey hair stuck out under his chin, and his grin revealed rotten teeth like burnt tree stumps. He was carrying a Spartan sword.

'Better do as Cato says,' said the man. 'He may not speak your Greek tongue, but his sword speaks a language you can decipher.'

Lysander stood back against the wall. The man who spoke Greek was clearly no simpleton. His eyes gleamed in the orange glow of the fire, and he plunged the iron back into the flames.

What can I do? thought Lysander, eyeing Demaratos's bonds. His friend wouldn't be of any use if it came to a fight. He'd have to talk his way out of danger. If only Timeon were here – he was always the persuasive one.

'Why don't you let him go? The battle's over – you won.'

'The battle may be over,' said the man, 'but the war has only just started. The Spartans will return.'

'No,' said Lysander. 'Our numbers are few. Nikos, the commander, is dead.'

The man snorted and turned the iron in the flames.

'Spartans treat their soldiers like slaves. There will be another Nikos.' He nodded to Demaratos, whose chest heaved with panic. 'But this son of Sparta will not be there to see that fight. The Gods will save special punishment for him, and the pain he will suffer here is only the start.'

He picked up the iron quickly and let it drop over Demaratos's chest. His friend screamed and the sound made Lysander's hair stand on end. Demaratos lurched on the bench, every limb straining to escape, and the smell of burning flesh filled Lysander's nostrils. He fought not to retch at the sickly aroma.

The man's face was like a statue, still as stone. His voice rumbled with a certainty that Lysander found unsettling, somehow far more terrifying than if he was shouting or cursing the Gods. He looked to the man called Cato. Could he tackle him without a weapon?

'What good can a hostage be to you?' he said in desperation. 'You say you know the Spartan ways. They won't bargain with you over the life of one boy.'

'You think I want a hostage?' said the man, his voice suddenly raised in pitch. 'This is not about bargaining. I've waited years for this moment. This is about revenge.'

'For what?'

'For decades of Spartan rule.'

The man plunged the iron back into the fire, turning it among the coals. There had to be something Lysander could say.

'Take me instead. This boy's nothing – an embarrassment to the barracks where he trains.'

Demaratos frowned in confusion through his daze of pain.

'I know who this boy is,' the man snarled. He held up his free hand. There, in his palm, was the Fire of Ares.

'He's Lysander, grandson of the Ephor Sarpedon, sprung from the line of the legendary Menelaos himself.'

Lysander suddenly felt cold. This man knew of the Fire of Ares' origins, all the way back to Menelaos, one of the first Spartan Kings who'd fought at Troy. 'No. No, he isn't . . .'

'Yes, I am,' whispered Demaratos. 'I'm the son of Thorakis.'

'And between the times of Troy, and now, there came another of that family whom every Tarantian despises. Aristarkus.'

Aristarkus? The name meant nothing to Lysander.

'They don't teach you about him in the barracks, do they?' said the man.

Was this some sort of trick? Lysander shook his head. His clothes were stuck to his body with sweat and his mouth was dry as sand. The point of the Tarantian's sword pressed into his throat. One wrong move and his blood would be spilling over the ground.

'And why should they,' continued the man. 'Aristarkus was an exile from your land – the illegitimate son of mighty Lykurgos, born of a Helot woman. A mothax, that's what you call them. He was sent here with the rest of them by Lykurgos himself. Cast out of Sparta for their impure blood. His cursed statue has stood on the temple steps for generations, a wretched reminder of our enslavement.'

Lysander felt his knees weaken as the man's story filtered through his brain.

'The statue with the Fire of Ares . . .' he muttered. 'Aristarkus was a mothax?'

'They're all mothakes!' laughed the Tarantian maniacally. 'You Spartans pride yourself on your bloodlines, your links to the past.' He prodded the iron towards Demaratos. 'Well, Lysander's blood here is as pure as ditchwater.'

Lysander's head was dizzy with the heat. If Aristarkus was a mothax, all his ancestors were. That meant Sarpedon too, his father Thorakis, his uncle Demokrates. Even Kassandra . . . none of them were Spartans of true blood. He needed to stall.

'And Aristarkus founded Taras?'

'Founded? No. Taras was here long before the half-breed Spartans came here. My ancestors fished these seas and farmed the vines in peace. What use did we have for weapons and war? No, we were put under the yoke by the invaders from Greece. They made us slaves, like their Helots.'

Now Lysander understood why Demaratos hadn't been killed in the market square. This man held him responsible for all Taras' woes. The strength of his hatred burned as fiercely as the forge.

'But the Fire of Ares is mine,' he said. 'It was given to me in Sparta.'

The blacksmith grunted. 'Aristarkus was exiled from Taras by his own men in the end. They grew tired of his strictness. It wouldn't surprise me if he ended up back in Sparta – a wolf always slinks back to its den.'

The man with the sword gabbled a few words, and the man with the branding iron replied.

'My brother says we should kill you both.'

Lysander held up his hands. 'Listen to me. This boy isn't Lysander – I am.'

The man tipped back his head and howled with laughter. 'I admire your bravery, Spartan, but I am no fool. Don't try me with lies.'

All this is my fault, thought Lysander.

'I'm telling the truth. I gave the amulet to this boy – Demaratos is his name – because I didn't want it any more. I felt I didn't deserve it, that it didn't belong around my neck. I was a mothax too, a Helot of the fields. The amulet was my father's, but since I've known of him, it's brought nothing but misery and pain. If I could, if it brought back the people whom I love, I'd go back to the fields and toil for the rest of my days. The amulet has been a curse.'

'You press a convincing case, twisting words like a lawyer in the courts,' said the man. 'But I don't believe you. This boy will die for the evil his ancestor wreaked.' He put down the branding iron and picked up a mallet. 'I'll break his bones, like Aristarkus broke the spirit of my people.'

Lysander sank to his knees. 'Please, you must believe

me. I'm the one you want.'

Demaratos moved his head slowly from side to side.

'He's lying,' he whispered. 'Let this impostor go, and get this over with.'

The man raised the mallet over Demaratos's lower ribs.

'This is for all my people.'

With a sharp swing, he brought the mallet down against Demaratos's side.

Lysander couldn't let Demaratos die in his place. There had to be a way to convince this man of the truth. But how could he do that with a sword at his throat?

The man lifted the mallet over his friend's kneecap next.

'Wait,' said Lysander. 'I can prove who I am.'

The Tarantian stopped, and the first frown of uncertainty crossed his face. 'How?'

'The amulet,' said Lysander. 'I can tell you what's written on it. It's in the old language – it says "The Fire of Ares shall inflame the righteous".'

The Tarantian huffed. 'Even I know this.' He turned back towards Demaratos.

'But I can draw the words themselves,' said Lysander. 'They're from the time of Troy.'

The man lowered his mallet, and looked at the Fire of Ares closely in the dim light. 'Go ahead – use that scrap.'

Lysander saw where he pointed. There was a piece of

iron lying against a stone trough, and he took it under the watchful eye of Cato. After clearing the stray pieces of straw from the ground in front of him, he etched a circle an arm's length across. Then, taking great care, he scratched around the outside the shapes of the ancient letters. He'd seen them so many times they were carved into his memory. All the time, the Tarantian observed him with a deadly calm stare.

When Lysander had finished he knelt back. The man with the mallet looked from the ground to the amulet, and back again.

The man shrugged. 'Righteous, eh! Very well, *Lysander.* If you are so inflamed with righteousness, I will let you save your friend.'

The Tarantian held the Fire of Ares above the fire behind the grate, then let go. The amulet dropped into the flames. 'Take your precious amulet, and you both go free.'

The brother, Cato, chortled through the blackened remains of his teeth.

The room suddenly seemed suffocating and small. Lysander stepped forward to the fire, where the jewel sparkled among the red-hot embers.

'Don't do it, Lysander.' Demaratos was staring intently at him, shaking his head. 'Run away. Don't – not for me.'

But other words were echoing in Lysander's brain. Those of Prokles.

Sacrifice is the Spartan way.

The heat licked his face and he clenched his fist, then stretched his fingers. He focused on the amulet.

Nothing else matters.

Lysander pushed his hand deep into the flames.

CHAPTER 23

It felt as though his whole forearm was being ripped apart. Lysander's vision went black, and he willed his fingers to close. He tore his hand out of the flames, and screams surrounded him. He fell to his knees and rolled into a ball, as the noises turned to whimpers; the sounds came from him. He opened his eyes. A smell like roasted pork sickened him.

He dared not look at his hand – he was sure it would be nothing more than a bleeding, melted stump, but he spotted a water bucket in the corner of the room and scrambled over on his knees and plunged his hand in.

Lysander wept in shame and dared not turn to face the room. He'd failed.

He didn't deserve the name of a Spartan. He felt the disappointment of his father and grandfather in the Underworld.

A hand touched the top of his head. Lysander expected a blade to cut his throat, and braced himself.

'Come, let me see,' said the man. There wasn't a trace of the former anger in his voice.

'I failed,' said Lysander.

'There is no failure in what you did.'

Still balled into a claw, the skin on Lysander's hand had gone. All that remained was black and red. His nails were peeling away. There was no blood, but he could see the scarring would be with him for ever. He turned over his hand.

'By the Gods!' cried the Tarantian. Lysander felt tears well in his eyes again, and blinked. Was it possible?

In the middle of his palm, hanging from the raw flesh, was the Fire of Ares.

Slowly, the amulet dropped away and landed on the floor, pulling off another layer of skin. In its place was a clear outline of the jewel and the letters that curled around the outside: *The Fire of Ares shall inflame the righteous*.

The Oracle had told Lysander: 'Fear not, your destiny is branded on your heart.' Lysander understood now what she had meant. The amulet's prophecy had become a part of him for ever, burned into his skin.

Lysander stood up, but couldn't take his eyes from his disfigured hand.

The Tarantian and his brother exchanged words, and both raised their voices in argument, though it was quickly settled.

'Go,' said their captor.

Lysander looked up into his eyes. 'What?'

'I gave you my word, and you have proved yourself. I have no wish to kill a boy who is followed by the Gods.'

Cato was already untying Demaratos, with his eyes warily on him. As soon as he was free, Demaratos stood unsteadily, tucking his arm over his smashed ribs. He staggered over to the water bucket where Lysander had plunged his hand, and frantically cupped the filthy liquid into his parched mouth.

Lysander faced the Tarantian.

'Thank you,' he said. The words felt strange in his mouth. This man had tortured them both, but he had given them back their lives when he could have taken them. Lysander helped Demaratos up again, but his friend seemed to have found new strength, and stood on his own. He glared at the Tarantian with undisguised loathing.

'Take heed, Spartans,' said the man. 'If I see your faces in Taras again, I will have no mercy. I swear that by the Gods. Go now.'

Lysander wasted no time and together he and Demaratos went out blinking into the morning light. There was a stable lad tending to a horse in the yard, but he was barely their age, and looked away nervously.

'Come on,' said Lysander. 'We have to get back to the forest. Aristodermus will be leading the others back soon for another assault.'

Despite his injuries, Demaratos managed to run alongside Lysander as they made their way through the backstreets of Taras. The town was coming to life. From beside the market hall, Lysander saw the port was busy, with men – Messapians and Tarantians alike – piling into boats of all sizes carrying weapons.

'What are they doing?' hissed Lysander.

'They must know that a second attack is coming,' said Demaratos. 'They're running away.'

But Lysander could see there was no panic in the preparations. No fear. Understanding spread through Lysander's brain like a gorse fire.

'They're not running away,' said Lysander. 'They're attacking.'

'By sea?' said Demaratos, then his eyes widened. 'They must have found out about the smugglers' cove. That's our only way out!'

Lysander made his way quickly out to the forest, with Demaratos by his side. His chest burned, but now it was a race against time. If the Tarantians reached the beach first, they'd overwhelm Moskos' marines and attack the forest from the rear. They'd have no way to get home.

And all the time, with the throb of pain in his hand, the revelation of his ancestors pulsed in his mind. Sarpedon was not a true Spartan. Even an Ephor had Helot blood!

In the distance, Lysander saw the Spartan forces approaching through the trees. At two hundred paces away, they spotted Lysander and Demaratos. A shout went up and the lines dropped into phalanx formation, spears at the ready. Lysander called to them as they came closer.

'It's us. Lysander and Demaratos.'

'Lower your weapons!' shouted Aristodermus. 'They're ours.'

Their tutor broke from the lines, and stormed towards them. His face was dark with fury, and he slammed his fist into Lysander's shoulder.

'How dare you disobey an order! You may think you're special, Lysander, but the truth is you're one of many expendable soldiers. Your injuries should tell you that.' He looked at Demaratos. 'And what happened to you?'

Demaratos pulled aside his tunic and showed the welts that scarred his body.

'I was captured. Lysander rescued me.'

Their tutor recovered himself.

'I told him to attempt no such thing, and he'll be flogged on our return to Sparta. For now, both of you get in line. We're retaking the town.'

He began to pace back to the phalanx.

'You'll find it empty of fighting men,' shouted Lysander defiantly.

Aristodermus spun around. 'What are you talking about?'

Lysander told him what they'd seen at the harbour. While he was talking, Sulla and Anaxander came from the ranks to investigate. 'They're heading for the smugglers' cove,' said Lysander.

'We've sent the women and children there for safety,' said Sulla, panic filling his voice.

'Then they're walking straight to their deaths,' said Aristodermus.

Lysander's hand was quickly bandaged by Leonidas, and Prokles dressed Demaratos's wounds, as Aristodermus addressed the troops. Agitated murmurs passed among the men when they heard of the Messapian and Tarantian plans.

'We must go at once,' said Cimon. 'There's no time for wasting.'

'We must maintain our order,' said Aristodermus. 'If we attack in disarray, they will vanquish us. The fight is no longer about land, or trading rights. Now you fight to protect your families.'

Running as fast as their tired legs could carry them, they skirted back along the edge of the forest, and followed the track towards the tunnels. Lysander took a sword and an ill-fitting helmet from one of the dead Spartans who lay at the side of the road. There was no time to fix on armour.

They filed in pairs into the rocky streambed, and entered the tunnels in single file. The clanging of their weapons reverberated off the dark walls and the stench of sweat was thick. Lysander tried to ignore the throbbing in his injured hand. His mind was focused on what they'd find on the beach side of the tunnel.

Would the enemy have reached there ahead of them? But more importantly, if they had, would he have the strength left for a final fight?

Midway through the winding passage the column slowed. There was Orpheus's body. Dark patches had gathered in his limbs where they touched the ground, and the blood had pooled under the skin. Beside him knelt Leonidas. As the other men pushed on, Lysander crouched beside the prince.

'Come,' he said. 'He wouldn't want you to delay.'

Leonidas nodded, and wiped the tears from his eyes.

'I'll kill every last one of them,' he said grimly.

'We'll come back for him afterwards,' said Lysander. 'Let's go.'

As they neared the exit, Lysander felt the ground shift beneath his feet. Sand. He stumbled out into the light.

The beach was almost as they'd left it since their landing. The ship was anchored just fifty paces offshore, floating evenly in the water.

'Moskos and his boys got her shipshape again,' said Demaratos.

Lysander could see the marine soldiers on the deck, waving to shore. He waved back.

'They probably thought we'd never make it,' said Prokles.

A strong wind was blowing across the bay, kicking up clouds of fine sand. At the far end of the beach, the wives and children of the Spartans huddled together.

They were unharmed, and the remains of Nikos' battalion dashed over to comfort them.

'We made it,' said Leonidas. 'They're safe.'

Lysander could see Moskos standing right on the prow of their ship, waving still.

'He's trying to tell us something,' said Lysander. Moskos began pointing out to sea, away from the bay.

A lone fishing vessel peeped around the headland, propelled over the choppy waves by four rowers. Lysander counted eight others in the boat.

'Is that their army?' laughed Aristodermus.

Another boat appeared in its wake, this time crowded to the beams with men. Then came two more ships, both carrying Messapians in battle array. Lysander saw the tips of metal pikes glinting. Suddenly the sea was full of boats, all carrying armed men, Messapians and Tarantians together. Their progress across the water, one stroke at a time, came with a menacing slowness.

'What do we do?' said one of the Spartan men.

'Take your families back through the tunnels,' said Aristodermus. 'Take shelter in the forest. We'll face off the enemies.'

A thunderous sound from behind shocked Lysander, and he turned to see a cloud of dust at the entrance to the tunnel. As it cleared, he made out a jumble of limbs and scarlet cloth trapped beneath a blood-spattered boulder. A shout from above drew his eyes upwards. At the top of the cliff face stood a group of three men carrying long pieces of wood.

Where did they come from? Lysander wondered. No matter, they were here now. They levered another boulder, which tipped over the lip of the cliff and landed by the first.

'They're blocking us in,' said Prokles, raising his spear.

With a quick step forward he released it, and it sailed through the air, punching through the belly of one of the Tarantians. With a gurgled cry, he fell forwards, crashing headfirst into the rocks below.

The children on the beach began to whimper with fear, and one of the women wailed. The other Tarantians on the cliff top backed away.

'The odds have shifted,' said Demaratos.

Lysander tightened his grip upon his sword hilt and faced out to sea. They might be trapped, but if this beach was to be his final resting place, he wouldn't give his life without a fight.

CHAPTER 24

'Ready your weapons,' shouted Aristodermus. 'Line up in front of the women and children.'

Lysander took his position alongside Leonidas and Demaratos in the centre of the shoreline, as the colony Spartans pushed their families to the far end of the beach, away from the approaching boats. Lysander's burnt hand was useless for gripping, so Leonidas strapped a shield tightly to his friend's injured arm. He counted around thirty vessels on the water heading for the other tip of the beach, each carrying between five and a dozen men. He guessed there were a hundred Spartans left, and many of those had injuries, just like him.

'Stay in the phalanx,' ordered Aristodermus. 'We don't stand a chance if we break formation.'

The first of the enemy boats nudged their way into the shallows, and the men began to disembark, shouting to each other in their tongue. All were heavily armed, with shields and swords taken from the dead on both sides.

'We should attack now,' said Cimon. 'While they're unprepared.'

'No,' said Aristodermus. 'If we commit ourselves, they'll send the rest of their men behind us and attack the families. We must wait until they are all on dry land, then deal the decisive blow.'

Gradually the enemy numbers increased, as the boats reached the shore and the men waded on to the sand. A Messapian, more grandly dressed than the others, with a plumed helmet and a double-ended spear, barked orders and formed the men into a line spanning the width of the beach. It was Viromanus, their leader. The enemy stood at least twenty across and ten rows deep. On the right were the Messapians, and on the left were the men of Taras.

'He knows what he's doing,' said Leonidas. 'He's put the men he can trust there to stop the line turning.'

Lysander, with his heart thudding in his chest, tried to calm himself by breathing deeply.

'They'll roll us back like a rug,' said one of the Spartans in the row behind. 'We've no chance.'

Aristodermus scoffed.

'While we have strength in our shield arms, we have a chance.'

The Messapian leader shouted two words, and his men began to step out.

'Ready, Spartans!' shouted Aristodermus. 'March on my count. One . . . Two . . . One . . .'

Lysander marched in time, and the line moved

forward. He kept his eyes locked dead ahead. He had been here before, with these friends beside him, and he knew he could trust each one of them with his life.

Aristodermus quickened the count, and Lysander paced in short strides across the sand. The unsteady ground was hard going, but the line didn't break. The Messapians had sped up also, and were shouting threats and curses as they approached.

'Save your breath, Spartans,' yelled Aristodermus.

Lysander picked up his knees as the phalanx moved into a jog. The enemy were twenty paces away. He had already chosen his target man — the Messapian leader with the plumed helmet. Strength pulsed through his sword arm.

'Ready!' shouted Aristodermus, the words barely audible over the war cries of the enemy. Lysander raised his sword, and charged.

Viromanus' spear-point slid over the top of Lysander's shield, and missed his face by a hair's breadth. The shaft scraped along his cheek.

Lysander was suddenly in the air. He landed in the middle of the enemy's second line, and slid his sword into the exposed flesh on the back of Viromanus' thigh. The Messapian leader screamed and dropped his weapon, clutching at the wound. His life blood poured out over his fingers, and his eyes were wide with horror behind the slits of his helmet.

Lysander sprang up as blows rained down on his shield from another Messapian, each one sending bolts of pain through his hand. He drove the shield upwards into the wide face of the soldier, then fell back into position beside Demaratos.

The phalanx was restored. Their only chance.

Lysander's heel dug into the sand as he leant into the enemy line with his shield. He stabbed over the top with his sword at the heads and necks of the enemy. Lysander concentrated on keeping the formation tight, pushing and thrusting, again and again. He lost track of the horrible wounds he inflicted, slicing into necks, cheeks, mouths and eye sockets. Men fell screaming at his feet, and soon he was pushing on over a carpet of the dead and dying.

Spartans make their own odds, he thought grimly.

The enemy line buckled, and Lysander found himself with room to take a breath. The left side of the Spartan phalanx was pushing back their adversaries, and the whole block of men wheeled about, to face away from the sea.

'Press on,' came Aristodermus' voice. 'Drive them back.'

Lysander obeyed, and shouldered into a Tarantian who was carrying a Spartan shield and spear. Lysander could tell from the way he held the shield away from his body that the man wasn't an experienced soldier. He feinted a low thrust with his sword. The man dropped his guard and Lysander half took off his scalp with a powerful swipe of his sword. Blood cascaded like spilt wine, splashing the pebbles at the Tarantian's feet.

Lysander sheathed his sword and unpeeled the dead man's fingers from his spear. The enemy line had broken up completely, and Spartans were plunging into the midst of pockets of men, wreaking slaughter with their swords and spears. The energy that coursed through Lysander masked the pain in his hand. A Spartan fell in front of him, clutching his face, and screaming. Above him stood a long-haired, bare-chested Tarantian, swinging a length of rope.

What harm can he do with that?

He lunged at Lysander and the rope whipped round. Something caught Lysander's arm and tore away. Suddenly there were deep gouges in his skin, oozing thick streams of blood. He ducked as the rope swung again. Thick, iron fish-hooks were tied on to the end of the rope, ready to tear flesh to pieces. The man shouted at Lysander and swung the deadly hooks again towards his legs. Lysander lowered his shield, and the hooks lodged in the surface. The Tarantian tugged at his end of the rope, but Lysander saw his chance and spun inwards, coiling the rope around his waist as he came closer to the enemy soldier. Using his momentum, he heaved his spear downwards through the Tarantian's unprotected torso. Blood appeared between his gritted teeth, as he fell on to his knees, and then backwards. Lysander put his feet on the dead man's chest and pulled out his spear.

'You should have stayed at sea, fisherman.'

He let the rope fall around his ankles.

The remains of the enemy were fighting in the shallows now, some up to their knees in the water. Lysander noticed that behind the men fighting, the Spartan ship lay still in the water. Where were Moskos and his marines?

He found Aristodermus, and pulled him from the fray.

'Look!' he said, pointing out to sea. 'Something's wrong.'

'Find Leonidas and Demaratos,' said Aristodermus. 'Take a boat and see what's going on.'

Lysander found both friends quickly and Prokles too, and explained what he'd seen.

'They're probably just cowering in the cargo hold,' said Demaratos.

Nevertheless, they loaded their weapons on to an abandoned enemy rowing boat. They pushed it out of the shallows, then jumped on board. Prokles and Leonidas took an oar each; Lysander's injuries prevented him rowing. Demaratos stood on the edge, watching the battle unfold on the shore. Lysander saw a wisp of black smoke rise from the far end of the deck of Moskos' ship.

'It's on fire!' said Lysander. 'Pull harder!'

They rowed alongside their ship, and as they rounded the prow, they saw a small boat hidden on the far side. A man was sitting, looking up towards the deck of their ship. Two ropes, presumably attached to grappling hooks, hung from the deck. He spotted Lysander and his comrades approaching, and began to scramble around in the little hull and to shout up wildly.

'Messapians!' said Prokles.

Two more faces appeared on the deck.

The smoke was thickening now, and black clouds were spiralling into the sky.

'They're not trying to steal the ship,' said Leonidas. 'They're trying to destroy it.'

The two Messapians from the deck lowered themselves over the side, and shimmied down the ropes. Immediately they were on their benches, oars in hand. Leonidas and Prokles pulled hard, grunting with the effort, and set off in pursuit.

'Get closer,' said Lysander, drawing his sword.

They drew level with the enemy after a few strokes, and Lysander put a foot on the edge of the boat, and leapt into the base of the Messapian vessel, slicing downwards through the arm of one of the rowers. The man screamed as the oar, and his arm, fell into the water.

The other man, who didn't have an oar, kicked the inside of Lysander's knee, and Lysander toppled backwards over a bench. The man lifted a small anchor with both hands, stood over Lysander and hurled it towards his head. Lysander rolled sideways as the chunk of metal crashed into the deck. Over the sound of splintered wood came the splash of water, and he was instantly aware of cold water gushing over his shoulders and neck. The anchor had smashed a hole in the boat's fragile hull.

The boat lurched to one side.

'Look out!' shouted Demaratos.

The Messapian landed on top of Lysander, crushing the breath from his chest. Lysander's hands instinctively sought his attacker's throat, and his fingers sank into the thick beard. He tried to roll over, but the boat came with him. He managed to take a lungful of air and suddenly they were both plunged into the water.

Lysander kept his grip on the Messapian's neck as they rolled over each other. Locked in a death grip, the Messapian's nails gouged at Lysander's face, but the stinging pain only made Lysander's hands clench tighter, crushing against his windpipe.

Lysander's head broke the surface and he gasped. The breath gave him the strength he needed to carry on, and the Messapian's hands moved more weakly.

Then they fell away all together.

Through the clear sea water, he saw the distorted, purple face of his enemy. The eyes were open, but unseeing.

Lysander lay back, utterly spent and let the waves take his weight while he caught his breath. Prokles was climbing up the rope on to the deck of the ship, with Leonidas right behind him.

'Need a hand?' said Demaratos.

Lysander rolled over slowly and trod water. His friend was leaning over the deck of their rowing boat, extending his arm. Lysander took it, and heaved himself aboard. Moments later, Prokles appeared at the edge of the Spartan vessel.

'We've put the fire out. It's lucky we got here in time. The damage isn't too bad.'

'Moskos and Sirkon. The others?'

Prokles shook his head. 'They're on the oar-deck. Throats cut.'

With Leonidas and Prokles safely back on board, they rowed to shore. The battle was over, and a great mass of the enemy were sitting on the sand, stripped of all but their tunics, their heads hanging. Even their sandals and footwear were in a pile, to prevent them running away.

'We did it,' said Leonidas.

'They'll think twice before attacking true Spartans again,' Demaratos added.

Lysander didn't feel the need to say anything. All that had stood between their slaughter or survival was their training, and they had triumphed. But he could not feel pleasure at the carnage displayed before him. Bring Spartans together in an army and they were killing machines. But in the aftermath, the bloodbath sickened his stomach.

Their boat reached the shallows, and banged into the bodies that drifted on the swell. Lysander noticed a face he recognised among them – the man who tortured Demaratos in Taras. A deep gash opened right into the middle of his chest. Lysander touched Demaratos's shoulder.

269

'Look, friend.'

Demaratos peered over the side of the boat.

'I would have spared him.' He turned away.

Lysander climbed out of the boat and noticed the red tinge of the water around his ankles.

Leonidas reported what they'd found on board the ship. Getting home without a navigator would be next to impossible, but Aristodermus didn't seem interested. He surveyed the remains of the enemy.

'What's wrong?' said Cimon at his side. 'Victory is ours.' Nikos' lieutenant had lost his right ear in the battle, and raw flesh glistened around the dark hole of his hearing canal.

'I cannot revel in another's shame,' said Lysander's tutor. 'I would have more respect for them if they'd fought until the death.'

CHAPTER 25

Aristodermus ordered a group of the prisoners to use oars to unblock the tunnel entrance. Two groups of two took an oar each and levered their paddles to dislodge the boulders. Their dejected faces poured with sweat as they groaned with the effort. After one oar had splintered, they got two more in its place, and finally moved the biggest boulders out of the way. Others joined their defeated comrades in lugging the smaller stones. Finally, the shattered bodies of the unfortunate Spartans were carried aside.

That could so easily have been me, thought Lysander.

With an armed Spartan for every two prisoners, they led their captives back through the cave passageway and on the road to Taras. They left the families at the forest.

Aristodermus was deep in discussion with Nikos' lieutenants for most of the way.

The citizens who'd remained in the town came out of their houses to witness the parade of their defeated menfolk. No one spoke as the vanquished forces were

271

marched towards the market square. Lysander noticed that his prisoners didn't lift their heads to meet any of the accusing or sympathetic stares.

The bodies had all been cleared, but the smell of battle still hung in the air – a sickly aroma of sweat and iron. Aristodermus mounted the steps of the temple and faced the crowd, looking out to the sea beyond. By his side stood Sulla. The plinth where the statue of Aristarkus had stood remained empty.

'Men of Taras!' he shouted. Sulla translated into the native language beside him, though Lysander suspected many of those gathered knew Greek perfectly well.

'This has been a dark episode in your lives,' continued Aristodermus. 'Many of your friends have died, many are terribly wounded. And for what?' He paused and looked out over the crowd, as Sulla related his words.

'I understand that you have grievances with your Spartan rulers, but bloodshed was not the answer. I am within my rights to have all of you put to death in front of your families, just as you would have slaughtered our people.'

Around the outside of the square, some of the spectators began to weep.

'But I am a merciful man,' said Aristodermus. 'Even if Sparta is not a merciful ruler. You will know, all of you, that Sparta is not a typical city. We do not seek to conquer and expand. When we fight, it is to protect ourselves, and our people. To make our borders safe.

Like a bear, we are slow to anger. But take heed, when roused, our anger is absolute. We do not rest until we have eradicated the source of that anger. Is that understood?'

All around the square, tired men nodded their heads.

'Split the prisoners, Messapians on this side . . .' he pointed, 'and Tarantians on this.'

Both Lysander's prisoners were Messapian, and he ushered them to the side of the square where the hall was. They looked at him with barely disguised hatred. When the Messapians were gathered together, there were around thirty.

'My anger is not against the people of Taras,' said Aristodermus. 'On those people this colony will depend. But Sparta will not brook invaders from foreign cities. They must be dealt with in the Spartan way.'

Lysander felt a sense of dread rising from his belly, through his chest and up his throat.

'Kneel Messapians!' shouted Aristodermus.

Cimon repeated the order. Some of the defeated soldiers obeyed immediately without question, others looked to each other. Cimon shouted the order again. All did as they were told bar one. Sulla went forward and drew his sword. The man spat on the ground and knelt. Aristodermus surveyed the men, and Lysander saw his lips moving silently.

'I need thirty-one volunteers,' he shouted. 'Men of Taras willing to show their allegiance to Sparta. Each

273

will be given a place on the new town council.'

A low murmur passed through the crowd of Tarantians. One by one, men detached themselves from the group, looking expectant.

But Lysander knew what they were volunteering for. A place on the council would come with a heavy price.

'Boys, give each of these men a sword,' said Aristodermus. Lysander went forward with the others from his barracks and gave his sword to a Tarantian. Only a little while before, he would have happily run it through Lysander's middle. Now, as he turned the hilt in his hand, he looked at it as though he couldn't fathom its purpose.

'You will buy back our trust with the blood of our enemies,' said Aristodermus. 'Kill these Messapian worms.'

The Tarantians looked at each other like lost children, and slowly walked towards the line of kneeling soldiers.

One or two of the Messapians on the ground began to weep and beg. Others shouted in their language – angry curses invoking the names of the Greek Gods. Cimon barked an order. Lysander turned away. The shouts of the Messapians were cut short with the blades of the swords. By the time Lysander turned back around, they were all lifeless.

Aristodermus pointed to the men who had carried out the killings. 'These citizens have proved themselves friends of Sparta. From this time on their families will carry the petitions of the people of Taras to the Spartan rulers here. But beware, if ever this sort of insurrection is attempted again, you will find us without mercy. Burn these bodies on a pyre before nightfall and go back to your homes.'

As the bodies were dragged into a pile at the harbour front, leaving trails of blood in the dust, Lysander and the others gathered around Aristodermus. He called out Nikos' lieutenants.

'The coming days will be hard. Trust is not engendered through fear and the sword. You must learn to live with these Tarantians not as your enemies, but your friends . . .'

'Friends?' said Sulla. 'They tried to kill us!'

'What choice did you leave them?' said Aristodermus. 'The taxes you levied against them were unfair – you treated them like slaves.'

'We rule here – they *are* our slaves.'

'But remember, comrade, a happy slave works twice as hard as one cowed by the whip.'

Lysander admired Aristodermus' philosophy, but it made him think of Kassandra's poor Helots back home. Tellios would show them no such charity, he was sure.

'These people don't understand our ways,' said Sulla, frowning.

Lysander felt anger surge up through him. 'Do you understand theirs?' he snapped. All heads turned to face him, and he expected a rebuke from Aristodermus. None came.

'You cannot expect people to bend to your will. Working together with the Tarantians, as equals, will make this society a happy one. Your families too, remember, were once not equals in Sparta.'

A murmur of approval went through the crowd.

'My wife is friends with a Tarantian woman,' said one of Sulla's soldiers. 'She says her cooking is actually quite good.'

The joke brought laughter, and the flicker of a smile even lightened Sulla's grim face.

'Very well,' said Aristodermus. 'I want you to initiate councils ten times in the year. Invite those Tarantians who have pledged themselves today, listen to their grievances. Give them a vote in the matters which affect them.'

'And what if they rise up again?' said Sulla.

'If you treat them with respect, they will not,' said Aristodermus. 'I will talk with the Council at Sparta, and suggest they send a new governor here twice a year to maintain order and settle any outstanding disputes.'

It was agreed, and having wished farewell to the colonists, Aristodermus marched Lysander and his comrades out of Taras, escorted by eight torchbearers to ward off the coming dusk.

'Do you think the peace will last?' Demaratos asked Lysander as they passed the outskirts of the town.

Lysander thought of the uneasy truce between the

Spartans and the Helots over the sea, and the distrust that still rankled between them. He'd lived on both sides, and could see that what really fed the hatred was nothing but plain and simple fear.

'Well?' said Demaratos.

'I hope so,' said Lysander.

It was dark as Lysander marched, barely able to keep his eyes open. His hand throbbed with each step. The Spartans took with them sacks of supplies for the journey home, sourced from Taras – fresh bread, pome-granates, hard cheeses and preserved lemons. Plus more fried fish, and cured hams.

Orpheus's body still lay in the tunnel where he had met his death.

'We can't leave him here,' Lysander said.

Aristodermus considered the body. 'We can't take him all the way home – his corpse will be ripe in another day. We'll bury him at sea.'

Using Orpheus's cloak as a makeshift stretcher, Lysander, Demaratos, Prokles and Leonidas took a corner each, and carried their fallen comrade back to the shore.

A boat remained from the fighting earlier that day, and they ferried themselves out to the main vessel in groups of six. It took only five trips. The high spirits of victory had seeped away with the daylight. Lysander – like most of the boys – was in a sombre mood. They'd won the battle, but lost fifty of their friends.

'Get a good night's rest,' said Aristodermus. 'We row at first light.' He extinguished the ship's lantern, throwing them into shadow.

Lysander listened to his tutor's feet creak up the steps to the top deck, and huddled down beside one of the oar-benches. Between the soft sounds of the other boys' breathing, and the gentle swell of the sea under the hull, peace reigned again.

But despite his weariness, Lysander couldn't sleep. He climbed stiffly to his feet, and crept between his comrades, out on to the deck.

A breeze caressed his face. The sky was clear and the stars crowded the firmament. Lysander looked back to shore. Although the ship rocked only fifty paces offshore, Lysander already felt they had left Taras far behind.

He'd thought this place would allow him to discover a sense of belonging, but all he'd found was more bloodshed. Men pitched against other men because of their lust for power. Honour came not from the red cloak. It came from ruling with a fair and even hand. The original mothakes who had left Sparta to find the freedom they yearned for had noble intentions, he was sure. But in the end they'd become just like those they despised: ruthless despots willing to enslave others. And he'd fought alongside them. What did that make him? Was there even such a thing as the right side?

Lysander went back below with his troubled thoughts.

The wind picked up a little in the night, and they unfurled the sail at dawn, making good progress.

With Moskos and his men dead, it was up to Phemus to navigate the vessel.

'Perhaps he was picked out by Zeus,' joked Demaratos. 'If it hadn't been for the lightning bolt, he'd never have learnt to sail.'

Lysander and Demaratos, unable to row, took shifts on the tiller, steering the ship, and gazed across the blue expanse.

Will I ever come back? Lysander wondered. He felt uncertain, troubled. *It feels like I'm leaving something behind.*

There was no denying that the people of Taras had been wronged by Sparta. Perhaps the amulet's prophecy wasn't specific to him only. The Fire of Ares had inflamed the blacksmith, leading him to slake his vengeance by torturing Demaratos. Was he the righteous one?

Lysander's body turned cold as realisation struck home.

'No!' he cried.

'What is it?' asked Demaratos in a panicked voice.

'The Fire of Ares!' said Lysander. 'How could I have forgotten it? It must still be on the ground in the forge.' He sank on to the deck. 'I'm a fool.'

'You're not a fool,' said Demaratos. 'There were other things more important . . .'

Lysander closed his eyes and imagined the red jewel

shining in its golden setting. After all his trials, he finally felt ready to wear the pendant again. But it was gone, lost for ever in a foreign land.

'I have something for you,' said Demaratos.

Lysander looked up. Swinging from Demaratos's hand, with the sun behind it, was the amulet. 'What . . . ? How . . . ?'

Demaratos laughed. 'I picked it up when I was drinking from the trough,' he said. 'It was just lying there on the ground.'

Lysander reached out, and touched the amulet.

'It's time for you to wear it again,' said Demaratos. 'You've earned it.'

He crouched down in front of Lysander, and lifted the leather thong over his neck. As soon as the familiar weight rested over his chest, Lysander felt invigorated. He stood up, and fingered the pendant. For so long the Fire of Ares had seemed a curse that brought with it misery and suffering. Now, the pendant was a reminder of all the sacrifices others had made. It made him who he was. It was a gift.

In the middle of the first day at sea, when they had reached the deep, dark waters, Aristodermus called for the sails to be lowered.

'This is as good a resting place for Orpheus as any,' he said.

The boys gathered in a semicircle by the vessel's port side. Leonidas and Prokles lifted the stiff body on to the deck-rail. Orpheus's cloak was wrapped around him, and pinned in place.

'He served Sparta well,' said Aristodermus. 'And we give him to Poseidon, God of the waves.'

Tears streaked down Leonidas's face as he let go of the body, and it dropped over the side of the ship. Lysander heard a splash and went to the edge. The body floated for a moment, then rolled over and disappeared.

'Goodbye,' he whispered.

A dolphin broke the surface of the water near where Orpheus had entered, then descended again. Lysander's friend was gone.

The wind stayed strong for two days, but dropped on the second night at sea. The other boys took to the rowing benches once again, but Lysander was excused because of his injured hand. He spent the time with Phemus, trying to learn the principles of seafaring and navigation. So many stars with names he would never learn.

He was on deck, with his arm outstretched, counting how many fingers rested between the horizon and the sun, when he spotted land just after dawn on the fourth day. In his other hand was a half eaten pomegranate. Its red flesh reminded Lysander of some of the wounds he'd seen in battle.

He called out 'Greece!' and Aristodermus came to his side.

They watched in silence as the coast rose from the blue water.

'Good to be back, isn't it?' said his tutor.

'It is,' said Lysander. Up ahead, was the place he'd been born into and fought for. It was Lysander's home. 'I never thought I would miss it so much.'

CHAPTER 26

They docked the vessel at Gytheion where a month earlier Lysander and his comrades had faced the Persian general Vaumisa and his armies. The sounds of masons' chisels and mallets rang in the air, as the people sought to repair the damage wreaked by fires. A free-dweller messenger was dispatched on horseback to announce their return to the Council.

'You look a ragged bunch,' said Aristodermus. 'Clean yourselves up, before we head back to the city.'

They washed as well as they could in the river. Half of Lysander's comrades had lost their cloaks, and those which were left were torn and filthy. They unloaded their remaining weapons and there were enough shields to go around. A boy helped Lysander change the bandage on his hand, then he strapped the shield in place. At least he would enter Sparta with his shield high on his arm.

It was a day of bright sunlight and blue skies as they marched along the river. They sang martial songs to keep their spirits high. Scouts on horseback met them several stadia outside the city limits, and galloped forth to proclaim their return in Sparta.

As they walked through Amikles, Helots and free-dwellers alike stopped and stared. Crowds had already begun to gather along the road that led up to their barracks. Many were men in red cloaks, with their wives at their side. Each expectantly scanned the faces of the returning boys.

Looking for their sons, Lysander realised. He chased away his own sadness. No mother and father would be waiting for him.

Aristodermus called them to a halt outside the barracks gate, and the crowd of parents descended. He heard Demaratos speaking to his father, a handsome Spartan who looked just like his son, only leaner and with flecks of greying hair.

'We saved the colony,' said Demaratos. 'I was badly injured, but still managed to kill eight or nine of them. Maybe ten . . .'

Lysander suppressed a smile. Some things would never change.

Helots were scurrying around the barracks entranceway, carrying platters of food, and jugs. Leonidas appeared at Lysander's side. His father, King Cleomenes, would not be at the barracks.

'My Helot tells me they're planning a feast in honour of our victorious return. Some special guests are coming apparently.'

'Who?'

'I don't know,' said Leonidas, smiling, 'but I hope Demaratos has kept enough of his stories back. He's currently killed twelve men; the number increases with every telling.'

Lysander laughed, and a plump woman ran out to Leonidas's side.

'Where is my Orpheus, Prince?'

Leonidas dropped his head, and said something in reply that Lysander couldn't hear. He watched the face of Orpheus's mother, expecting it to crumple into tears. Instead, she lifted her chin, and placed a hand on Leonidas's shoulder.

'Don't worry for me. It's you I feel sorry for, not having shared such a brave death.'

All around the entranceway, mothers and fathers were hugging their children, or standing apart in childless pairs. Not all were as composed as Orpheus's mother, and Lysander saw many leaning on each other.

He heard a familiar whinny, and spied Pegasus, Sarpedon's horse, being held by a Helot groom. Did that mean . . .

Someone tapped him on the shoulder and he turned to see a familiar face.

'Kassandra!' he cried.

Kassandra's face broke into a wide smile. She threw her arms around his shoulders and he winced as his injured hand was pressed against his chest.

'Cousin!' she said. 'I didn't know . . . I asked the

messenger . . .' Her eyes fell to his hand. 'Oh, Lysander! What happened?'

'It could have been much worse if it weren't for you,' said Lysander.

A blush rose to Kassandra's cheeks.

Lysander nodded over at Prokles, who was embracing his father.

'He did his job well.'

'What are you talking about, Lysander?'

'I couldn't work it out, at first . . .' said Lysander. 'Where Idas got his gold. But then I remembered where he'd been just before we set off. I sent him to tell you I'd been delayed at the Council.'

Kassandra looked at her feet. 'I couldn't let you go. Not like that. If you had died and I'd never managed to say sorry, I would have lost everyone who was dear to me.'

'I thought that you didn't want to speak to me,' said Lysander. 'That day, when the column moved off, and you turned your back . . .'

'Don't, please,' she said. 'It's behind us now. Our family has suffered much grief. Now it's time to be thankful for what we have.'

'I was a different person then,' said Lysander. 'I didn't know who I was, or where I was going. I felt trapped between two worlds: Helot and Spartan. Both seemed like prisons to me.'

'And do you know now?' she said. 'Who you are, I mean.' The crowds of barrack boys swirled around them, red cloaks shifting in the breeze.

286

Lysander thought for a moment. 'I'm Lysander,' he said. 'Son of Thorakis and Athenasia. Friend of Timeon and Demaratos. Cousin of Kassandra.'

'Can you be all those things at once?'

'I can try,' he said. 'That's the role the Gods have given me.'

He thought also, *I'm a descendant of Aristarkus. And so are you.* Could he tell her?

Demaratos came between them, took Kassandra's hand and kissed it.

'Greetings, Lady Kassandra. I trust Lysander has told you all about how we drove the Messapians out of Taras.'

'He hasn't even started!' said Kassandra.

The thudding of hooves interrupted them, and people in the crowd mumbled, 'It's the Ephors.'

'Make way!' shouted a Spartan on the lead horse. 'Make way!'

The celebrations ceased as a path opened up to the barracks.

Myron and four others trotted towards the open gates on horseback. Lysander recognised Tellios, and the other two Ephors.

'Who's the other man?' he whispered to Kassandra as they dismounted and entered the barracks gate.

'I don't know,' said Kassandra. 'He looks familiar, though.'

Kassandra stared after them, and Lysander saw her jaw set hard.

'What's wrong?'

'It's the settlement,' she said quietly. 'Every day I have bad news through my messengers. Tellios has put a team of overseers in place, and they're little better than thugs. My cook is the sister of two Helot labourers. She says that the overseers are beating the workers for no reason at all. One has already been crippled, Tellios' men were so severe. I don't understand it.'

Lysander told Kassandra what Tellios had said to him before he left for Taras: about how he would work the Helot slaves into the ground.

Kassandra lifted both hands to her face. 'I always knew he and Sarpedon disagreed on many things, but I had no idea he would carry his grudges after Grand-father's death.'

'He means to have vengeance at the Helots' expense,' said Lysander.

'There must be a way we can stop him,' said Kassandra.

Lysander shook his head. 'While Tellios is one of the most powerful men in Sparta, there's nothing you or I can say.'

The stranger and Myron had gone inside, but Tellios was still at the gates, looking back at Kassandra and Lysander. He raised his hand as a greeting. 'The feast is laid out,' he called. 'Will you come to celebrate the *safe* return of the barracks?'

You'd rather I lay dead on a foreign shore, thought Lysander.

Kassandra turned away. 'You go in,' she said. 'I couldn't share the same table as that man. It would sicken me.'

After the families were dismissed, a feast was laid out in the barracks training yard, but Lysander had lost his appetite. He watched Tellios over the tables, chewing on a piece of bread. Every so often, the Ephor would catch his eye and smile.

'Not hungry?' said Demaratos at his side. He tore a chicken leg from the roasted carcass.

'No,' said Lysander.

'Come on,' said Demaratos. 'There's someone I'd like you to meet.'

Lysander followed his friend to the side of the yard, where Myron and the stranger were talking to Aristodermus.

'What are we doing?' said Lysander. 'We can't interrupt them!'

'Don't worry,' said Demaratos.

The three men turned as Lysander and Demaratos approached. Aristodermus pointed to Lysander.

'This is the young man who disobeyed my order, abandoned his post, and entered the enemy territory before a major assault, jeopardising the other members of the army.'

Myron and the other man stared at him without emotion.

'I told him that he would be flogged on his return,'

Aristodermus went on. 'We need to set an example for the others.'

Lysander lowered his head.

How could he? After all we've been through!

'That's probably the right choice . . .' said the stranger.

'Very well,' said Aristodermus.

'But that's not what we're going to do.'

Lysander looked up and saw that Demaratos was grinning.

'Lysander, meet my grandfather, Ajax, the new Ephor of Amikles.'

'The vote took place while you were all away,' said Myron. 'Ajax is Sarpedon's replacement for the next year.'

Ajax bowed his head slightly. 'Your grandfather was a fair ruler, and a good man. I owe you my gratitude. Not many would have risked their lives to save Demaratos.'

'Thank you,' said Lysander. 'He has saved my life many times as well.'

A Helot walked past, carrying a sloshing jug of water. He stopped in front of a line of others, including Idas, and began filling their separate flasks, so that they could dilute the wine of the guests.

'Spoken like a true Spartan,' said Ajax. 'With two like you at the front of every phalanx, our city will never fall. Now tell me, Lysander, is there anything I can do for you?'

'I have everything I need,' said Lysander.

'Nonsense. There must be something. Take your time, and name your wish.'

Lysander thought for a moment.

'Clumsy Helot!' someone shouted.

Lysander turned and saw Tellios standing over Idas, who was crouched on the floor picking up a fallen cup. The Spartan kicked him viciously, knocking him back to the ground as he tried to stand. Idas' face burned with shame and anger – emotions that Lysander understood all too well.

'That's enough!' called over Lysander. 'Idas, get inside the barracks and clean yourself up.'

Idas' chest heaved, and his small fists bunched. *Don't do it*, prayed Lysander. *You have many years ahead of you.*

Idas stormed off back into the barracks building. As Lysander watched, Tellios appeared at his side. 'I trust you'll have that boy whipped,' he whispered.

'Consider it done,' said Lysander coldly.

'Perhaps I was wrong about you,' said Tellios, leaning in close. 'You seem to have straightened out your *priorities*.'

Lysander managed to smile. 'Of course.'

After Tellios had gone back to the table, Lysander found Ajax again, talking alone with his grandson. A plan had formed in his head.

'I'm sorry to disturb you,' he said, 'but if your offer is still open, there is one thing you could do . . .'

The next day, Lysander walked across the ploughed
fields of Sarpedon's estate towards the Helot settlement
that used to be owned by his grandfather. Aristodermus
had sent Lysander and Demaratos off with a smile:
'Take as long as you need; Sparta owes you a great
debt.'

They'd stopped to pick up Kassandra on the way, and
Lysander had been happy to see the villa back to
normal, full of life, with her belongings unpacked once
again. Yesterday's celebrations had passed without an
opportunity to tell her of Lykurgos' half-Helot son
Aristarkus, and what he had discovered of their
common heritage. But Lysander's enthusiasm to share it
with her had waned with the afternoon sun. What
good would it do for Kassandra to know that she too
was part mothax? That everything she believed in was
false.

With his good hand, Lysander guided the reins of
Pegasus as Kassandra rode. His other was wrapped in a
clean bandage and a sling. Though the swelling had
gone down, and the scabs had hardened, Lysander
knew that his limb would bear the scars of Taras for
life. The Fire of Ares' prophecy would be with him
always, indelibly marked in his skin.

Demaratos came behind them. The narrow streets
smelled of rotten food and human waste. Even by the
standards of the settlement where he used to live, this
was dreadful. Every so often a face would appear at one

of the doorways, then duck out of sight again when the person spotted red cloaks.

'Why are they so frightened?' asked Kassandra.

They heard cries of pain from ahead, and quickened their steps. They reached an open space, where a building was half constructed. The cries were coming from a middle-aged man who cowered on his knees. A man in free-dweller's clothes stood above him, thrashing him with a stick.

'I told you to make sure the mortar was dry before beginning the roof supports,' he shouted.

'But sir,' said his victim, 'we can't help the rain. You wanted the building finished.'

Another blow landed across his back, and the Helot sprawled on the ground.

'Don't be clever,' said the free-dweller. 'Plautus, teach this Helot how to obey orders.'

Another free-dweller, who'd been sitting on a stool picking his teeth, stood up and kicked the prone Helot in the gut. He writhed on the floor with a whimper.

'What's going on?' shouted Kassandra. 'Stop that at once!'

The free-dweller backed away, breathing heavily.

'Who are you?'

'I'm Lady Kassandra, owner of this settlement,' she said. 'And I order you to leave.'

The Helot scrambled up and limped to one of the buildings nearby, where a woman was hovering.

The second free-dweller snorted.

'Tellios, Ephor of Limnae owns this land. We take orders from him alone. Now, be on your way.'

'I suggest you do as she says,' said Demaratos, stepping forwards threateningly. 'As of yesterday, Tellios is no longer in charge.'

'Who says so?' said the overseer.

'Ajax, the new Ephor who governs Amikles,' said Kassandra. 'Tellios has no power here. The Council of Elders has decreed his temporary authority ended. If you doubt it, take it up with the other Ephors.'

'Of course, if you wish to *talk* about it here . . .' said Lysander, unsheathing his sword, 'we can oblige.'

The overseer took a step backwards, tripped over and landed on his behind in the mud. His friend Plautus helped him to his feet, and together they backed away.

'We'll speak to Tellios,' he said. 'We'll see about all this.'

Demaratos knocked the stick from the man's hand with his sword. With a yelp the two overseers turned and fled between the buildings.

Faces dared to appear at doorways again.

'Come out,' called Kassandra. 'We mean no harm.'

Gradually, the Helots emerged from their homes. Word travelled down the alleyways, and soon the square was filled with people.

Kassandra nodded to Lysander, who climbed on part of the half finished masonry. Pride coursed through him.

'Some of you may know me,' he said, smiling. 'My name is Lysander, son of Thorakis the Spartan. But also son of Athenasia, the Helot. I have lived in a settlement such as this one, and I have lived in a Spartan barracks.' The faces around looked at him with suspicion. With his good hand, Lysander untied his cloak, and threw it into the mud. The crowd gasped.

'I stand before you not as a Spartan, or a Helot, but as a human being like yourselves,' he announced. 'Now I carry a sword, where I used to wield a sickle. With one I cut down men, with the other crops. But this land needs both food and workers to survive.'

A grumble passed through the people who had gathered.

'Sparta would be nothing without your toil. There would be no food to feed the soldiers and we would all starve. And without the protection of shield and spear, this land would be prone to invasion after invasion, plunder and pillage.'

Surveying the tired and twisted wretches before him, Lysander felt their sorrow like it was his own.

'I know that your lives are difficult, and that sometimes your masters treat you badly. I am here to tell you now that this will not happen again on this settlement while I live. Just as my Spartan grandfather looked after my Helot mother, I will make sure you are cared for. There will be no more beatings. No more hunger. When you are ill or injured, you will be spared work. We will employ a new overseer, not as a scourge and punisher, but as my guarantee that things will change.

'You,' he said, pointing to the man who had received the beating, 'the job is yours until the next full moon. The Lady Kassandra will employ a manager with whom you can speak.'

'It can't be true . . .' said one of the Helot women. She came forward and took Lysander's hand, placing it against her forehead. 'Bless you, son of Athenasia.'

'This is only the start,' said Lysander. 'But one day, like harvesting a crop, we will reap the benefits.'

The Helots cheered. Among the crowd, a child began to cry, its wail cutting above all other sounds. Lysander spotted a young woman rocking the baby on her shoulder.

The crowd surged around him, and he felt himself lifted on to the shoulders of the Helots. They bounded across the clearing, calling out his name.

'Lysander! Lysander!'

From his vantage point, he saw Demaratos offer his hands to the struggling mother. For a moment, she paused, but his friend spoke some quiet words. She smiled and extended her arms with the screaming child.

Supporting the head, Demaratos took the baby in his arms, and nestled it against his red cloak. Almost at once it hushed, its tiny fists gripping at the wool.

If that one baby feels no fear, thought Lysander, *that's a start.*

He turned around, and looked back towards Sparta. This small city – just five villages clustered around the acropolis — had held his life under its sway for nearly fourteen years. Growing up, he couldn't remember a time when he didn't understand what a red cloak meant. Danger. Fear. Power.

But now he wore one himself its meaning had changed. It symbolised comradeship, duty and above all courage.

If it weren't for the courage of others I wouldn't be here. Not only the Spartans who had stood beside Lysander in the phalanx, like brave Demaratos and Leonidas, and wise Orpheus. But his parents too: his father Thorakis who died on the battlefield and entrusted the Fire of Ares to his brother; his mother who strove to keep him safe in the settlement.

And how different his life would have been if Sarpedon had never entered it. His grandfather had placed him in the agoge, and given him a chance of a life beyond the drudgery of the fields. When the reckoning had come, he'd chosen to meet the shades rather than see his grandson die.

And Lysander couldn't have survived in the barracks without Timeon, the friend who'd not batted an eyelid when Lysander donned the red cloak of their oppressors. He'd met life with a steady grin, even when times were hard. He too had paid the price for being Lysander's friend, murdered in the night by the Krypteia. But Lysander knew that one day he'd meet Timeon again in Hades, when he'd walk across the fields and see that smile again.

Lysander imagined his friends in the Underworld lifting their faces to the sun.

'I'll make you proud,' he whispered. 'I swear.'

'We should be heading back,' said Demaratos. 'Aristodermus said we have marching practice this afternoon.'

Lysander climbed down from the Helots' shoulders. His friend handed back the baby to its mother. The Helots were smiling, and talking excitedly, their work forgotten for a short time. Two of the women were speaking to Kassandra.

Honour the dead by caring for the living, Chilonis had said. She was right. The red cloak could mean compassion as well.

Sparta had set Lysander on this path. He'd thrown off his shackles, and made his own destiny. Now it was time for the Fates to spin their threads. Whatever they threw at him, Lysander could take.